THE
GIRL WITH
KALEIDOSCOPE
EYES

THE

GIRL WITH

KALEIDOSCOPE

EYES

A STEWART HOAG MYSTERY

DAVID
HANDLER

WILLIAM MORROW
An Imprint of HarperCollins*Publishers*

THE GIRL WITH KALEIDOSCOPE EYES. Copyright © 2017 by David Handler. All rights reserved. Printed in the United States of America. No part of this book may be used or reproduced in any manner whatsoever without written permission except in the case of brief quotations embodied in critical articles and reviews. For information, address HarperCollins Publishers, 195 Broadway, New York, NY 10007.

HarperCollins books may be purchased for educational, business, or sales promotional use. For information, please e-mail the Special Markets Department at SPsales@harpercollins.com.

FIRST EDITION

Designed by Diahann Sturge

Library of Congress Cataloging-in-Publication Data has been applied for.

ISBN 978-0-06-241284-3

17 18 19 20 21   RS/LSC   10 9 8 7 6 5 4 3 2 1

For Shaun English, who taught me what friendship means

THE

GIRL WITH

KALEIDOSCOPE

EYES

CHAPTER ONE

The Silver Fox was waiting for me in a back booth at Wan-Q, the retro nonchic Cantonese restaurant that was two doors down from the rear entrance to the Essex House on West Fifty-Sixth Street. It was very quiet in Wan-Q at 4:00 on a rainy December afternoon. I paused just inside the door next to the burbling Buddha fountain to remove my trench coat and fedora. Wan-Q's owner, Benny, who was a burbling Buddha himself, hung up my coat while I helped my basset hound, Lulu, off with the pert duck-billed rain cap that I'd had made for her by C.C. Filson. Lulu is susceptible to sinus problems in damp weather. Snores like a lumberjack when she gets stuffed up. I know this because she likes to sleep on my head.

Benny led me to one of the high-backed wooden booths in back. Wan-Q was discreetly lit, which is to say dim. It helped keep your eyes from dwelling on the tacky, circa-1957 tiki bar décor. Wan-Q's extensive menu of "tropicocktails" offered such exotic classics as mai tais and zombies, but no one went to Wan-Q to drink. Its lunch and dinner menu featured bygone finger food treasures such as egg rolls and fried wonton with a gooey red sweet-and-sour dipping sauce. But no one went to Wan-Q to eat.

In fact no one went to Wan-Q at all.

Wan-Q was, by unwritten accord, the designated safe haven where literary and theatrical people could meet in public without meeting in public. If, say, a celebrated Broadway star was trying to maneuver his way into, or out of, the bed of a dewy-eyed ingénue, he'd meet her, or him, in a booth at Wan-Q. If a Hollywood studio executive was in town to try to lure a big-name editor out to the West Coast they'd talk terms in a booth at Wan-Q. It was understood that you became legally blind the moment you walked in. If you saw someone there you didn't see them and they didn't see you. If you wished to be seen then you had lunch at the Russian Tea Room, drinks at the Algonquin or dinner at Elaine's, where I'll have you know that Lulu once had her very own water bowl. But that was way back when the *New York Times Sunday Book Review* had hailed me as "the first major new literary voice of the 1980s." It was 1992 now. Governor Bill Clinton of Arkansas had just ousted Poppy Bush. In a few weeks Bill, his wife, Hillary, and their daughter, Chelsea, would be moving into the White House. The eighties were over and out.

And so was I.

The Silver Fox was seated in the last booth on the left smoking a Newport, drinking straight bourbon—no umbrella drinks for the Fox—and wearing those oversized round glasses of hers that made her look like the world's most devious owl. Her real name was Alberta Pryce, and she was the top literary agent in New York. My literary agent. She was a tiny woman, barely five feet tall, and seventy-two years old that year. Over the course of her forty years in publishing she'd represented such luminaries as Norman Mailer, William Styron, Irwin Shaw, Katherine Anne Porter and Daphne du Maurier. She was known as the Silver Fox because of her sculpted helmet of silver hair and because she was sly, tough and brutally honest. I'd been with her since I published my first short story in the *New Yorker* back when I was two years out of that college up in Cambridge that nobody mentions by name. She'd run her own agency for decades until she accepted a lucrative offer two years back to join the Harmon Wright Agency as head of its literary department. It was, she'd informed me at the time, no longer possible for an independent agent to compete with a colossus like HWA, which had offices in New York, Los Angeles, London, Paris and Tokyo.

I sat across from her. Alberta was wearing a black pantsuit and a white silk blouse. Black and white was the official dress code for all HWA agents. Harmon Wright, who'd been born and raised Heshie Roth in the rough-and-tumble Bedford-Stuyvesant section of Brooklyn, didn't like to see his people in anything else. I wore the chalk-striped navy blue suit that I'd had made for me in London by Strickland & Sons, a pink shirt and a blue-and-gold striped tie.

Lulu circled around three times at my feet before she curled up there. I ordered a Chinese beer for me and a plate of fried shrimp for Lulu, who actually does go to Wan-Q to eat. And has mighty strange eating habits.

"How are you, dear boy?" Alberta asked, peering at me through her glasses.

"Fine and dandy."

"And how is the incomparable Miss Merilee Nash?"

"Also fine and dandy, as far as I know."

She shook her head sadly. "I'm sorry to hear that you're not together."

"That makes two of us, Alberta." Lulu grunted sourly. "Correction, three of us."

"I may have something for you," she informed me, sipping her bourbon.

"So you said on the phone." The waiter brought me my beer. I took a sip. "Whom do you want me to meet with? And why are we being so secretive?"

She stubbed out her Newport. "Just promise me that you'll keep an open mind. Can you do that?"

"For you? Of course. But who is this person?"

"HWA's new vice president of Literary Synergy, whatever the devil that is. Do *you* know what it is?"

"I only know that I hate the word *synergy.*"

"As do I, dear boy." Her eyes flickered as someone arrived at our booth.

I looked up—and an involuntary shudder went right through my body. Now I knew why the Silver Fox had been so secretive.

"I believe you two already know each other," she said uneasily.

We most certainly did. The last time I'd encountered Boyd Samuels he'd been a bearded wild man who wore ostrich-skin cowboy boots and snorted lines of coke all day long in his office in the Flatiron Building. In those days, twenty-five-year-old Boyd Samuels had been the hottest literary agent in town. Also a ruthless scam artist who'd treated the honorable profession of publishing as if it were a sidewalk game of three-card monte. Before he flamed out, he'd perpetrated the biggest literary hoax in modern publishing history and pulled me right into it with him. By the time I managed to extricate myself a total of four people had lost their lives. Maybe you read about it.

"How are you doing, amigo?" he asked, flashing an uncertain grin at me.

"I was doing quite well right up until a minute ago."

"I see you've still got your pooch."

Lulu let out a low growl from under the table. She's mighty protective of me. She also doesn't like to be called a pooch.

Boyd sat across from me next to Alberta, setting his black Samsonite briefcase beside him. He now dressed like a crepuscular twenty-four-karat Harmon Wright Agency thug—black Armani suit, white shirt, black tie. His hair was cropped short, his face clean-shaven. His manner was subdued, bordering on respectful. He looked lean and hungry, which was the way Harmon Wright liked his agents.

Our waiter brought Lulu her fried shrimp and took Boyd's drink order—a club soda with a twist.

"Alberta, why are we taking a meeting with this amoral sociopath?" I demanded to know. "Boyd Samuels is a lying weasel. Boyd Samuels is a supreme waste of human skin."

"I'm sitting right here. I can hear every word you're saying, amigo."

"I'm well aware of that. And I'm *not* your amigo. Come on, Lulu, we're out of here."

In my dreams. Lulu had fried shrimp in front of her. She wasn't budging.

"Just hear him out, Hoagy," Alberta urged me. "Can you do that?"

"All right, as a personal favor to you. But how on earth did he land a job at HWA? Is he holding one of Harmon Wright's grandchildren hostage?"

"Harmon believes in second chances," she responded, sipping her bourbon. "And a client of Boyd's has brought us something that, in my opinion, warrants a conversation."

"Not interested."

"Aren't you even the least bit curious to hear what I've got?" he asked.

"The only thing I'm curious about is how you stayed out of jail. You should have been locked up for ten years."

"You're right, I should have been," he conceded readily. Boyd had blamed his criminally unscrupulous behavior on an addiction to cocaine, prescription painkillers and NyQuil. A sympathetic judge had let him skate with a stint in rehab and community service. "But I'm clean and sober now, Hoagy. I run seventy miles a week, and I'm learning how to like myself. You drank the Haterade when it comes to me. I accept that. I accept that I made some mistakes. I know I have a big hill to climb before I can regain your trust."

"You can't regain something you never had in the first place."

"You're not going to make this easy for me, are you?"

"That's not what I do."

"Okay, let's talk about what you do." He opened his briefcase, produced a manila file folder and removed a single sheet of typing paper, sliding it across the table toward me. It appeared to be a Xerox copy of a letter. "A client of mine received this by express mail over the weekend."

There was no letterhead of any kind. No name or address at the top of the page to indicate to whom the letter had been sent. It had been typed on an old-fashioned manual typewriter, the kind you don't see much anymore unless you get a letter from me. I still write everything on my solid steel 1958 Olympia portable, the Mercedes Gullwing of typewriters. Pretty much everyone else had switched to Macintoshes, those boxy plastic word processors that were the color of cat puke.

Dear Olive Oyl—

I have a story to tell. My story. And I'm ready to tell it. I need your help. Please think it over, will you? I haven't much time left, and I want to make things right among the three of us. There is a great deal that you and your sister don't know and ought to know. Everyone ought to. Please tell Alberta Pryce that I have written to you. And please ask her to contact Stewart Hoag. He will know how to proceed. Trust no one else. I will be in touch soon.

Love,

Dad

I read the letter over twice. The typeface looked strangely familiar to me. The words *Love, Dad* had been signed by hand. The signature was a tight scrawl. No flourish at all. I sat back and said, "Okay, now what?"

Boyd's eyes narrowed. "Now I tell you who my client is. I'll give you a small hint. She's a lifestyle brand. Her name is on three bestselling cookbooks."

"I don't do cookbooks."

"*And* a design for living book."

"I don't do 'design for living' books either, whatever those are."

"She has her own line of clothing, linens and home furnishings. Hosts one of the highest-rated syndicated daytime talk shows on television. She's tall, blonde, gorgeous . . . Do you still need to hear the magic words?"

"It would help."

"My client's name is Monette Aintree."

My stomach tightened right up, which was its way of telling me *Casey Jones, you'd better watch your step.* I took a sip of my beer before I said, "Are you telling me that you think this letter is from *Richard* Aintree?"

"I'm positive it is," Boyd assured me.

I looked at the Silver Fox, who was studying me very guardedly from behind her round glasses, then back at Boyd. "Monette lives out in L.A. these days, doesn't she?"

He nodded. "In Brentwood. Has a fabulous place on Rockingham, north of Sunset. Her phone number is unlisted. I have no idea how he got her address, but he got it."

"Where was this letter postmarked from?" I asked, studying it again.

"Edison, New Jersey."

"And what's with this 'Olive Oyl' business?"

"According to Monette," Alberta said, "that's what Richard used to call her way back when she was a skinny little girl."

"Monette swears that she's never mentioned it in print," Boyd said. "In fact, she swears she's never told a soul. No one else in the whole wide world knows about that nickname. Except for her sister, Regina, that is. Which is where you come in."

"I'm in?"

"Kind of. You were practically a member of the family, weren't you?"

"Reggie and I were close," I acknowledged. "But that was a long, long time ago. I haven't seen her in over ten years, and she and Monette weren't exactly on speaking terms. Reggie thought Monette was a pathological liar. No doubt still does. That's not something she'd change her mind about. I never met Monette. And I sure as hell never laid eyes on their father."

"No one has, dear boy." Alberta drained her bourbon and signaled our waiter for another. "Not since he disappeared off the face of the earth on the third of December 1970. Twenty-two years ago almost to this day. I was the last person in publishing who had any contact with him, you know. It was the day after Eleanor's funeral. I put him in a Checker cab on Fifth Avenue, he said goodbye and was never seen again."

I sat there in silence with my head spinning. Maybe I'd better give you a little background here. In the world of contemporary American fiction there is a holy trinity of coming-of-age masterpieces that are studied by high school English students year after year after year: *The Catcher in the Rye* by J. D. Salinger, *To Kill a Mockingbird* by Harper Lee and *Not Far from Here*, Richard Aintree's nostalgic, heartwarming tale of a twelve-year-old boy's encounter with life and death in a small New England town during World War II. Oddly enough, all three authors were notable recluses—though J. D. Salinger and Harper Lee were practically pub sluts compared to Richard Aintree, who was as legendary a missing public figure as there was in modern America. Think D. B. Cooper, Bigfoot and the late Elvis Presley all rolled into one. The celebrated author had totally disappeared off the face of the earth after the suicide of his wife Eleanor, the Pulitzer Prize–winning poet. So-called sightings of him had popped up in the tabloid press for years. Back in the seventies three different people said they'd spotted him living out of a van in Berkeley. Someone else swore that he was working on an oil rig in Odessa, Texas. Hunter S. Thompson of *Rolling Stone* became convinced that Richard Aintree had undergone extensive plastic surgery to change his appearance and was living in a coastal village in Baja, writing erotic novels under an assortment of female pen names. But Thompson's journey down there in search of the elusive literary giant, which he chronicled in his brilliantly hallucinogenic book *Fear and Loathing in Todos Santos*, failed to produce any sign of Richard Aintree. To this day, the man remained an enigma. No one knew where he was. Not his family. Not his friends. No one. Many people speculated that he might be dead. If he *were* still alive he'd be well into his seventies by now.

"Monette could have written this herself," I pointed out, gazing down at the letter. "Bought an old typewriter, copied his signature. How do we know it's not a hoax?"

"Monette swears it's not," Boyd said.

"She's lied before. She spent years lying about him."

"She's not lying. I believe her."

"May I keep this letter?"

"Absolutely. I brought it for you."

I folded it and slid it into my breast pocket, glancing over at the Silver Fox. "What do *you* think? You were the man's agent. You discovered him."

"I've never cared for that expression," she said, lighting a fresh

Newport with a gold lighter. "Agents don't discover talent. It reveals itself to us."

"Is it for real?"

Alberta stared down into what was left of her drink. "I dug some old business correspondence of Richard's from out of my files. It sure looked to me as if it had been typed on the same sort of machine as this letter—a Hermes 3000 portable from the late 1950s. That's what Richard used. He wrote *Not Far from Here* on it. But I'm hardly an expert on such matters."

"Did you try Mrs. Adelman at Osner's?"

Osner's, the typewriter repair mecca on Amsterdam and West Seventy-Ninth, services the vintage machines of many of the great writers of our time—Isaac Bashevis Singer, Philip Roth, William Goldman, me.

Alberta nodded. "I took the letters up to Mrs. Adelman and asked her to compare them. She examined them very carefully with a magnifying glass."

"And . . . ?"

"She's convinced that this letter was typed on the very same machine—which means that Richard still has it with him, wherever he is." Alberta let out a sigh. "I'm deeply skeptical, same as you are, but part of me does wonder if perhaps Richard has finally decided it's time to come in out of the cold," she said softly, her eyes glistening a bit. "Perhaps his health is failing. I can't imagine he's had an easy time of it." She took a drag of her Newport, staring off into space for a moment. At my feet, Lulu had begun to snore softly. A few more people had drifted into Wan-Q, though it remained discreetly quiet. "I can still remember the first time I met him. It was in the summer of 1966. He was a professor of contemporary literature at Yale. A very buttoned-down sort. Salt-and-pepper crew cut, smoked a pipe." She signaled our waiter for another bourbon. The Silver Fox could put it away. There wasn't an author in New York, man or woman, who could keep up with her. "He was also a pompous ass who had a nasty chip on his shoulder. It bugged him that Eleanor was a vastly more important writer than he could ever hope to be. Eleanor had already won her Pulitzer by then and had been named the Consultant in Poetry to the Library of Congress, which was what they called America's Poet Laureate before 1985. Eleanor was also a genuinely warm, giving person. She had those two teenaged girls of theirs whom she doted on. A lovely old farmhouse in the countryside north of New Haven. She was a passionate bird-watcher and gardener. Made her own jam and gave me a jar every year at Christmas. Eleanor was my favorite client. I adored her. I can't imagine that anyone liked Richard. I always felt that it was his bruised male ego that drove him to write *Not Far from Here*. He hated being known around the Yale campus as Mr. Eleanor Aintree." Our waiter arrived with her fresh drink. Alberta thanked him and took a sip. "I read his first draft because Eleanor begged me to. I wasn't exactly crazy about it, but as a favor to her I invited him to come into the city and meet with me. So he rode in on the train and sat across my desk staring down his nose at me while I gave him my editorial input. In my opinion he'd made his young protagonist, Titus, too sickeningly sweet. I felt that Titus needed more of a streak of the devil in him. I also suggested that Richard come up with a new title. He'd originally called it *The Summer When God Died*, which to this day still ranks as the single worst title I've ever heard in my life. Richard didn't agree with one word I said. In fact, he felt that a money-grubbing agent had no business making editorial suggestions at all. He was quite condescending. I told him, 'It's your decision, but I can't send this manuscript out in its present form and I highly doubt that any other agent of my stature will take it on, seeing as how the only reason I'm willing to is that I'm very fond of your wife.'"

"Damn, you've got a pair of balls on you, Alberta," Boyd said admiringly.

She stubbed out her Newport. "He went home and thought it over. Six months later he sent me his revised manuscript, which was now called *Not Far from Here.* I felt it was a significant improvement and told him that I'd see what I could do. I warned him that it wouldn't be an easy sell. It was a first-person coming-of-age novel with a twelve-year-old protagonist. Furthermore, Saroyan had already turned over a lot of the same soil in *The Human Comedy*, which I still believe is a vastly superior novel. But I agreed to send it out. The first eight editors who saw the manuscript turned it down cold, which all eight of them would regret until the day they died. I finally placed it with a young editor at Lippincott who offered us a nice little advance of $3,500. She had no great expectations for it. I certainly didn't. But from the moment that the bound galleys of *Not Far from Here* began to circulate in the summer of '68 it was an instant publishing phenomenon. Lippincott had to go back to press ten times within a matter of weeks. I've always felt that timing had a lot to do with it. The Vietnam War was raging. Bobby Kennedy and Martin Luther King Jr. had been assassinated. Blacks were rioting in city after city. Students were rioting at the Democratic National Convention in Chicago. Everyone was angry at everyone else. Readers were desperate to travel back to a friendly New England village where everyone knew and liked everyone else. Nostalgia. That's why *Not Far from Here* spent twenty-six weeks atop the *New York Times* bestseller list. And why I was able to make what was, at the time, the largest six-figure paperback sale in publishing history. I also had huge offers from every studio in Hollywood, but Richard refused to sell the movie rights. He did not want his beloved creation tampered with. He also, as you might imagine, became an even bigger ass."

"Is that when he and Eleanor started having problems?" I asked.

"They changed," she replied, pursing her lips. "Both of them. And it wasn't just because of *Not Far from Here*. They became very outspoken leaders of the antiwar movement on the Yale campus. Led sit-ins and demonstrations. Got themselves arrested a couple of times. Also started fooling around with marijuana, and didn't stop there. They fell in with the Timothy Leary crowd up in Millbrook that was experimenting with LSD. Within a few short months they'd become a pair of middle-aged hippies who were stoned all of the time. 'I feel so free,' Eleanor told me on the phone one day. She slept with every passionate young poet who wanted her. And Richard slept with every pretty young thing who wanted him. Meanwhile, Lippincott was desperate for another novel from him. When I asked him if he was working on one he told me, 'I'm beyond that now.' And Eleanor told me that poetry was 'an outmoded form of expression.' Instead, they became performance artists, I guess you'd have to call them. They rented a rather slummy apartment in the East Village and became part of that strange underground scene at Andy Warhol's Factory. Took more and more LSD, drifted further and further from the life they'd known. And then one night, while Richard was fast asleep in bed next to her, Eleanor went up onto the roof of their building and flung herself off it. She left no note, although Richard said she'd been depressed for several weeks because she'd wanted to start writing again but couldn't remember how. They found LSD in her system as well as marijuana and alcohol. Eleanor's death was . . . it was tragic. A great loss for American poetry. And for me personally. She was my friend," Alberta said softly. "Richard and the girls buried her at her family's plot in Rochester. Monette was in her junior year at Bennington. Reggie had just started at Yale. The next day, at Richard's insistence, we met with my lawyer in his office on Fifth Avenue and arranged for all future paperback and foreign earnings for *Not Far from Here* to go directly into a trust fund for the girls. Then I walked Richard downstairs and we stood there together on the sidewalk. It was a crisp, cold December day. The street vendors were selling roasted chestnuts. Richard told me that he was going to visit his friends Scott and Helen Nearing at their farm up in Harborside, Maine, for a few weeks. I put him in that Checker cab, wished him well and sent him on his way. The Nearings said he never showed up. He simply disappeared off the face of the earth. That was twenty-two years ago." Alberta tossed back the last of her bourbon. "He abandoned those two girls. They were, for all intents and purposes, orphaned. Eleanor had an older sister up in Rochester. She and her husband did what they could to help. Her husband was an accountant and was able to take care of their finances. *Not Far from Here* remains one of the top-five-selling mass-market paperbacks in the world each and every year. It has sold nearly thirty million copies to date. But Richard's disappearance left those girls grief stricken and lost. And Monette was so angry that she sat down and wrote that hateful 'memoir' of hers."

Monette's corrosive tell-all account of her childhood, *Father Didn't Know Best*, detailed her years as a silent victim of sexual abuse by Richard that dated all of the way back to when she was seven years old.

"Monette was still at Bennington when she wrote it," Alberta recalled. "She sent the manuscript to me. I refused to touch it because I didn't believe one word of it. And I didn't even like the man. To me it was nothing more than a troubled young girl's cry for help. But it was so salacious that *Father Didn't Know Best* turned Monette into a major public figure. Not to mention a polarizing one. The literary establishment hated her. The tabloids loved her. She was an attractive young blonde who craved attention. Reggie was not at all pleased."

That much I knew from personal experience. Richard Aintree didn't respond to any of the accusations that Monette made against him in *Father Didn't Know Best*. He stayed silent, wherever he was, but Reggie didn't. She denounced every word of her sister's book in letters to the editor of the *New York Times Sunday Book Review*, the *New York Review of Books*, *Time*, *Newsweek*— anyone and everyone who reviewed *Father Didn't Know Best*— blasting it as "a vicious lie from start to finish." When Reggie and I were going out together she and Monette hadn't spoken in years. Monette certainly didn't mend any fences when she performed a 180-degree pivot and wrote her "cleansing" follow-up bestseller, *Where Did I Go Wrong?* in which she denounced the culture of victimhood that had led her to write *Father Didn't Know Best*, which she now acknowledged had been riddled with fabrications and falsehoods. Undaunted by Reggie's even angrier denunciations, Monette continued to traffic in her own celebrity with shameless zeal. She was on tour in Los Angeles promoting *Where Did I Go Wrong?* when she met Patrick Van Pelt, the ruggedly handsome former Notre Dame wide receiver turned television actor, who in those days was playing a softhearted private eye with a moustache. They got married, had two kids and soon after that Monette penned a pair of mommy self-help bestsellers, *The Let Go Muscle* and *The Goldilocks Zone*, that earned her so much face time on *Good Morning America* that she landed *Me, Monette*, a syndicated daytime talk show of her very own. *Me, Monette* wasn't exactly a critical favorite, but criticism had never deterred Monette. She was rich. She was famous. She was . . . what was it Boyd had called her? A lifestyle brand.

"Alberta, I have to ask you something in the interest of mental hygiene," I said. "After all of those horrible lies that Monette spread about Richard, why on earth would he write to her and not Reggie?"

"Why does he do anything?" she answered with a shrug. "But I agree. It makes no sense. Reggie's the one who defended him. I've always had a soft spot for her. When she came to me with her first volume of poems I was happy to represent her. And when you two took up together I was ecstatic." Alberta smiled at me fondly. "You were my golden children, you know."

"That's ancient history, Alberta."

"It seems like only yesterday to me."

"That's because you're so old."

"I can put this cigarette out in your eyeball, you know."

"No, you can't. Lulu would pounce on you."

"And do what, lick me to death?"

"Be careful what you wish for."

"Monette happens to be one of HWA's biggest earners," Boyd interjected. "She makes us a ton of money. So does Patrick." For the past three seasons, Monette's husband had been starring as a professional surfer turned high school guidance counselor in the mega-hit TV series *Malibu High*, which was *Beverly Hills 90210* meets *Baywatch* meets *Mr. Novak*. And served as a showcase for a lot of hot, hard-bodied teens who seemed to wear very little clothing to school. "Monette and Patrick are very important HWA clients, not to mention one of Hollywood's A-list super couples." His face dropped. "Or I should say they *were* until this small marital dustup of theirs."

Page-one tabloid shit storm was more like it. Patrick Van Pelt, age forty-five, was having a very public affair with one of his hard-bodied young co-stars, super sexy Kat Zachry, age nineteen, who was currently three months pregnant with their love child. The producers of *Malibu High* were furious about Pat 'n'

Kat. The network was furious about Pat 'n' Kat. But no one was more furious than Monette, who'd kicked her cheating horndog of a husband out of the house and filed for a divorce. The proceedings promised to be very public, very ugly and very, very expensive. It seemed that she and Patrick hadn't signed a prenup. They'd thought it would be unromantic.

I studied the Silver Fox from across the table. "Seriously, do you think this letter from Richard is genuine?"

"Seriously?" She stared down into her glass. "I don't know."

"It's *got* to be." Boyd stabbed the table with his index finger for emphasis. "No way Monette would try to fake something this huge."

"Sure, she would. She has a proven track record as a liar."

"So she played a little loosey-goosey with the truth back when she was a kid. She came clean about it in her second book."

"And profited handsomely from it in her second book."

"You say that like it's a crime, amigo. This is America, remember? Besides, she's a class act. Why would she make up something like this?"

"Damage control," I replied. "Monette has been trapped inside of the Pat 'n' Kat tabloid freak show for weeks. That damned story's bigger than Charles and Lady Di, bigger than Donald and Ivana, bigger than Bubba's latest bimbo eruption, Shannen Doherty's latest meltdown . . ."

"I keep forgetting," Alberta said. "*Who* is Shannen Doherty?"

"Monette is being publicly humiliated day in and day out by her very famous husband. If her legendary father suddenly reappears after all of these years she'll seize control of the narrative and bump Pat 'n' Kat to the back pages. Me, I'd call that a shrewd career move by a woman who has a history of making shrewd career moves."

"You must admit that the timing is rather fortuitous," Alberta said to Boyd. "Kat Zachry and her swelling belly are on every tabloid front page in America. That naughty girl seems to be loving every minute of it, too."

"She's a bare-knuckle opportunist," Boyd acknowledged. "She's also an HWA client."

"Of course she is," I said.

"Mr. Harmon Wright has very high hopes for Kat Zachry."

"Of course he does. What sort of a client is Monette?"

"Demanding," he answered. "Some might call her bitchy. Not me. I get along with her fine. If her father's really planning to resurface *and* if he's ready to talk about where he's been for all of these years, then we are talking about a major, major literary event."

"I'm hearing a lot of *if*s. What I'm still not hearing is where I come in."

"I already have a firm, seven-figure offer from a major publisher for the exclusive rights to the inside story."

"Told by . . . ?"

"Monette, which is to say *you*. Her father mentioned you by name in his letter. He wants you involved. And why wouldn't he? You're the top ghost in the business. Plus you have that former connection with Reggie."

"Not interested," I said.

"Did I mention that I've negotiated her a nice, fat kill fee? If the old guy changes his mind, Monette is still guaranteed $250,000. As her co-author you'd be entitled to a third of that."

"You told me you could guarantee Hoagy a $100,000 kill fee," Alberta said. "One-third of $250,000 is only $80,000 and pocket change."

Boyd grinned at her. "I was just checking to make sure you were paying attention, Alberta."

"Do that again and I'll put my cigarette out in *your* eyeball."

Now he grinned at me. "I am loving this, aren't you? Somehow, I just knew we'd cook up another scam together."

"Let's get one thing straight. If I agree to do this it'll be strictly out of respect for Alberta."

"And let's not forget the $100,000, dear boy."

"Are you thinking that Richard will show up—if he shows up—at Monette's place out in L.A.?"

She nodded. "We'd want you out there as soon as possible."

Lulu's tail thumped on my feet. She loves L.A. The weather's warm and dry, and the sushi plentiful.

"HWA will cover it," Boyd said. "Airfare, car rental, whatever you need. You can stay in Monette's pool house. I hear it's very nice."

"I'll have to talk to Reggie before I give you my answer."

"Of course you will, dear boy."

"How does she feel about it?"

Alberta lowered her eyes. "We were hoping you'd find out. She and Monette don't speak."

"They still hate each other after all of these years?"

"I can't say for certain. But they're still sisters, so it's a pretty safe bet."

"Do you know where Reggie's living these days?"

"At the Root Chakra Institute—a five-thousand-acre meditation retreat that she owns in the hills outside of New Paltz. Money, as you'll recall, was never Reggie's problem."

"Is she doing any writing?"

"She hasn't sent me a poem in a long, long time." The Silver Fox gazed at me through her owlish glasses. "What do you say, Hoagy? Are you in?"

"I'll think about it."

"Don't think about it for too long," Boyd Samuels said to me sharply. "This is a go project. If you turn us down, I'll have to find somebody else, and I have no idea where to look. Let's face it, there's only one Stewart Hoag."

"Thank God for that. I'd hate to run into another me."

MAYBE YOU'VE HEARD of me. Then again, maybe you haven't. It's been a while since I burst onto the scene as that tall, dashing author of that fabulously successful first novel, *Our Family Enterprise*. I won literary awards. I spoke at smart, prestigious gatherings of smart, prestigious people. I got a lot of attention. *Esquire* was keenly interested in what my favorite flavor of ice cream was (licorice, and it's damned hard to find). *Vanity Fair* wanted to know who my favorite actor was (a tie between Mitchum and Howard, as in Moe). *GQ* applauded me as a man of "easy style" and wanted to know what I wore when I worked (an Orvis chamois shirt, jeans and mukluks). Hell, for a while I was as famous as John Irving, only he's shorter than I am, and he still writes.

Or maybe you've heard of me because of Merilee. Ours was a match made not so much in heaven as in Liz Smith's column. Liz thought we were perfect for each other. And we were. I was, as you may recall, the first major new literary voice of the eighties. Merilee was Joe Papp's loveliest and most gifted leading lady. We did London, Paris and most of Italy on our honeymoon. Bought a magnificent eight-room apartment in an art deco building on Central Park West, a red 1958 Jaguar XK150 and a basset hound, Lulu. I kept my drafty old fifth-floor walk-up on West Ninety-Third Street as an office. Went there bright and early every morning to work on novel number two only to discover that there was no novel number two. Writer's block, they call it. Trust me, it's not a block. It's a void. And a terror that you no longer know how to do the only thing you know how to do. I crashed and burned in style. Drank too much. Snorted way too much

Colombian marching powder. I drove my friends away. Worst of all, I drove Merilee away. She got the eight rooms overlooking Central Park West, the Jaguar, the Tony for the Mamet play, the Oscar for the Woody Allen movie. Me, I ended up right back where I'd started—in my drafty fifth-floor walk-up. Just me, Lulu and my ego, which is so large that it recently applied for statehood.

A failed novelist has a severely limited menu of career choices. You can teach, except I can't. The academic world makes me want to hit someone. I don't know why. I'm usually a peace-loving man. You can try your hand at screenwriting, except I can't do that either. The movie business gives me acute nausea. You can go into television, which gives me acute nausea *and* hives. That leaves only the French Foreign Legion for lost literary souls—ghostwriting celebrity memoirs.

I'm not terrible when it comes to being an invisible pen for hire. In fact, I've done the Claude Rains thing on three number-one bestsellers so far. My background as an author of fiction certainly helps, since celebrity memoirs should never, ever be mistaken for nonfiction. So does the fact that I used to be a celebrity myself. I know how to handle stars. They don't frighten me. Hell, they can't do anything to me I haven't already done to myself. On the downside, my second career has proven to be more than a bit hazardous to my health. Celebrity memoirs tend to be about juicy secrets, past and present. There are people near and dear to those celebrities who want those juicy secrets to stay safely buried. And will do anything to make sure that they are. And I do mean anything.

Still, I've survived. And Merilee and I have managed to reach a civilized détente, which is to say that we get along quite well as long as we aren't together. But I'm not exactly a kid anymore. That year found me staring forty right in the eye. Not only was forty winning but I was growing more and more certain that I would never, ever write a second novel. I was also growing increasingly fed up with the ghosting game. A memoir used to represent the culmination of a lifetime of achievement by someone who mattered. A great movie star. A transformative political leader. A pioneering business titan. But that was then. To be considered memoir-worthy these days all you had to do was ring your married boyfriend's front doorbell, shoot his clueless wife in the face and—faster than you can say Joey Buttafuoco—you went from being an anonymous suburban teenager to being the world-famous Long Island Lolita. Fame? It's just a shot away. Practically every publisher in New York was throwing major bucks at any woman on the planet who had big hair, big boobs and a reasonably plausible claim to having been up close and personal with Bill Clinton's pecker. The Silver Fox had dutifully called me twice in the previous few weeks with highly lucrative tell-all offers. I said no to both. Electile dysfunction is not my thing. Neither are dinosaurs. I'd also said no to penning a memoir for Barney, the stuffed purple-and-green T. rex likeness that was the hottest phenomenon in kid vid that year.

That's what was, or I should say wasn't, happening on that particular rainy December afternoon when the Silver Fox asked me to meet HWA's new vice president of Literary Synergy at Wan-Q.

I had the cab driver drop me at West Ninety-Third and West End. Lulu and I walked the remaining half block toward Riverside, me with my hands buried deep in the pockets of my trench coat, Lulu picking up speed as we got closer to home. The rain had stopped, and a cold, blustery wind had picked up. I could see the clouds breaking up in the dusky western sky over the Jersey Palisades.

There was nothing in my mailbox except for an extremely early Christmas card from my accountant and a discreet past-due notice on my dues for the Racquet and Tennis Club.

My apartment smelled of the dried remains of Lulu's favorite canned food, 9Lives mackerel for cats and very weird dogs. I hung my trench coat and hat in the narrow hall closet, scooped the desiccated mackerel into the trash and rinsed out Lulu's bowl while she stood there in the kitchen with her large black nose pointed directly at the refrigerator. She wanted a treat. Her idea of a treat is an anchovy. She likes them cold out of the refrigerator. The oil clings better. I gave her one. She wanted two. I said no. She woofed at me. She has a mighty big bark for someone with no legs, and I have mighty touchy neighbors. So she got two. Don't ever try to out-stubborn a basset hound. You'll lose.

There isn't much to my apartment. My desk with my Olympia set atop it. My books and records. My stereo. One good leather chair. One not-so-good corduroy loveseat. And a bedroom that's barely big enough to hold a bed. I put some Erroll Garner on the stereo, unfolded the letter that Monette Aintree had supposedly received from her father and looked at it. As the Little Elf had his way with "I Cover the Waterfront," I poured myself a jolt of eighteen-year-old Macallan and sipped it, gazing at the framed letter that hung on the wall directly over my desk, the one that I'd received in the mail two months after *Our Family Enterprise* had been published. It was one of my most prized possessions. A fan letter that had been typed on plain white typing paper and folded into a square so that it would fit inside the small, square envelope it had arrived in. The envelope was right there inside the frame next to the letter. My address had been typed on it. No return address. Just a postmark from Missoula, Montana. The letter read:

Your book doesn't suck. I think you are genuinely tal-
ented. Very few are. Don't fuck it up.
                                        —*Richard Aintree*

I took the frame down from the wall, set it next to Monette's letter and removed my magnifying glass from the top drawer of my desk, feeling my pulse quicken as I compared the two letters. I'm no NYPD crime lab scientist but they sure looked to me as if they'd both been typed on the same Hermes 3000. The capital letter *I* was out of proper alignment. Struck the page a bit higher than it should. And the space bar had an irregular jump to it— what Mrs. Adelman called "a hitch in its giddyup." The scrawled signatures looked identical, too. I sat there for a long moment, staring at the two letters. Then I grabbed a couple of worn paperbacks from the bookshelves, *Sneaky People* by Thomas Berger and *Giles Goat-Boy* by John Barth. Drank the last of my Macallan. Put on my shearling greatcoat and the dark brown Statler from Worth & Worth. Turned off the stereo and lights and headed back out into the cold New York City evening.

As I made my way to Broadway I noticed yet again how many Yushies were swarming all over my charmingly old-fashioned Upper West Side neighborhood. In the past year I'd lost my mom-and-pop Jewish deli, my Chinese laundry, Greek shoe repairman, Polish butcher, German baker and Italian fishmonger. All had been driven out by deep-pocketed chain stores like the Gap and Banana Republic that catered to the Young Urban Shitheads. Trendy sidewalk cafés with one-word names like Zoot or Toot had started springing up, too, the kind that served foamy, overpriced cocktails and mesquite-grilled everything. There was no getting around the horrifying reality. My home turf was *chic.*

But at least one thing hadn't changed. My favorite pair of street vendors were still anchored on the northwest corner of Broadway and West Ninety-Second. The two of them looked out for each other. Flopped together at an SRO somewhere on Amsterdam. One was a longhaired kid with a scraggly moustache who sold used LPs and yammered nonstop at the people walking by, trying to convince someone, anyone to show an interest in his wares. The other was an old man in a tweed overcoat who sold used paperback books and never spoke or made eye contact with anyone. Just sat on a battered folding chair by his meager little display of books and scribbled madly away in a lined yellow legal-sized pad. The city is home to many mad scribblers. Last year there'd been a middle-aged lady with uncombed hair and bare, filthy legs who sat on a stoop down the block from my apartment scribbling day after day. I used to buy sandwiches for her until she disappeared one day and never returned. I share a special kinship with mad scribblers. I'm victimized by the same chaos inside my own brain. Teeter on the edge of the very same cliff. One good shove and I could easily be one of them.

So I pay homage. Donated the two used paperbacks I'd brought with me and reclaimed the two paperbacks that I'd brought him the day before—*Don Martin Steps Out* and *Don Martin Bounces Back*, illustrated collections by *Mad* magazine's maddest artist, whom I consider one of the underappreciated comic geniuses of the past thirty years. The mad scribbler accepted the five-dollar bill I put in the cigar box before him without looking at me or thanking me. He never seemed to notice that I kept donating and buying back the same books. Or that I ignored the hand-lettered sign that read: ALL BOOKS FIFTY CENTS. He was a rather well-dressed old man. His Harris tweed coat and red cashmere muffler were stylish and in good condition. I know this because they used to belong to me. I gave them to him a few weeks back when the weather turned cold. He was a tall, gaunt old man with a full white beard, long, greasy gray hair and a battered nose that looked as if it had been broken many times.

I gave the kid an extra twenty dollars. "You may not see me for a while."

"Cool. Oh, hey, can I interest you in the Brothers Gibb on vinyl today?"

"Not today. Not ever."

The kid grinned at me. "Have a good one."

Lulu immediately growled at him. She hates that expression.

The two of us strolled down to West Seventy-Ninth and then over toward Amsterdam, Lulu ambling a step ahead of me, her nose, ears and tummy to the ground. We ate dinner at Tony's, a neighborhood Italian place that hasn't changed its menu or décor in twenty-five years. I had their homemade sausages with a plate of pasta in garlic and olive oil, and a bottle of Chianti. Lulu had the fried calamari. As I ate, I found my thoughts starting to drift their way back through the years to Reggie. What we'd had together. Why it had gone bad. But I reined those thoughts in. It was not healthy for me to let them roam free.

Afterward, I strolled back uptown on Central Park West and found myself in front of what had once been my building, gazing up at those eight glorious windows that overlooked the park. The lights were on. Merilee was there. Good. I intended to phone her when I got home.

Lulu had other ideas. She let out a low whoop, went barreling into the grand lobby and started pawing at the elevator door.

George, the evening doorman, always had a soft spot for Lulu. Me, he didn't like. He held up a big white-gloved hand to stop me as soon as I set foot in the lobby. "Where do you think *you're* going?"

"She's home, isn't she?"

"Maybe she is, maybe she isn't." He called her on the house

phone and informed her that I was there. Listened briefly, then hung up and reluctantly acknowledged that I could go up.

Lulu started whooping again in the elevator. As soon as the elevator doors slid open, she tore her way down the tile corridor to her mommy's open door and circled around and around her, whimpering, her tail thump-thumpeting. Divorce is always hardest on the children.

Merilee knelt in the doorway to stroke her and hug her. "Oh, sweetness, how are you? Yes, I've missed you, too. Yes, I have."

Then she stood and we looked at each other and I got lost in those green eyes of hers the same way I have since that night we first met at the Blue Mill a million years ago. Merilee Nash, pride of the Yale School of Drama, will never be mistaken for a fashion magazine cover girl. Her nose and chin are too patrician. Her forehead is way too high. Plus she's no slender, delicate flower. She has broad, sloping shoulders, a muscular back and strong legs. Standing there in her size-ten stocking feet she was just under six feet tall. Her waist-length golden hair was brushed out and gleaming. She had on a silk target-dot dressing gown that was identical to my own. In fact, it *was* my own until she stole it and I had to buy myself another one. Holding on to my clothes had been a genuine problem when we were together. She always looked better in them than I did. Under the gown she wore a pair of white pima cotton PJs with blue piping. Men's PJs, because she insists they're better made. She sews the fly shut, in case you're wondering.

"What an unexpected pleasure, darling," she said in that magically cascading voice of hers.

"Is this a bad time?"

"A slightly hectic time, but not bad. Never bad. May I get you a whiskey?"

"No, I'm all set."

She stowed my coat and hat in the hall closet and stood there inspecting me. "My God, I forgot how good you look in a navy blue suit."

"You look good in everything. And I haven't forgotten."

"Don't flirt," she said, coloring slightly.

"You started it."

"Did not."

"Did."

She'd furnished the apartment in Mission oak after I'd gone, but not just any Mission oak—signed Gustav Stickley Craftsman originals, each piece spare, elegant and flawlessly proportioned. There was an umbrella stand and a tall-case clock in the marble-floored entry hall. In the dining room she had a hexagonal dining table with six matching V-backed chairs around it and a massive sideboard with exposed tenons and pins. The living room, with its floor-to-ceiling windows overlooking Central Park sixteen stories below, was anchored by a seating area consisting of two Morris armchairs and a matching settee of oak and leather. The coffee table was heaped with scripts.

I sat in one of the chairs. Merilee curled up on the settee. Lulu promptly joined her there and plopped her head in Merilee's lap, gleeful argle-bargle sounds coming from deep in her throat.

"Is your daddy taking good care of you?" Merilee asked her. "Are you getting enough to eat?"

"She's been supping in fine fashion," I said, feeling my chest tighten. It was painful to return to this place, this life where I once belonged.

The phone rang. And rang. Merilee ignored it.

"Do you need to get that?"

She shook her head. It stopped ringing. All was quiet again—until a horrible grinding noise came out of the kitchen.

"Merilee, are you milling your own grain in there?"

"It's my fax machine, silly man."

"I can't believe I was married to someone who owns a fax machine."

"Hoagy, you are a hopeless trog."

I glanced at Grandfather's Benrus. It was nearly nine. "Who's faxing you at this time of night?"

"My agent's sending me the final details of my deal. I suppose I ought to see what they are." She climbed out from under Lulu, padded into the kitchen and came back with a sheet of paper, peering at it. "My goodness, that's quite a lot of zeroes, unless I'm seeing double."

"Here, let me . . ." I glanced at it. "My goodness, that's quite a lot of zeroes. What are they for?"

"If we can agree on the dollars, which it appears we have, I'll be leaving on a jet plane to play Brett in a remake of *The Sun Also Rises*. I still have some issues with the latest draft," she said, gesturing at the pile of scripts on the coffee table. "But it's quite good, and the director is someone with whom I've always wanted to work. Not that I was his first choice, of course."

"Who was?"

She sat back down with Lulu. "Meryl, who else? She's everyone's first choice for everything. It's a good thing that she can only be in one movie at a time or they would have no need for Sigourney, Glenn, Michelle, any of us."

"Who's playing Jake Barnes, dare I ask?"

"I'll be starring opposite *People* magazine's Sexiest Man Alive."

"Dear God, please don't tell me you're flying off to Paris to film *The Sun Also Rises* with Patrick Swayze."

"No, silly. He was last year's. This year's is Nick Nolte."

"Oh, him."

She gazed at me through her eyelashes. "Why, Hoagy, are you a teensy bit jealous?"

"Not at all. I'm just not happy about you flying to Paris without me. Paris is ours."

"You're right, it is. And I'm not. Flying to Paris, that is. I'm going to Budapest."

"What's in Budapest?"

"Paris is. It seems that it isn't in Paris anymore. Not when they want a vintage look. Budapest stands in for it."

"When do you leave?"

"Tomorrow morning," she said as she stroked Lulu, whose tongue was now lolling out of the side of her mouth.

"Shouldn't you be packing?"

"I'm still a trouper at heart, darling. It takes me five minutes to pack for six weeks on the road. I've spoken on the phone with Nick several times. He's intelligent and serious. I'm looking forward to working with him."

"I can't remember, did you ever work with Patrick Van Pelt?"

She arched an eyebrow at me. "America's number-one television hunk? No, I never have. Larry Olivier he's not, but Patrick's had an amazing career out there. Why, I'll bet he hasn't missed a leading man's paycheck in fifteen years. That is not easy to do, believe me. Mind you, one does hear things . . ."

"Things? What things?"

"That he's difficult, not to mention a p-i-g. Knocking up little Kat Zachry was certainly not an enlightened move. She's nineteen years old. He should have kept his sword in his scabbard."

"I've missed your quaint little expressions."

"Are you sure you won't have a whiskey, darling? It's awfully chilly out, and I have the Macallan you like."

"All right."

She dislodged Lulu, who was dozing contentedly now, and went to the sideboard in the dining room. Came back with my single malt in a heavy vintage bar glass that fit comfortably in my hand. "Why this interest in Patrick Van Pelt?" she asked as she settled back on the settee with Lulu.

"Actually, my interest is in Mrs. Patrick Van Pelt."

"Monette Aintree?"

"It seems that her father may be about to reappear in her life."

Merilee's eyes widened in shock. "You're kidding."

"No, I'm not. She's received a letter from him that appears to be authentic. He wants to come in from the cold. There's quite a story to be told. I may get involved in the telling of it. It'll mean going out to L.A. for a while. It'll also mean . . ." I sipped my Macallan. "I have to go see Reggie."

"Oh, her." Merilee smiled at me sweetly. "You're such an old-fashioned gentleman. I love that about you. You and I aren't a couple anymore and yet you still came here to ask me if I mind you visiting her."

"Actually, I was wondering if I could borrow the Jag. She's living at a meditation retreat outside of New Paltz. The only way to get there is by car and you know how allergic Lulu is to rental cars. She starts sneezing and can't stop."

"You want to borrow my Jag?"

"I still like to think of it as our Jag."

"I still like to think of myself as an innocent young slip of a girl. That doesn't make it so. The Jag is *mine*. But since I'm going away you may as well use it. I keep it in the same garage. Keys are in the bowl in the entry hall." She studied me, her eyes narrowing. "Besides, it might do you good to see Reggie."

"Why do you say that?"

"Because I don't believe you ever got her out of your system."

"Sure, I did."

"Nay, not so. Do you remember your author photo for *Our Family Enterprise*? You standing on the roof of your brownstone in that beat-up old leather motorcycle jacket you used to wear?"

"Actually, it was a 1933 Werber A-2 flight jacket that I found in a vintage clothing store in Provincetown. And I still wear it."

"You look all full of hoo-hah and vinegar in that photo. Tough, defiant, sure of yourself . . ."

"Your point?" I asked, starting to think I should have just asked Avis if there's such a thing as a hypoallergenic car.

"You don't look that way anymore, darling."

"How do I look?"

"Like someone who has doubts."

"That's to be expected. I no longer have the courage of my ignorance. I'm ten years older."

"Are you any wiser?"

"No, I wouldn't say that I am. I was much smarter then."

Her green eyes locked onto mine. "Has it occurred to you that this long creative dry spell of yours has coincided with Reggie's departure from your life?"

"We split up before I started *Our Family Enterprise*. She wasn't in my life when I wrote it."

"Like hell she wasn't. She inspired you to write it. You dedicated it to her."

"Only because I didn't want to dedicate it to my parents. My father in particular." I sipped my Scotch, gazing out the windows at the darkness of Central Park and the lights of Fifth Avenue beyond it. "Merilee, you're not suggesting that Reggie was my muse, are you?"

"I'm suggesting that some part of you, deep down inside, has never let go of her. You and she still have some unfinished business. For all I know maybe you belong back together."

"We don't. Once was plenty for me."

"I'm suggesting that you ought to attend to it. This is your chance, Hoagy."

"Merilee, I don't want to get back together with Reggie. I'm over her."

"No, you're not. Women know these things. Men don't. You're clumsy oafs." Merilee studied me across the coffee table, her brow furrowing. "I'm trying to help you, Hoagy. I'm thinking about your future. *Our* future, if we have one. You haven't written one single word that you're proud of since the day we met. Don't you think I know that? Don't you think that hurts me deeply? I want to bring out the best in you. Somehow, *she* did. Figure out how she did it. And get her out of your system—however you need to do that."

I stared at her. "You make it sound as if you want me to . . ."

"However you need to do that," she repeated. "I'll be in Budapest until the seventeenth of next month. I'll leave a message on your machine when I get settled there to let you know how you can reach me. You know how I hate it when we're out of touch." Her green eyes shined at me. "Good luck, darling. I genuinely mean that. For Richard Aintree's sake, for your sake and for ours."

CHAPTER TWO

It was sunny and bracingly cold the next morning as I worked the Jag through the sluggish traffic on the Henry Hudson Parkway. Merilee's Scottish-born mechanic in East Hampton kept its 3.4-litre S engine tuned to perfection. I love that damned car. When I'm behind the wheel of the XK150 it's still my season in the sun. I'm *me*.

I wore my shearling greatcoat and my shearling-lined ankle boots from Tanino Crisci since the Jag didn't have a very effective heating system, what with it being a vintage British-made rag-top. Actually it had no heating system. Lulu was curled up in the biscuit-colored leather passenger seat in her Fair Isle sweater vest.

As I drove I found myself remembering when Reggie and I first met at the Antioch Writers' Workshop back in the summer of '76, back when Nixon, Watergate and Vietnam were still hanging over all of us like a poisonous, odorless miasma. I was two years out of college and convinced that I was pretty hot shit. I'd published two short stories in the *New Yorker*, had drinks in the lobby of the Algonquin with the legendary Alberta Pryce and now the Antioch people were inviting me out to the farm country of Yellow Springs, Ohio, to teach short story writing for a week. Regina Aintree, who'd just won the Walt Whitman Award for her first collection, *Don't Go Home*, was there to teach poetry. She was young and gifted. She was also big-time literary royalty.

We were billeted at the same quaint little inn in Yellow Springs, walking distance from the Antioch College campus. I showed up way late. Missed the mandatory meet-and-greet the evening before classes began. Barely even got there in time to teach my first morning class. I had to ride my bad black 1973 Norton Commando 850 all night in order to make it. When I pulled in shortly after 8:00 am, I was wearing my vintage Werber leather flight jacket, a grease-stained T-shirt, torn jeans and Chippewa engineer boots. I was unshaven, windblown and filthy. The innkeeper, who was aghast, gave me a cup of coffee. I smoked unfiltered Chesterfields in those days. I lit one with Grandfather's Ronson Varaflame chrome lighter and as I stood there in the parlor, drinking my coffee and smoking, Reggie came downstairs from her room wearing a tight little tank top with nothing underneath it, tight jeans, an exotic assortment of bracelets and necklaces and a pair of rubber flip-flops. She was barely five feet tall and built like a nimble ballerina. She had a thin, pale face with an aristocratic nose. A long curtain of shiny, jet black hair marked by a single streak of premature white that made her appear as if she'd been struck by lightning. And she had amazingly huge blue eyes. When she made it to the foot of the stairs, she stopped, looked at me and stared, those huge eyes of hers widening. I looked at her and stared. Right away, I knew my life had just changed.

"Finish your coffee, Stewie," she commanded me in a voice that was unexpectedly husky. "We'll be late for class."

"I should wash up before I go."

Reggie squinted at me as if she were regarding me from a great distance. "Why on earth would you want to do that? Come on, I'll show you where your classroom is." Then she took me by the hand and walked me to the Antioch campus, which was very peaceful on a warm summer morning. "Do you have any idea what the subject of your first lecture will be?"

"No idea at all. Haven't given it a thought."

"Neither have I. I like to plunge in headfirst. Otherwise the fledglings will get bored. They can get bored at home for free, right, Stewie?"

"Right. By the way, my friends call me Hoagy."

"As in Carmichael?"

"As in the cheesesteak."

"I'll meet you after class, Stewie. Don't try to find me. I'll find you."

And she did, because we were about to become a couple. It was already understood. Same as it was understood that she was never, ever going to call me anything but Stewie.

I took her for a long ride on my Norton that night through the meandering farm roads outside of Yellow Springs. She loved to go fast. Loved the feel of the wind on her face. She didn't believe in wearing a helmet. That made two of us. When we made it back to the inn shortly before midnight, she informed me that she possessed two hits of orange sunshine. We dropped them without a second's hesitation and strolled hand in hand back over to the campus so that we could lie on the vast expanse of lawn and gaze up at the moon and the stars. I remember that we argued like crazy over which flavor of Fizzies we'd thought was the best when we were kids. My favorite had been strawberry. Hers was cherry. She informed me that her mouth still tasted of cherry if I cared to check it out for myself. And I did. And she was right. And my own, she assured me, still tasted like strawberry. God, dropping acid was fun. Without question the most fun I ever had with my clothes on. Or off. We shed ours and lay there naked on the damp grass, gazing into each other's eyes in the moonlight. Reggie's huge blue eyes shimmered so vividly that I fumbled around in the pocket of my jeans for Grandfather's lighter and flicked it on, the better to behold the magic. I saw an entire universe in those eyes. Constantly shifting mirrors of color. Op art and pop art, swirling paisleys, primitive cave paintings. I saw flowers bloom, wither and die. I saw R. Crumb's Mr. Natural and Flakey Foont truckin' along in their bulbous, oversized shoes. I'd dropped acid many times before, but I'd never, ever experienced anything like Reggie Aintree's eyes.

She was the girl with kaleidoscope eyes.

We had wild, amazing sex on the lawn until shortly before dawn, when we decided we should put our clothes on and head back to the inn, where we took a shower together, singing "The Crystal Ship" by The Doors at the top of our lungs and waking up everyone in the place and causing quite some scandal.

Neither of us was invited back to Antioch.

We were inseparable after that. New York City was home for both of us. I had my crappy fifth-floor walk-up on West Ninety-Third Street. She had a dark little room on the third floor of the Chelsea Hotel. The city was grimy, impoverished and dangerous in those days. Gangs roamed the parks. Drug dealers and prostitutes worked any corner they felt like. Homeless people slept in doorways and vestibules, wrapped in blankets and despair. The garbage never got picked up. No one who was sane wanted to live there. Just crazies like us. We hung out at Max's, CBGB and the Mudd Club. Also an after-hours dance club up in Spanish Harlem that she dared me to take her to one night. She was always daring me to be as fearless as she was. Dropping acid that first night at Antioch? A definite dare. Putting on a parachute and jumping out of a plane together somewhere over an airfield near Chester, Connecticut? Another definite dare. She could be a real stinker that way. That's what I used to call her. Stinker.

She dared me to get started on my novel, too. Did I write it to prove to her that I could? That would be overstating it. I had plenty of other people to prove it to. My father, my mother, myself. But Merilee wasn't wrong. It was Reggie who gave me the push. Trouble was that absolutely nothing about my faltering attempts to write it was nearly as exciting as *she* was. Reggie was the most intensely alive person I'd ever met, a 105-pound whirlwind of spontaneity. Sparks flew off her. Her poems were just like she was—bursting with raw, unfiltered emotion and energy. Often, she'd dash them off longhand in a single burst of creativity. And then she'd go raring off on another adventure.

Reggie was always on the move. If she wasn't a poet-in-residence for a semester here or a guest lecturer there then she was busy trying to save someone or something somewhere. The Irrawaddy river dolphins in Laos. The elephants in Thailand. The mahogany trees in the Brazilian rain forest. If women were fighting for their rights in Moscow or Glasgow or Maputo, she'd be there. If Native Americans were getting kicked off their ancestral lands in Wyoming by a giant oil company she'd be there. She was my very own pint-sized Joan Baez.

And that became a problem for me. When she was around, my life was Mr. Toad's Wild Ride. She turned everything so completely upside down that I couldn't write. When she was gone my life was so painfully empty that I couldn't write. The operative words here: *I couldn't write*. After months of tormenting myself, I realized that I could either be with Reggie or I could write my novel.

I chose the novel.

Stopped seeing her. Stopped returning her calls. Stopped answering the door when she buzzed my apartment. I even stopped going to the places where I might run into her.

I did the right thing. My novel proved to be an even greater critical and financial success than I imagined was possible as I lay alone night after night for three long years, staring at the cracks in my bedroom ceiling. I also did the wrong thing. I broke off a relationship with a rare and special woman who was the love of my life. Until I met Merilee, that is. And I seem to have messed up that one, too. Possibly there's a pattern there. Possibly there's no possibly about it.

Reggie and I never saw each other again. Or spoke, although she did leave me a phone message after the novel came out, thanking me for the dedication and telling me she'd liked the book. Actually, what she said was, "Not bad, asshole."

I got off the New York State Thruway at New Paltz, where there's a SUNY campus and a quaint little village of narrow streets crammed with coffeehouses and delis. New Paltz had been a counterculture stronghold back in my own college days. And it hadn't changed a bit, I discovered as I eased the Jag through town. The sidewalks still swarmed with scruffy, longhaired students wearing peacoats, flannel shirts and ripped, faded jeans. The morning air was richly scented with patchouli and pot. Thanks to the immensely popular Seattle grunge bands Nirvana and Pearl Jam and their throwback look, it was as if the revolution were still happening.

Here's something that hadn't occurred to me back in 1969: that Neil Young would someday come to rival Ralph Lauren as an American fashion icon.

On the outskirts of town I took the right-hand fork and crossed a bridge that went over a rushing river. Then the road narrowed and there seemed to be nothing but apple orchards and dairy farms. Five miles outside of town I spotted a wooden sign for the Root Chakra Institute, turned off onto a dirt road that twisted its way deep into the woods, and there it was.

It was not cozy or welcoming. It was a circa-1920s stone edifice that resembled a state reformatory where bad little boys and girls got sent to learn the errors of their ways. The Silver Fox's assistant ran a check on the place for me and reported that it had, in fact, been a Jesuit seminary before Reggie bought it and turned it into a spiritual retreat and learning center that offered an array of workshops during the summer months. He didn't know what went on there in December. Standing there, I had a pretty good idea what. Nothing. The parking lot was deserted except for one VW. It was so quiet that my citified ears buzzed.

The main entrance hall was exactly what you'd expect from a Jesuit seminary. Austere. In the administrative office a young woman informed me that Reggie was in the meditation solarium, which I'd find at the end of the hiking trail that was marked with blue arrows. She didn't tell me that it was a steep, two-mile climb from the main building. That part Lulu and I had to figure out for ourselves.

The meditation solarium was a two-story, octagonal-shaped hilltop aerie. The first floor was constructed of stone and rough timbers. The second floor was a steel-trussed glass dome. The entryway served as a mudroom. A down jacket hung from one of the hooks on the wall. A pair of small, well-worn hiking boots was parked on the floor beneath it. There was a furnace room, judging by the quiet roar coming from behind a door marked DO NOT ENTER. A cast-iron spiral staircase led up to the dome.

I called out Reggie's name. She didn't answer. No one did.

I looked down at Lulu. Lulu was looking up at me.

I took off my coat and boots. We climbed the spiral staircase and reached a closed door.

I called out Reggie's name. She didn't answer. No one did.

The door wasn't locked. I opened it. It was quite warm inside the meditation solarium. Also quite breathtaking. Thanks to that glass dome, it enjoyed unobstructed panoramic views of the slate gray Hudson River and the bare, rolling hills miles beyond it.

Reggie Aintree was seated in lotus position on a prayer rug with her eyes closed. She was naked. Her body looked exactly the way I remembered—trim, taut and lovely. Her smooth flesh glowed. The only thing different about her was the long, shiny black hair that draped her thin, aristocratic face. It now had three streaks of white, not one.

Lulu moseyed over and mouth-breathed on her.

Reggie immediately opened her huge blue eyes. Lulu's breath has that effect on most people. She squinted at me same as she used to, as if she were regarding me from a vast distance. The squint may have been the same but her eyes were not. I used to see mischievous gaiety in those eyes. Utter fearlessness. Now I saw disillusionment and despair.

"Stewie, is that really you?" she asked me after a long moment, her voice sounding rusty and thin.

"In living black-and-white."

"Forgive me, I've been in silent meditation for . . . It's been five days, I think. Maybe six. I've lost track. I was very close to Mom again. I could feel her aura." She smiled at me faintly. "It's been ages and ages. It's good to see you."

"Good to see you, too, Stinker. How have you been?"

"Okay, I guess. And you? Still wandering helplessly, day by day?"

"And the nights, too. Don't forget the nights," I said, gazing at her. The Reggie that I'd known had been a study in perpetual motion. This Reggie exuded a deep stillness. And the closer I studied her face the more I noticed that time had, in fact, etched it with creases and lines. "Tell me, how is it possible that you haven't gained a single ounce in all of these years?"

"It was a snap. I picked up a parasite in Mumbai and had uncontrollable diarrhea for a month. I still have to watch what I eat or it'll go right through me." Reggie turned and found herself nose to nose with Lulu, who was studying her with keen interest. "So this is the famous Lulu, also known as Her Royal Earness, who loves chilled anchovies and once had her very own water bowl at Elaine's."

"How do you know all of that? Don't tell me you read Liz Smith."

"Of course I do. Besides, I always wonder how you're doing. You were my first true love." Reggie looked me up and down, arching an eyebrow. "One of us is overdressed for the meditation solarium."

"It is rather tropical in here, now that you mention it." I took off the jacket of my barley-colored tweed suit and hung it from a hook by the door.

"Stewie, why are you wearing cufflinks that say SSH?"

"Those are my initials, remember? Stewart Stafford Hoag."

"Allow me to rephrase that. Why are you wearing cufflinks?"

"Certain traditions are important to hold on to."

"I liked you much better in that old motorcycle jacket you used to have."

"Flight jacket. And I still have it."

"Does filmdom's favorite forehead like the way you dress?"

"She does, as a matter of fact. And must you call her that?"

"Yes, I absolutely must."

"Why is that?"

"Because it bothers you. And you're still overdressed, Mr. Fancy Pants. This is a clothes-free space."

"I'm not stripping."

"My house, my rules."

Same old Reggie. Everything was a dare. "Fine, we'll talk outside when you've finished meditating. I can wait."

"You're in for a long wait."

"How long?"

"Eight hours."

"You're going to sit here like this for eight straight hours?"

She nodded. "Either strip or wait. It's entirely up to you."

I stripped. To those of you out there who aspire to a career in ghostwriting, I should mention that if it's dignity you're after, then you ought to grab yourself a nice judgeship.

"You used to be in better shape," she observed after I'd shed my clothes.

"That's not entirely fair." I sat cross-legged on the floor facing her, paying no mind to the shooting pains in my knees. "When you first met me I still possessed the physique of a topflight inter-collegiate track-and-field star."

"You did?"

"Don't tell me you've forgotten that I was once the third-best javelin hurler in the entire Ivy League."

"Somehow that slipped my mind," she said as Lulu sprawled out between us. "Are you doing any writing these days?"

"Some people call it writing."

"What do you call it?"

"I call it crap. How about you?"

She lowered her gaze. "No, not for a long time."

"How come?"

"I lost my mojo."

"Think it'll ever come back?"

"I don't think about it at all. I can't or I go bonkers." She held out her bare arms so that I could see the thin white scars on the inside of her wrists.

"When did you do that?"

"Three years ago. Not to worry, I'm better now."

"Good, because that's the coward's way out."

"I happen to come from a family of cowards, remember?"

"Your mother was tripping. That's different."

Lulu had begun to doze with her mouth open, imbuing the

snug warmth of the meditation solarium with a strong scent of the Brooklyn Navy Yard.

"Not a terrible place you have here, by the way," I said, gazing out at her view of the Hudson River.

"It keeps me busy," she said, brightening a bit. "My accountant hates it because I lose a steady million dollars every year, but it's super gratifying. I can bring together knowledgeable people to debate pretty much any subject I'm interested in—overpopulation, ground water pollution, the World Wide Web, women's reproductive rights—"

"Back up, the World Wide what?"

"It's coming, Stewie. Up until now, computers have been information islands unto themselves. But a British computer scientist named Tim Berners-Lee has figured out a way to link millions of them together. They'll be able to share information and talk to each other, and before long they'll be—"

"Taking over the world. Okay, you're scaring me."

"Don't be such a wuss. And you're going to love e-mail, which is coming sooner than you think. Put every extra dollar you have into a company called America Online if you know what's good for you."

"I've never known what's good for me. And I don't have any extra dollars. Or cents."

Reggie studied me curiously. "Does she know that you're here?"

"Who, Merilee?"

"Yes, Merilee."

"She encouraged it, actually."

"Why did she do that?"

"She thinks I never got over you."

Reggie blinked at me in surprise. "You did, didn't you?"

"I certainly thought so."

"Are you two back together?"

"We tried Paris together for a week last spring. It didn't work out at all. And Lulu was miserable."

"How come?"

"She doesn't speak French."

Reggie let out a guffaw. She took my hand and squeezed it. "I've missed you, Stewie."

"You could have picked up the phone."

"So could you."

"I didn't think you'd want to hear from me."

"You did break my heart into a million little pieces," she acknowledged, dropping my hand. "And I hated you for a long time. But I moved on. Only, it turns out that I suck at the whole girlfriend thing."

"Since when?"

"Since it turns out that I don't know how to pretend I'm happy. That seems to bother most men. You need to feel like saviors. You also prefer something in a younger model. I'm not exactly a hot young babe anymore."

"You look mighty good to me. In fact, I'm finding it very difficult to keep my eyes off those perky nipples of yours."

"You're flattering me now. It's working, too, damn it. You're such a sweet-talker. And I forgot how handsome you are."

"Now who's sweet-talking whom?"

"I mean it, Stewie. When I opened my eyes and saw you, all of the breath went right out of my body. I've had this incredibly powerful feeling all week that someone was about to come into my life. It never occurred to me that it would be you." Her eyes bored into mine. "What are you really doing here?"

"Chasing a wild goose."

"I don't know what that means."

"It means I'm here on a fool's errand."

"Are you getting paid to do it?"

"Yes, I am."

"Then you're not a fool, you're a hooker. You should be wearing hot pants and fishnet stockings."

"It's about Monette."

Reggie's face darkened. "My sweet, darling sister? I've been reading all about her idiot husband and his pregnant teenybopper. Patrick sure has a thing for lowlife *People* cover girls, doesn't he? First Monette, now Kat Zachry. But what does that have to do with me?"

"I take it you haven't been in touch with Monette."

"Not for years. Why? What's happened?"

"Your dad has written a letter to her. Or so it appears. He told her that he wants to come in out of the cold. And he wants me to help her tell his story."

"Why you?"

"Possibly because of my connection to you."

"I don't believe one word of it," she said with a shake of her head. "Sounds like classic Monette bullshit to me. She's spent her entire life making up stories about Dad."

"You think she's concocted a fake letter from him?"

"I don't have a doubt in my mind."

"It appears to have been typed on your dad's old typewriter. How can that be?"

Reggie shrugged her smooth bare shoulders. "She has it. She must have taken it when we cleaned out his apartment together."

"You don't remember?"

"I'm afraid not. I was stoned a lot in those days."

"The author of the letter used a nickname for Monette that your dad gave her when she was a girl."

Her eyes narrowed slightly. "Olive Oyl?"

I nodded. "Monette claims there are only three people on the planet who know about it—your dad, her and you."

Reggie let that sink in for a moment before she said, "You're not asking me if *I* wrote the letter, are you?"

"Did you?"

"Do you honestly think I've been sitting up here in the woods with my dad's old typewriter hatching some bizarre hoax? Why would I do that? How can you even think it?"

"I've been a celebrity ghost for a while now. My mind burrows into all sorts of strange, sick places. Has your dad been in touch with you?"

"No."

"Do you know where he is?"

"No."

"I find this whole thing very odd. If it's for real, I mean."

"It's not."

"Just for the sake of argument let's say it is, okay?"

She let out a sigh. "Okay . . ."

"Why would he reach out to Monette? She's the one who made a name for herself by blasting him in print. You were his loyal defender. Wouldn't you be the one who he'd write to?"

Reggie considered this for a moment. "No, that part makes total sense, actually. If he'd chosen me I'd have tossed his letter in the trash and caught the first flight for Bangkok. He'd know that Monette would make a big fucking deal out of it, because that's what Monette does." She gave me that long-distance squint of hers. "You're going out there, aren't you? You're flying out to L.A. to find out if it might actually be for real."

"I'm chasing a wild goose, like I told you. Want to come?"

"Not a chance. I have no desire to see Monette again."

"Don't you want to meet your niece and nephew? They must be in high school by now."

"It was good to see you again, Stewie," she said, her huge eyes shining at me. "I thought it would hurt, but it doesn't. I guess that means I'm all grown up now. Or something. Let's have dinner in the city some night, okay?"

"Okay." I climbed slowly to my feet, shaking the numbness out of them. Lulu stirred, yawning hugely. "I'll be in touch."

"I'll be right here." Reggie closed her eyes, returning to her silent meditation.

I gathered up my clothes and got dressed downstairs, then headed back down the path with Lulu. The Jag was the only car in the parking lot now. The VW was gone. Lulu hopped in and got herself settled in the passenger seat. I started it up with a roar and sped on out of there. When I made it back to New Paltz, I stopped at a gas station, fished my AT&T calling card from my wallet and called the Silver Fox at her office to tell her that I was in.

The next morning I flew out to L.A.

CHAPTER THREE

I flew first class. HWA was picking up the tab, and Lulu has been known to get truculent if she has to fly coach.

I never trust my Olympia to baggage crews. I carried it on board along with the antique doctor's bag that I use for toting around Lulu's bowls and supply of 9Lives and anchovies. I'd dressed casually in a blue chambray shirt, khakis, kid leather ankle boots and my battered old Werber flight jacket, which is an ideal weight for December in Los Angeles, where the forecast called for a high of seventy-three going down into the fifties that night.

The stargazing in first class was exceptional that morning. I was privileged, privileged to witness Pauly Shore, the slow-talking MTV stoner comic, logging face time with Richard Simmons, the screechy, hyperkinetic TV exercise guru. The two of them bore such an eerie yin-yang physical resemblance to each other that I began to wonder what might happen if we encountered air turbulence and they accidentally bumped into each other. Would they fuse into one giant, jiggling, protozoan blob? Happily, Richard went bounding off to yammer with one-half of the sizzling hot hip-hop duo Salt-N-Pepa. I think it was Salt, but I can't swear that it wasn't Pepa.

I took a pass on our in-flight movie, a smarmy $65 million

Bruce Willis flop called *Hudson Hawk*, and contented myself with that morning's *New York Daily News*, which carried a page-one banner headline that read "WHO'S YOUR DADDY?" above a photo of Kat Zachry and her noticeable tummy strolling down a West Hollywood street in a loose-fitting camisole and sweatpants. The *New York Post*, not to be outdone, went with "KAT IN THE HAT" and a photo of her in an L.A. Dodgers cap as she and her tum-tum were getting out of a BMW convertible in a coffee shop parking lot. The *Daily News*, citing "sources close to the production of *Malibu High*," disclosed that it was becoming "increasingly difficult" to shoot around Kat's "increasingly obvious" pregnant state, which was "an obvious taboo" for a character who was a high school senior. According to the *Post*, several evangelical Christian and family values organizations were calling for a nationwide boycott of the top-rated show unless the network fired the young actress for her "immoral" behavior.

The Gray Lady of American journalism, the *New York Times*, went with the breathtaking news that bestselling lifestyle author and TV talk show personality Monette Aintree, elder daughter of legendary novelist Richard Aintree, had just signed a seven-figure book contract that would team her with "former literary wunderkind" Stewart Hoag on a project that would, according to her publisher, "surely rank as one of the major literary events of our time." No details about the book's subject were disclosed. Monette Aintree's literary agent, Boyd Samuels, vice president of Literary Synergy at the Harmon Wright Agency, would neither confirm nor deny that it would concern itself with her famous missing father.

I set the newspapers aside, vowing that I was not going to obsess about those smug shitheads at the *Times* calling me a "former literary wunderkind." One of these days I would write another novel, an even better one than my first, and they would fall all over themselves raving about how great I was. Until then, I wasn't going to let them ruin my morning. Instead, I spent the flight reading a collection of short stories by John O'Hara, which is something I do every few years just to remind myself what good writing is.

A uniformed driver was waiting for me by the baggage carousel at LAX to take me to Monette's home on Rockingham Avenue in Brentwood. He collected my bags and led Lulu and me to a black Cadillac Brougham that was parked outside in the loading zone, where the warm Southern California air was scented with a rich mix of jet engine exhaust and morning smog. I instructed him to drive me instead to a converted prop warehouse on La Brea, one block south of Olympic. Dirk Weir, the brother of an old college classmate, owned a garage there that supplied movie producers with specialty vehicles for period shoots. I would need my own wheels while I was in town, and what you drive when you're in L.A. is as vital as the air that you breathe. Or can't breathe, as the case may be.

The limo driver dropped us there before he continued on to Monette's house with my luggage. I moseyed through the bustling garage in search of my wheels. Strolled past a white 1956 T-Bird that was a dead ringer for the one Suzanne Somers drove in *American Graffiti*, then an immense, mouthwatering 1930 Duesenberg dual-cowl phaeton before I found the ride that I'd reserved—a truly classic 1947 Indian Chief Roadmaster, complete with sidecar. The bike was in beautiful condition. Brilliant red enamel body and fenders. Gleaming chrome everywhere else. A sport windshield, leather saddlebags.

Lulu jumped into the sidecar and let out a whoop of delight.

"She's got good taste, I'll give her that," said Dirk, who had a ponytail and was missing several teeth. He was grinning as he handed me the key.

I climbed on. Worked the choke, gave the throttle a quarter turn and stepped down hard on the kick start. The 1,212 cc side-valve air-cooled engine roared to life unlike any engine before or since.

"It's got new points and plugs," Dirk assured me after I was done revving it like a gleeful kid. "Shouldn't give you any trouble."

"Can I take it on the freeway?"

He nodded. "It'll cruise smooth as silk at sixty-five. Helmet?"

"Never use them."

After I'd signed the paperwork, I eased on out of the driveway and headed north on La Brea, getting used to the feel of it and drawing wide-eyed stares from the other drivers on the road. Lulu, who, let us not forget, has an actress for a mother, rode with her nose high in the air, loving the attention. I don't believe I'd ever seen her happier.

When I got to Melrose I stopped off at Pink's for two chili dogs and a root beer because I can't go to L.A. and not stop at Pink's. Then I continued north on La Brea to Sunset Boulevard and hung a left, making my way past Laurel Canyon and Crescent Heights toward the Sunset Strip, the glitzy, fabled onetime home of Ciro's and Dino's and the Pink Pussycat. These days the Strip was home to Spago, Wolfgang Puck's A-list Hollywood restaurant, Tower Records and a smattering of rock and comedy clubs that were meant to be seen after dark. They looked tacky and tired in the midday sunlight. But, mostly, the Strip was famous for its gigantic billboards. If you wanted to find out who was hot all you had to do was cruise the Strip. Calvin was hot. You couldn't miss the strikingly naughty black-and-white Herb Ritts photo for Calvin Klein jeans that featured a semi-naked waif model named Kate Moss straddling a semi-naked white rapper who went by the goo-goo handle Marky Mark. But nobody was as hot that season as Whitney. There was Whitney on one huge billboard promoting her smash hit film, *The Bodyguard*, a treacly interracial romance that starred her opposite a semi-catatonic Kevin Costner. And there was Whitney on another huge billboard promoting her smash hit soundtrack album for *The Bodyguard*. It was a mighty impressive feat considering that Whitney had no acting chops and possessed a singing voice that was of no value whatsoever unless you wished to shatter bulletproof glass from a half mile away. Loud. Whitney could sing really loud.

When Sunset crossed over into Beverly Hills at Doheny, the billboards gave way to palm trees and the color palette switched over to lush green. There was a center divider that was lavishly planted and immaculately shorn. And, on my right, there was the elegant Beverly Hills Hotel. Just past the hotel, at North Whittier Drive, Sunset made an extremely sharp right bend that was famous to anyone who remembers the music of Jan Berry and Dean Torrence. I took it good and slow, still getting used to the Roadmaster and its sidecar. It handled well as I took it through the curves into Holmby Hills. When I hit a red light at Beverly Glen a young, caramel-tanned blonde on a Vespa who was wearing a bikini, a windbreaker and no shoes pulled up next to me and blew Lulu a kiss.

We had officially arrived in L.A.

Sunset skirted along the northern edge of UCLA before it dipped under the San Diego Freeway into Brentwood. I rode past Bundy Drive and Kenter Avenue before I found North Rocking-ham, where I made a right and started my way north of Sunset into a canyon of ultra-high-end estates surrounded by mani-cured carpets of green lawn. Not so much as a blade of grass or a leaf was out of place. They were the usual L.A. mash-up of Spanish, Mediterranean, Tudor, Gothic, Cape Cod and Greek revival, along with a smattering of modern architectural non-masterpieces. Monette's house was set so far back on a corner lot behind a six-foot-high stone wall that I couldn't see it from the street. There was a wide wrought iron front gate and, around the corner, a narrow service gate for tradespeople and other lowly serfs. An LAPD black-and-white was parked outside the front gate with two uniformed officers sitting in it. Four other cars were parked there that belonged to four tabloid photographers who were standing around smoking four cigarettes and chatting aimlessly.

My arrival at the front gate on the Indian Chief with Lulu riding shotgun caused a bit of a stir. The paparazzi snapped my picture and shouted at me, demanding to know who I was. I didn't respond. It's not my job to do their job for them. A cop got out of the cruiser and asked me if I was expected. When I told him that I was, he buzzed the house on an intercom that was built into the wall next to the security code keypad. A voice responded. I said my name into the intercom, the gate swung open and with that I entered what I would quickly come to think of as Aintree Manor.

It was quite some spread. Five, maybe six acres, which is the Ponderosa by Southern California standards. It was also a Merry Olde England theme park. The long, curving driveway was made of aged cobbles that had thatches of weeds growing between them in an artfully haphazard way. After the cobbled driveway had made its way past a formal rose garden, topiary garden and tennis court, it crossed over what appeared to be an old stone bridge spanning what appeared to be an actual babbling brook, before it finally arrived at a massive Georgian manor house of weathered brick with periwinkle blue shutters and ivy and honeysuckle growing up its walls. The house had a conservatory appointed in gleaming copper. Everyone should have one of those. A matched pair of crouching marble lions flanked the front door. Everyone should have two of those. The driveway changed over to pea gravel as it neared the house and widened out enough to accommodate a dozen or more cars, though there were none there now. I pulled to a halt, shut off the bike and climbed off. Lulu hopped out of her sidecar. I climbed the bluestone front steps and rang the doorbell, half-expecting Bertie Wooster to come flying out of the door with a red-faced Honoria Glossup in hot pursuit, waving a mashie niblick at him.

But it was the housekeeper who greeted me. Unless, that is, she was the live-in dental hygienist. She was dressed like one in her short-sleeved yellow smock, matching yellow pants and spotless white Nikes. She was a Latina in her early twenties, about five foot seven, slim and quite lovely with gleaming dark eyes, flawless skin and shiny black hair that was tied back in a ponytail.

"Welcome, Senor Hoag. I am Maritza. I shall make you settled," she said, slowly and carefully. Her English was fair. She was working hard at making it more than that.

"Nice to meet you, Maritza. Make it Hoagy, okay?"

"As you wish, Senor Hoagy."

"And the short one with four legs is Lulu."

Maritza's face lit up. "Such a pretty, pretty girl." She knelt down to pet Lulu, then drew back, her eyes widening. "*Dios mio*, her breath . . ."

"She has rather strange eating habits."

"When I unpacked her food I expected she would be a cat. I mean no offense."

"None taken, I assure you. Are those photographers always camped outside?"

She nodded. "Day and night. You are seeing only the small crew because they know the senora is not here. When she returns from work, there are many more. She will be home from taping today's show by six o'clock. Senor Joey and Senorita Danielle ride the bus home from Brentwood School and shall be here by four o'clock. I can show you around now, if you would like."

"I would like. How long have you been working here, Maritza?"

"I arrived from Guatemala City six month ago. I am very happy here. Senora Monette is so kind to me. I wish to take classes soon at Santa Monica City College. I should like to be a school-teacher someday."

I nodded, wondering if she were here illegally. Many of the live-ins on Park Avenue in New York were. The same was true here in sunny Southern California. It was a mixed blessing. It got them away from a bad situation at home, but it also turned them into modern-day indentured servants.

The two-story entry hall featured a marble bust of a bygone nobleman who wore six, seven, eight vintage straw hats stacked high atop his head in a manner that I suppose was meant to be whimsical. Next to him there was a blue porcelain urn filled with walking sticks and umbrellas. The floor was made of wide oak planks. Old ones by the look of them. There was a tall clock, an ornate gold mirror, a long bench that looked a lot like a repurposed church pew. A grand, winding staircase led up to the second floor. The stairway walls were lined from floor to ceiling with framed covers of *TV Guide*, *People*, *Parade* and other magazines featuring the famous lady of the house as well as her famous husband, who was currently residing elsewhere. It was the sort of display that you'd expect to find in someone's workplace, not home. I found it a bit odd. I would have opted for formal oil portraits of dead English gentry. Or possibly Jimi Hendrix posters.

"If you will follow me, please," Maritza said.

We followed her, Lulu's nails clacking on the oak floor as Maritza led us into an immense, sun-drenched living room where the walls were painted red, the curtains were white lace and the rugs were Persian and stylishly worn. There was a great deal of decorative molding and wainscoting. A chintz-covered sofa and two armchairs faced the marble fireplace. There was a glass coffee table piled with copies of magazines such as *Town & Country* and *Architectural Digest*. Fresh flowers were displayed in vases here, there, everywhere.

"Nice little place. How old is it?"

"It was built three years ago, I believe," Maritza replied.

The conservatory, which was off the living room, had a Steinway grand piano. The walnut-paneled library had two walls of bookcases lined with leather-bound tomes and an eighteenth-century mahogany writing table set before tall windows framed by purple velvet drapery. Matching leather sofas and a pair of armchairs faced a marble fireplace. In the billiard room I discovered yet another marble fireplace. They sure had a lot of fireplaces considering that it's seldom cold enough in Los Angeles to curl up in front of one. Hanging over this fireplace was a framed photograph of Patrick Van Pelt yukking it up with Burt Reynolds on the set of a 1970s action comedy that they'd made together. The billiard room, I gathered, was his room. There was an antique pool table with leather pockets. A ten-foot-long carved mahogany bar with an ornate mirror behind it and glass shelving that was stocked with leaded glass decanters filled with a generous assortment of what I imagined to be good liquor. Unless it was just colored water. You never know about these things when you're in L.A. It felt a whole lot like the bar of a proper gentlemen's club in there. Except, that is, for a low-slung sofa from the 1950s over against one wall that had arms and legs of tubular chrome and leopard-skin upholstery. It didn't go with the rest of the décor at all. Looked like something you once might have romped around on with Eartha Kitt.

Maritza noticed me studying it. "Is Senor Patrick's. The senora does not like it, but he insists."

I nodded, wondering why it hadn't departed the premises with Patrick. Or ended up in pieces out in the street. Possibly he had every intention of moving back in. Possibly Monette had every intention of letting him. There's just no telling with married couples. I happen to know more than I want to about these things.

The dining room was suitably huge and formal with stenciled walls, more lace curtains and more decorative molding. The dining table, which could seat two dozen healthy eaters, was covered with a spotless white linen tablecloth. For a centerpiece there was a pitcher of heavy cut glass filled with fresh-cut pale pink camellias. The kitchen was open, airy and decidedly more country casual than the rest of the place, or at least Monette Aintree's idea of country casual, which is to say that the floor was slabs of slate and the exposed beams in the cathedral ceiling were rough and hand-hewn. Old chestnut by the look of them. Assorted baskets and bunches of dried herbs were hanging from the beams in a manner that was way too artsy and self-conscious to come across as casual. The rustic table that anchored the kitchen was of scrubbed pine. The kitchen cupboards were of scrubbed pine as well. The counters were butcher block. The stove was a mammoth AGA. The stainless-steel refrigerator and freezer looked adequate enough to supply the needs of a modest-sized hotel.

French doors led from the kitchen to an outdoor dining area that was set under a grape arbor. We were making our way out there when a buzzer went off somewhere.

"Please, one moment. It is the dryer." Maritza darted through a doorway off the kitchen into the laundry room. A door next to the laundry room led to a bedroom. Hers, I imagined.

She returned quickly and outside we went. Beyond the patio dining area there were some lemon trees, very pretty, and the babbling brook that I'd crossed on the old stone bridge went babbling on by.

"Is that brook real or fake?"

"It has a generator and pump to move the water around. But it is real."

"Spoken like a true Los Angeleno, Maritza. You talk the talk."

She flashed a cautious smile at me. "Thank you. I pick up much from watching Regis and Kathie Lee."

"That's a scary thought."

"Also Kermit the Frog and the Cookie Monster."

"Okay, that was a much better answer."

A bluestone path lined with rose bushes led to the swimming pool, which was quite large and inviting. Teak lounge chairs with spotless white canvas cushions were lined alongside the pool in a manner that you would associate with a four-star resort hotel. On the other side of the pool was the pool house, which was built of old brick just like the main house.

As we approached it, I heard the rusty creak of a gate being opened. It was the narrow service gate that I'd noticed when I arrived, located adjacent to a fenced enclosure where the trash barrels were kept. A squatly built Latino, maybe thirty, came in toting a bag of peat moss over one shoulder. He wore a sweat-stained short-sleeved khaki shirt, jeans and work boots. In a leather holster on his belt he carried a pair of pruners.

"*Hola, bonita!*" he called out to Maritza, grinning broadly. "*Hola, Senor!* I am Hector. I make everything look nice here. And you are . . . ?"

"He is called Hoagy," Maritza informed him coldly. "Here to help the senora."

"Glad to know you, Hector." I shook his hand. He had a grip of iron. On his left wrist he wore a Rolex Submariner with a steel-linked band. Nice timepiece for a gardener. "The short one's Lulu."

"She won't leave messes in my flowerbeds, will she?"

"Wouldn't think of it."

He turned back to Maritza and said, "Tell me, how is it possible that you look even more beautiful today than yesterday?"

"The senora told you not to speak to me, remember?"

"But the heart wants what it wants," he protested, winking at me.

She turned her back on him and marched toward the pool house.

Hector let out a huge laugh, heading off with the bag of peat moss.

"Is Hector your man friend?" I asked when I caught up with her.

"No, he is not. He is a married man. And I do not trust him. You see that fancy watch he has on? He told me Senor Patrick gave it to him as a present."

"Why would Patrick give Hector a Rolex?"

"So Hector will keep his eye on the senora for him is why."

Maritza used a key to unlock the pool house. She opened the shutters to reveal a décor that was Early Nothing, which made for a welcome change after all of the high-octane fauxness of the main house. There was a seating area with a loveseat and an armchair covered in blue canvas. A kitchenette with a bar sink, mini fridge, microwave and coffeemaker. A tiny kitchen table. A manila envelope lay on the table.

She handed me the key. "For you."

"Do I need to keep my door locked?"

"The senora likes for her guests to know they have privacy." Maritza also handed me a business card that had numbers scrawled on it. "The security code," she explained. "So you may come in the gate without buzzing."

She'd already stowed Lulu's provisions in a kitchen cupboard. I opened the fresh jar of anchovies and gave Lulu one so she'd feel at home, then put the jar in the mini fridge, which was stocked with milk, orange juice, Perrier, Dos Equis and a bag of freshly ground French roast coffee beans.

I filled Lulu's water bowl and set it on the floor, then followed Maritza through a doorway into a small bedroom that was thoroughly crammed with a queen-sized brass bed, two nightstands, dresser and desk. She'd unpacked my suitcases and garment bags for me. My suits, jackets and slacks were hanging in the closet along with my silk target-dot dressing gown. My dove gray trilby and handmade straw Panama fedora awaited me on the top shelf, my shoes in a neat row on the floor down below. My shirts, ties, socks and underwear were neatly folded in the dresser drawers. The items from my toilet kit were laid out in the adjoining bathroom. Grandfather's straight-edge razor and strop, my Floris No. 89 talc, toothbrush and so on. The bathroom was considerably nicer than the one in my apartment, but you come to expect that in Los Angeles. If having a nice bathroom is important to you, then L.A. is the place for you, not New York.

"Thank you for doing all of this, Maritza. It really wasn't necessary."

"You have such nice things," she said as she kept moving around the bedroom, careful to make sure that I was never between her and the door. I wondered if someone had given her a reason to be so careful. I wondered who that someone might be. "And the senora wishes you should feel at home."

"In that case you'll have to do something about *that*," I said, meaning the cat-puke-colored plastic Macintosh word processor that was parked on the desk.

"You will need it for your work, no?"

"No, I will not. And I won't be able to sleep a wink with it staring at me. Please remove the printer and fax machine as well. All I need is my Olympia," I said, rescuing it from the closet floor where she'd stowed it. "Is that princess phone on the nightstand a private line or an extension?"

"It is private. Yours alone. Senorita Danielle and Senor Joey have their own lines also. Danielle is on the phone constantly. She has many friends."

"How about Joey?"

"He does not believe in friends. Spends all of the time alone. He wishes to be a writer someday."

"Poor kid. We'll see what we can do about that."

"I shall let you get settled." Maritza returned to the living room. "This came for you by messenger an hour ago." She handed me the manila envelope from the kitchen table, then bent down and patted Lulu on the head again before she left us.

It was addressed to me care of Monette Aintree at this address on Rockingham Avenue. The return address was the *Malibu High* production office on the Radford lot in Studio City. Inside the manila envelope was a letter-sized envelope with my name written across it with a black marking pen. I opened it and removed a business letter that had been typed on *Malibu High* stationery with an IBM Selectric:

Dear Hoagy—

> *Real anxious to talk at you as soon as possible, dude. If you have time please meet me this afternoon at our location shoot. We're at the Devonshire Grand Prix in Pacoima. Get off the San Diego Freeway at Devonshire and hang a right. It's about a mile from there. Just ask a production assistant to point you to my trailer. Does 3:00 work for you? I should be available around then. Be a dude and please don't say anything to Queenie about this, okay?*

> *See you soon,*
> *Patrick Van Pelt*

He'd signed it with that same black marking pen.

I glanced at my grandfather's gold Benrus. It was 1:45.

I took off my flight jacket and opened some windows. Sat down on the brass bed and used my calling card to check my messages at home in New York. I was well within my contractual rights to stick Monette with the cost of any and all long-distance calls that I made, but if I did that then she'd have a record of them. I didn't want her or anyone else to know with whom I was in contact. Just one of those little things I've picked up along the way as a ghost.

I had messages galore thanks to the *Times* story that morning. Calls from not only three different *Times* reporters but reporters from *Time*, *Newsweek*, *USA TODAY* and the *Washington Post* as well as segment producers from all three of the network evening news shows. Everyone wanted me to call them back, which I had no intention of doing. Boyd Samuels had left a message, too: "Just wanted to make sure you got out there okay, amigo. Call me if you need *anything*, understand? You are my top priority right now!"

Comforted. I felt incredibly comforted.

There was no message from Merilee in Budapest yet.

I changed from my khakis into a well-worn pair of jeans. Put my jacket back on, tucking Patrick's letter into my pocket. Then I let Lulu out and took off, locking the pool house door behind me.

BACK IN THE postwar boom years, the San Fernando Valley had been the pot of gold at the end of America's rainbow, a sun-kissed dreamland of orange groves and crystal-clear blue skies. As I crested at Mulholland on the San Diego Freeway, what was laid out before me on this December afternoon was a wasteland of tract houses and shopping centers as far as the eye could see, which wasn't very far due to the thick, peach-colored smog that hung low and heavy over the valley floor. I could taste it on my lips as I made my way out into the sun-baked flats of Van Nuys and Panorama City, the Indian Chief cruising steady and smooth at sixty-five. Lulu sat happily in her sidecar, enjoying the wind and the admiring looks of the drivers who sped by us. Many of them waved at us, as if we were day sailors at sea. I waved back. Kids made funny faces. I made funny faces back.

I got off at Devonshire, as instructed, and rode past a wider array of fast food franchises than I'd ever known existed before I spotted a huge sign for the Devonshire Grand Prix, which turned out to be a go-kart raceway. Or make that former go-kart raceway, because it was no longer in business. Boarded up. Padlocked. Gone. There was a vast trash-strewn parking lot where weeds grew in cracks in the pavement in a decidedly non-artful manner. But there was no *Malibu High* location shoot. No lights. No cameras. No action.

I pulled into the empty lot, shut off my engine and climbed off, pulling Patrick's letter from my pocket to give it another look. Yes, I had come to the right place. Yes, I'd arrived at the correct time. Patrick hadn't included his phone number on the letter. I decided I'd call Maritza to see if she had it. There was a payphone in front of the car wash next door. I started my way toward it on foot, Lulu ambling along next to me.

That was when a black Trans Am pulled into the raceway's parking lot. I came to a halt, thinking that Patrick had sent someone to deliver me to a different location. Last-minute changes happen all of the time. I waited there for the Trans Am's driver to pull up alongside of me and roll down his window. Except he didn't do that.

He sped up.

And headed right for me.

My first response was to freeze in disbelief. But then my paternal instincts took over. *Lulu.* Bassets are scent hounds that were bred to hunt rabbits. Lulu's sense of smell is second only to that of a bloodhound. Her first step is second only to that of a potted philodendron—which explains why I reached down, scooped her into my arms and dove all in one swift motion. I came down hard on my right shoulder and cheekbone just as the Trans Am sped past us, missing us by inches. My cheek burned instantly from smacking against the rough tar. So did my right knee. I lay there with Lulu squirming indignantly in my arms as the driver hit the brakes and turned around, gunning his engine. I couldn't get a good look at him. The Trans Am's windshield was tinted. And its California license plate was conveniently splattered with mud. I scrambled back up onto my feet with Lulu and readied myself as he started back at us, burning rubber . . . Only this time he swerved around us and kept right on going to the driveway, where he made a screeching left on two wheels, took off down Devonshire and was gone.

There was no mistake. I'd come to the right place. And I'd been given a message. Scram. And don't let the door hit you in the ass.

Message received.

"WHAT HAPPENED TO your cheek?" Monette Aintree wanted to know.

"Lulu and I had a small disagreement. She can get a bit fierce."

Elliot Schein let out a nervous chuckle, which was something I was about to discover he did a lot. Monette Aintree stared at me with chilly disapproval, which was something I was about to discover she did a lot.

It was nearly 6:00. Darkness had fallen. They were seated under the grape arbor at Monette's glass and wrought iron dining table, sipping white wine. Maritza was in the kitchen making dinner. It was peaceful out there on the patio. So quiet I could hear Elliot's breath wheeze in and out. Monette's pudgy producer/manager was not in the greatest cardiovascular health.

"I love that kooky motorcycle you rode in on," he said to me.

"It handles well. And style points for your use of the word *kooky*. Very Maynard G. Krebs."

"It so happens that I used to represent Bob Denver."

"Lucky you."

"Luck had nothing to do with it, my friend. I had to fight off three other managers with my bare hands. One of them needed a neck brace and a tetanus shot by the time I was done with her."

I'd been back at Aintree Manor for nearly an hour. When I returned I'd encountered four times as many photographers as when I'd left. Translation: The lady of the house was in the house. Her white Toyota Land Cruiser was parked out front near the crouching lions. I'd gone directly to my pool house, stripped and showered. My cheek stung a bit. My knee stung a lot. I dabbed at both wounds with a cotton ball soaked in hydrogen peroxide that I found in the fully stocked medicine chest. My right shoulder ached. I washed down a couple of aspirin with a cold Dos Equis from my mini fridge and gave Lulu her supper. She was hungry and super pumped. Danger is her middle name. Mine, as you may recall, is Stafford. Not that we'd been in serious danger. The driver of that Trans Am hadn't been sent to kill me. If he had I'd be dead right now.

My jeans had a three-inch tear in the right knee. I hung them from a hook on the back of the bathroom door. Stropped Grandfather's razor and shaved. Dressed in my navy blue blazer, vanilla gabardine slacks, a white shirt, blue-and-yellow polka-dot bow tie and my spectator balmorals. I pulled the brim of my trilby low over my right eye, but it didn't help. Monette had spotted that fresh scrape on my cheek right away when I'd found her there under the grape arbor with Elliot.

She stood up as I approached, as did Elliot. Monette was a tall woman. Not as tall as I am but nearly six feet tall in her low-heeled pumps, which made her a good eight inches taller than Elliot. She stuck out her hand, which was quite large, and gave me a firm handshake.

"What were you and Lulu disagreeing about?" she wanted to know.

"The usual. She likes Richard Gere."

"And you don't?"

"I think he has the emotional range of a napa cabbage."

Monette studied me curiously. "You're not exactly the sort of person I was expecting."

"Thank you."

"That wasn't intended as a compliment," she said, raising her chin at me. Monette Aintree was a regal presence, no question about that. She was self-possessed, strong-willed and accustomed to getting her way. She held herself very erect in her cream-colored silk blouse and charcoal pleated slacks. Her back was straight, shoulders squared. She had long, shiny blond hair and the same aristocratic features as Reggie, albeit a bit more pronounced, as in almost but not quite masculine. Like Reggie, she had blue eyes. Unlike Reggie, hers were an unusually pale shade of blue. And when they grabbed hold of mine they didn't waver or blink. They held on, assessing me, challenging me.

Elliot Schein, who was in his late fifties, resembled two extremely large green marshmallows as he stood there stuffed inside his matching lime green Nike warm-up jacket and pants. Elliot was freckle-faced and had a shock of red hair that was so toweringly frizzy that I couldn't decide whether it was a perm or a rug. I didn't want to think about it long enough to decide. He was a nervous little guy who blinked a lot and, as I mentioned, chuckled a lot. In his pudgy left hand he was clutching a mobile phone with a built-in antenna.

"We're drinking Sancerre," Monette informed me. "Will that do?"

"Always has."

"I'll get you a glass. I want to see how Maritza is doing with dinner."

As soon as she'd gone inside Elliot hurriedly called someone on his mobile phone. "Can you hear me . . . ? No . . . ?" He struggled to his feet and hurried over in the direction of the pool. "How about now . . . ? Good, did you take care of that little problem? Good, good. Righto, bye." He rang off and returned to the table, plopping himself down in his chair. "Small hiccough in today's taping," he explained. "Monette was interviewing a diet doctor who happened to use the phrase *pregnant pause* in passing—meaning nothing untoward—but the studio audience jumped on it and went 'Oooh . . .' on account of this Pat 'n' Kat bullshit. I just made sure our sound editor took it out. We do not need to be feeding the beast."

"No, you do not."

Elliot Schein was a showbiz legend. He'd been a small-time manager of stand-up comics in New York back in the early seventies when one of his clients had come up with the idea for *Coming Soon*, an ingenious low-budget film comedy that was nothing more than a dozen hilarious ten-minute previews for major Hollywood motion pictures that didn't actually exist. They were equal-opportunity spoofs of big-budget sci-fi spectaculars, low-budget slasher fests, hard-boiled cop films, romantic comedies, disaster epics, you name it—complete with soaring music, basso profundo narration and a campy B-list of has-been performers like Mr. T, Erik Estrada and Charo. Elliot scrounged up the financing for *Coming Soon* and served as its executive producer. It was such a huge box-office smash that it spawned two hit sequels and prompted Elliot to move to L.A. to launch his own production company. He was currently producing three successful prime-time sitcoms as well as Monette's syndicated daytime show, which he and Monette jointly owned. Elliot was a multimillionaire power player, yet he still came across like a small-timer. He also came across like someone who cared about Monette. There was concern on his face as he gazed at her through the kitchen window.

"I'm glad that you're here," he confided to me. "Monette really, really needs for this project to happen."

"Why is that?"

"Because she's in trouble. Her last two books lost so much money that her publisher just flat out rejected her newest proposal. She wanted to do a gardening book. Had a photographer all lined up and everything." He shot a worried glance at me. "You didn't know?"

"Somehow, Boyd Samuels neglected to tell me that part."

"I don't like that guy."

"No one likes that guy. And you?"

"What about me?"

"What aren't you telling me?"

Elliot swallowed uneasily. "Our show's bleeding stations from coast to coast. Twenty good-sized markets have bailed on us in the past two weeks. This mess with Patrick is killing her image. Who wants to take lifestyle advice from a woman whose husband just ditched her for a nineteen-year-old tramp? Monette is in real trouble, my friend. She needs a game changer in the worst way. This business with her father could be it, am I right?"

"It could be."

He folded his hands across his belly, studying me. "Everybody I talk to tells me you're the best. Top of the list. King of the hill. A-number-one."

"You're not going to break into 'New York, New York,' are you?"

"You'd better be."

"Or what?"

"Or I'm going to be very upset. And you do not want to be around me when I'm upset."

At my feet, Lulu let out a low, protective growl. Me, I had nothing to say. It never occurred to me that Elliot Schein had gotten to where he was by being a cuddly teddy bear. He'd felt it necessary to make absolutely sure I knew it. I'm accustomed to such threats by members of a celebrity's inner circle. They wash right over me.

Monette returned with my wineglass, poured me some Sancerre and said, "Dinner will be ready in about thirty minutes." She was sitting back down with us when Elliot's mobile phone rang.

"This'll just take a second," he said, answering the call. "Hello . . . ? Wait, I can't hear you." He got up and waddled off in the direction of the pool again. "Can you hear me . . . ?" And waddled still farther. "How about now . . . ?"

"All of the movers and shakers *must* talk on those silly things," she said drily. "They remind me of little boys playing with walkie-talkies."

"Hang on, I'll try the other side of the pool . . . !"

Monette gazed at me in that direct, unblinking way of hers. "How long are you prepared to stay?"

"As long as it takes. But if that letter's genuine, and I have every reason to believe it is, then your dad will reach out to you again very soon. You're absolutely sure that no one other than you, he and Reggie know that he used to call you Olive Oyl?"

"No one else knows about that."

"Not even Patrick?"

"No one," she repeated, her gaze hardening. "I understand that you're to be well compensated no matter what happens."

"Your plumber doesn't give away his time for free. Neither do I."

"No, of course not." She softened slightly. "I didn't mean for that to sound . . . I'm just not sure I understand what sort of a book will come out of this."

"You don't have to be sure. That's where I come in."

"Perhaps you can explain something to me . . ."

I sipped my wine, which was dry and quite good. "I can try."

Elliot returned to us, mobile phone in hand, and said, "That young comic of mine from Iowa? The one with the cowlick? He's having an anxiety attack over the network's notes on his pilot script. I gotta go hold his head while he vomits. Will you kids be okay without me?"

"We'll be fine, Elliot," she assured him.

He handed me his business card. "Holler if you need anything. There's nothing I won't do for this lady. I'll call you later, hon," he promised, wheezing as he padded off in the direction of the driveway.

I heard his car start, followed by the sound of tires on gravel. A moment later the front gate opened and there was a great deal of shouting from the paparazzi camped out on the street. Then he drove off and all was quiet again.

"I feel so bad for our neighbors," Monette reflected. "This is normally such a quiet neighborhood."

"What did you want me to explain to you?"

Monette reached for her wineglass, staring down into it. "I came home late last evening from Burbank. Our postproduction meeting went on until practically ten o'clock. I didn't feel like taking the freeway. I was tired and people drive too damned fast. So I came over the hill on Coldwater. It takes a bit longer but it's a more relaxing drive. Or it usually is . . ." She sipped her wine. "I was up near Mulholland by Coldwater Canyon Park, starting my way down the hill, when I realized that someone was *right* up on my tail. There are a lot of steep twists and turns up there, and very little traffic at that time of night. He flicked his brights on and started honking at me, forcing me to go faster than I wanted to. And then I swear he tried to shove me over the edge of a cliff. He would have, too, if I hadn't hit the brakes when I did."

"What happened when you hit the brakes?"

"He veered around me, stopped and started to back up—until I made him think twice about it."

"How did you do that?"

"I got out and pointed my loaded Beretta at him."

"I'm sorry, you did what?"

"This city isn't safe anymore. We have to protect ourselves. Carjackers, they tap your bumper on a deserted street and when you get out they steal your car out from under you. It's happened to three of my co-workers. But it's not going to happen to me. I own two Berettas. I keep one in my glove compartment and the other in my nightstand. Why are you looking at me that way? Surely you keep a gun in your apartment in New York City for your personal protection."

"No, I don't. Lulu's all the personal protection I need. So you pointed your Beretta at him and . . . ?"

"He floored it and took off."

"Did you call the police?"

Monette shook her head.

"Why not?"

"The media would have gotten wind of it. I do not need that kind of publicity right now."

"Are you sure he wasn't just a cowboy with too many beers in him?"

"Positive. He tried to run me off the road. I just don't understand why."

"What was he driving?"

"A Trans Am."

"Was it black?"

"Might have been. I'm not positive. Why do you . . . ?"

"Because I had an encounter with a black Trans Am myself this afternoon," I said, fingering my cheek. "A letter from Patrick was waiting here for me when I arrived. He wanted me to meet him at a location shoot in Pacoima. The letter was on *Malibu High* stationery, arrived by studio messenger. It looked authentic enough. But when I got there nobody was around—until a black Trans Am pulled into the parking lot and tried to take me out." Lulu snuffled indignantly at my feet. "Us out."

Monette's eyes had widened with alarm. "I won't blame you one bit if you catch the next flight home."

"Not to worry, I don't scare that easily. Any idea who was behind the wheel?"

"None," she said with a shake of her head. "What I do know is that Patrick wants me spooked. He loves it that those paparazzi are lurking outside my gate. Loves the idea of me feeling trapped and desperate. I have a great deal more money than he has, you see, and he thinks he can stampede me into a divorce settlement that isn't in my own best financial interest. He's wrong. I'll never cave just because of a few nasty headlines. Never." She stared across the table at me with her steely pale blue eyes. "I'm going through a painful time, Hoagy. It hurts, morning, noon and night. But I'll get through this. I have to. My children are counting on me."

I thought about what Elliot had just confided to me about Monette's faltering multimedia career, wondering yet again whether it was possible that this proud, ambitious woman had concocted the letter from Richard Aintree herself. "How did you feel when that letter from your father showed up?"

"May I be honest?"

"It would be nice."

"I was frightened. I'm being forced to confront some very deep feelings that I've kept safely bottled up for most of my adult life." She gave me her unblinking stare again. It was a bit disconcerting, though I was starting to get used to it. "How does Reggie feel about it? You've spoken with her, surely."

"I have. She told me she felt nothing at all."

"Did you believe her?"

"I did and I didn't. I don't know her very well anymore. In fact, I don't know her at all. May I speak frankly?"

"It would be nice," Monette answered tartly.

"I was always under the impression that you two detested each other."

"Not really." Monette brushed her hair back from her face with her fingers, which were long and slender. "I'll admit that I used to resent her a tiny bit, but mostly I admired her. Reggie was genuinely gifted, in the same way that Mom and Dad were. Me, I've had to work incredibly hard to carve out a place for myself. Reggie was a pretty little girl, too, and this world of ours loves pretty little girls. It doesn't love gigantic, strong-willed women. Mind you, Reggie's plenty strong-willed herself, but she comes across as frail and helpless. I come across as a great big bitch." Monette studied me over the rim of her wineglass. "I was always under the impression that you were the great love of her life."

"That was a long time ago. We were kids."

"You and Merilee Nash used to be married, didn't you?"

"Right up until she divorced me."

"Are you two still involved?"

"We'll always be involved."

"But not you and Reggie?"

"No, it's good and over between us."

"Why don't I believe you?"

"You're not alone. Merilee doesn't either. How about you? Are you still in love with Patrick?"

"I don't see how I was ever *in* love with him. He's a no-good lying prick. But he can also be very charming. He's incredibly good at that."

"There's a reason why they call them actors."

We fell into silence for a moment. It was so quiet there on her patio in the early evening darkness that I could barely hear the chirping of the paparazzi out on Rockingham.

"Reggie and I got along fine when we were girls," Monette recalled. "We looked out for each other. We had to, because Mom and Dad weren't Mom and Dad anymore. They'd become different people. *Stoned* people. Would you like to hear something crazy? I'm now the same age that Mom was when she threw herself off that roof. My own children are nearly as old as Reggie and I were when it happened. Being a mother, I still can't accept what she did to us. I can't imagine abandoning my children that way. I'd do anything for my children, Hoagy. Anything except leave them."

"She had a lot of LSD in her system. That drug can do nasty things to people."

"You've taken it?" She studied me curiously. "What is it like?"

"Sometimes it's fabulous. Other times you get trapped inside of a loop and you can't get out."

"Do you mean like a panic attack?"

"Yes."

She nodded to herself. "I know what those are like. My life has been all about one frightening experience after another. And, I hope, imparting what I've learned so that other women will know they're not alone. I should never have written *Father Didn't Know Best*. But I was a desperate mess and my therapist—a complete fraud who ended up losing his license to practice—told me that I showed every sign of being someone who was repressing memories of sexual abuse. He urged me to embrace whatever fragments of memories, dreams or fantasies popped into my head. To stop fighting and *believe* them. And so I did. I kept a journal, also at his urging. The rest is history. Reggie never forgave me. But when I published *Father Didn't Know Best* I genuinely believed that Dad had sexually abused me. And then, after working with a new therapist who *wasn't* a quack, I genuinely believed that he hadn't. So I wrote about that, too, which made Reggie even more furious. She called me a 'soulless parasite.' She never understood that I was simply trying to figure out who I was, and that I had a lot to learn. I still do. I'm always discovering new things about myself. It just so happens that I do my discovering in public. And now . . ." Monette let out a long sigh. "Thanks to Patrick and his pregnant teenager, I'm a national joke. Johnny Carson makes fun of me every night in his monologue. Not Patrick, not Kat, *me*. Why am *I* the one who's being ridiculed?"

"Because you're rich, famous and beautiful. You're Monette Aintree. Tell me, how are Joey and Danielle holding up?"

Monette's eyes flickered. "Danielle's an absolute dynamo. A straight-A student, gifted pianist and an exceptional middle-distance runner. Last month she organized a food drive for a homeless shelter in Venice. She's a special girl."

"But . . . ?"

"She's so determined that she scares me sometimes. Danielle has a Rolodex, can you imagine? What fifteen-year-old girl keeps a Rolodex? Whenever she meets someone at school who has a parent in the movie business she writes down their contact information. She's planning to intern in Elliot's office next summer. Always planning. I can't remember the last time I saw her smile."

"And how about Joey?"

"Joey's exceptionally bright, but he's flunking half of his classes and I practically need a crowbar to pry him out of his room. All he ever wants to do is sit in there with his nose buried in a book listening to that depressing music group, Nirvana. He's turning seventeen on Saturday. When I asked him what he wanted to do for his birthday, he said he didn't care. What boy who is Joey's age doesn't care about his birthday?"

"Is he seeing someone?"

"If by that you mean is he seeing a therapist, the answer is yes. A woman in Beverly Hills who came highly recommended. But he's been very resistant. Hates going." She tilted her head at me slightly. "I'm glad that you're here, actually. It'll be good for him to spend some time around a mature man."

At my feet, Lulu started coughing.

Monette frowned. "Why is she doing that?"

"Because she doesn't know how to laugh. You may not be by the time this is over."

"I may not be what?"

"Glad that I'm here."

"I'll take my chances. You see, Hoagy, I already know something about you that you don't." That unblinking gaze of Monette's grabbed hold of mine. In an ice-cold voice she said, "You're not going to disappoint me. You wouldn't dare."

THE FOUR OF us ate at the big scrubbed-pine kitchen table under the exposed, hand-hewn chestnut beams with those bunches of herbs and dried flowers suspended artfully over our heads. Dinner was a Provençal-style beef stew served over buttered noodles with asparagus and a salad of romaine lettuce and red onion. We passed around the brightly colored serving dishes that Maritza had set on the table before she made herself scarce. Monette stayed with the Sancerre. I switched to the Côtes du Rhône that was offered. Joey and Danielle drank mineral water.

"Those are impressive beams," I observed, gazing up at them. "Where did they come from?"

"A carriage barn in North Stonington, Connecticut," Monette informed me. "My builder keeps an eye out for such things. Most of the paneling and molding came over from Cornwall, England. And those aged cobbles out in the driveway are from Philadelphia."

"How about the weeds in between them?"

Joey snorted quietly, which constituted the first reaction I'd gotten from him since he'd come downstairs from his room and refused to shake my hand.

"I don't do that," he'd said scornfully.

"Because you're making a statement or because you're afraid of germs?"

"I don't believe in societal conventions."

"Good. We'll get along fine."

"Dream on," he'd said, before retreating into silence.

Mostly, he kept his eyes fastened on his plate. After Maritza left the kitchen, that is. He couldn't take his eyes off the pretty young housekeeper when she was moving around the table depositing the serving dishes. Given that he was about to turn seventeen I ranked his fixation as somewhere in between a schoolboy crush and raging hormonal lust. Maritza did nothing to encourage his stares. But she had to know. Women always do.

Joey was a gangly, splayfooted kid with a melon-sized Adam's apple, a generous assortment of pimples and a wispy see-through moustache. Pale by L.A. standards. He wore his stringy blond hair down to his shoulders and didn't appear to wash it very often, which was a Kurt Cobain thing. So was his stoop-shouldered posture, rumpled flannel shirt, fraying T-shirt and baggy old jeans. He also wore a studied air of tragic disillusionment mixed with burning artistic purity and anger. Whole lot of anger.

Unlike Joey, Danielle was extremely poised and polite, not to mention pretty in a tall, leggy, sun-kissed California-girl way, complete with long, shiny blond hair and big blue eyes. Grunge was absolutely not, repeat not, Danielle's thing. She was done up all Ralph Lauren preppy casual in her blue oxford-cloth button-down, argyle vest, stonewashed jeans and suede loafers. Her short, upturned top lip gave her young face a slightly rabbity look. But it was the determined set of her jaw that I really noticed. That and her analytical gaze as she studied me from across the table. Monette hadn't been exaggerating. There was a complete absence of girlish playfulness in those fifteen-year-old eyes.

"Joey wants to be a writer someday," Monette said to me as we ate. "Mr. Hoag is a famous novelist, Joey."

"If you're so famous how come I haven't heard of you?" he demanded.

"Actually, that says more about you than it does me."

"Oh, yeah? Like what?"

"That you aren't as well read as you think you are."

"Wow, what a witty put-down. Not."

"Mind your manners, Joey," Monette scolded him.

"Manners are for assholes."

"Have you decided what you'd like to do for your birthday?" she asked him, forcing a bit of good cheer into her voice.

He heaved a suffering sigh. "Mom, how many times do I have to tell you? Birthdays are an outmoded ritual."

"We could have a pool party. You could invite some people."

"Like who?"

"Your dad, if you'd like."

"You'd let him come?"

"I would if it's important to you."

"Dad can go to hell. I don't ever want to see him again."

"Well, what *are* you going to do?" Monette pressed him. "Just sit in your room all day reading?"

"Sounds good to me," he said, shoveling stew into his mouth. His table manners tended toward slurpy.

"Who are you reading these days?" I asked him. "Wait, wait, don't tell me. You've transitioned out of your Asimov-Clarke-Bradbury phase, made a brief stopover at Vonnegut, whom you consider overrated, and now you've arrived at . . . Ayn Rand."

He blinked at me in surprise. "How'd you know that? I just finished *Atlas Shrugged*."

"What did you think of it?"

"Simplistic, whiny crap. I suppose *you're* going to tell me it's brilliant."

"Hardly. You're talking to the man who labeled her work 'intellectual porn for bed wetters' in the *New York Review of Books*. I still get hate mail from Alan Greenspan. That man never forgets. Have you read Kerouac yet?"

"Jack Kerouac?"

"No, Steve Kerouac. You need to read *On the Road*. How about *Stop-Time* by Frank Conroy?" On his blank stare I said, "He's someone who'll speak to you. So is Dorothy Parker. You need Mrs. Parker in your life, same as you need Frank Zappa and Warren Zevon. And you need to read poetry. Have you read your aunt Reggie?"

He shook his head.

"How about your grandmother?"

Again he shook his head.

"Your grandmother was a great American poet. And Reggie's a stone-cold genius. How can you not be reading them? What about your grandfather's novel? Please tell me you've read *Not Far from Here*."

"Well, yeah, in English class," he said defensively. "Everyone does."

"And . . . ?"

Joey shrugged his shoulders. "It was okay."

"Try again. Something a bit less lame this time."

"I thought it was corny crap."

"I thought it was sweet," Danielle said. "The ending made me cry."

"That's because you're a sap," he said to her. "You still get weepy over Shirley Temple movies."

"I'd rather watch Shirley Temple than those stupid monster movies of yours," she shot back. "How many times have you seen *The Beast from 20,000 Fathoms*?"

Joey ignored her, considering me from across the big table. "So what's your deal? Are you banging our mom?"

Monette let out a horrified gasp. "Joey, that was totally inappropriate! I've told you why Mr. Hoag is here."

"How do you feel about that?" I asked the two of them. "The possibility of your grandfather coming into your lives after all of these years. Are you looking forward to meeting him?"

"Not really," Joey said. "Why would I be?"

"Well, I am," Danielle said. "He's a really famous literary figure. Almost mythical. And he's my grandfather. So, yeah, I'd love to meet him."

"You're just hoping he'll write you a letter of recommendation to Yale," Joey jeered at her.

"What's so wrong with that? He used to be a professor there. A recommendation from him would mean a lot." To me Danielle said, "I intend to go to Yale when I graduate from Brentwood. It's vital that I get into Yale. Sometimes I lie awake at night wondering what will happen to me if I don't."

"You'll go somewhere else and you'll be fine."

She shook her blond head at me. "No, I won't. I have to get in."

I studied her more closely. This was one tightly wound girl. "Your mom said you're a middle-distance runner."

"Last spring Danielle ran the second-fastest four-hundred-meter time of any high school girl in the entire city," Monette said proudly. "She's running cross-country this semester. Wins every meet by hundreds of yards. The second-place finisher is so far behind you can't even see her."

"That's very impressive, Danielle. But all of that slogging over hill and dale can take the turbocharge out of your kick when you switch back to four hundred meters. Keep doing some sprints so your legs remember how to."

Danielle eyed me curiously. "You ran track in high school?"

"And college. I was the first alternate on our mile relay team."

"What does 'first alternate' mean?" Joey asked.

"It means I was our fifth-best quarter-miler."

"That's not saying much," he scoffed.

"You're right, it's not. But it wasn't my main event. I was a spear chucker. Third best in the Ivy League."

"Really?" Danielle's eyes widened with newfound interest. "Where did you go to school?"

"Cambridge."

"You went to *Harvard*? No way! Harvard's a huge part of my career plan."

"You have a career plan?"

"Totally. Yale for undergrad followed by an MBA from Harvard. After that I'll go to work for a film studio to gain development and production experience, and then I'll go out on my own. I intend to be producing my own movies by the time I'm thirty."

I set my fork down, dabbing at my mouth with my napkin. "Forgive me, but that doesn't sound like a career plan. It sounds more like a sickness."

Danielle blinked at me in shock. "Why would you say that?"

"These movies that you plan to produce—what are they going to be about?"

"How should I know?"

"That's my point. You don't know. You've left that part out."

"What part?"

"The part where you figure out what really matters in life. You need to hang out at a sidewalk café in Paris drinking wine and thinking deep thoughts for at least a year. You need to see the cloud formations over the Isle of Skye in the Scottish Hebrides. You need to stroll arm in arm in Venice at midnight in the rain with some guy who you're crazy in love with."

Danielle wrinkled her nose at me. "You're weird."

"Thank you. That's the nicest thing anyone's said to me in weeks."

"Actually, I'm starting to tolerate him," Joey said grudgingly. "Mr. Hoag, would you *like* to bang our mom?"

THE LIGHTS WERE on in the pool house. I didn't recall leaving them on. When I unlocked the door I discovered that Maritza had let herself in to tidy up. She'd washed out the fragrant remains in Lulu's mackerel bowl. Brought me fresh, thirsty towels. Also absconded with my torn jeans, which were no longer hanging from the hook on the bathroom door. I hadn't expected her to do any of this. Wondered why she had. Was she spoiling me or spying on me?

I sat down on the edge of the bed and called my answering machine in New York. Nine more reporters had called me. So had Boyd Samuels—just to make absolutely, positively sure I was settling in okay.

There was no message from Merilee in Budapest.

I took two more aspirin for the dull ache in my shoulder, got undressed and climbed into bed with Lulu and John O'Hara.

That was when my phone rang.

"Stewart Hoag? This here's Patrick Van Pelt," said the voice on the other end of the line. Not that he needed to identify himself. His folksy, regular-guy voice was instantly recognizable. "Did I get you at a bad time?"

"Not at all. And I got your message this afternoon."

"What message?"

"The one that you gave me at the Devonshire Grand Prix."

"Don't know what you're talking about, dude."

"You didn't send me a letter asking me to meet you there?"

"Nope. Sure didn't."

"It was on *Malibu High* stationery. A studio messenger delivered it."

"I don't know anything about it. Wasn't me who sent it."

"Well, then who was it?"

"How the fuck would I know?"

"Do you know anyone who drives a black Trans Am?"

He fell silent for a moment before he said, "It's a popular ride."

"Does that mean yes or no?"

"I was wondering if you and me could get together. I figure we should meet each other."

"Really, why is that?"

"You're working on a project with Queenie. You're sleeping under my roof. I have an interest in what goes on there."

"Personal or financial?"

"Exactly. We should talk about that. Dudes talk to each other. I'm a dude, you're a dude. You *are* a dude, aren't you?"

"Was the last time I checked. Fine, let's get together. How about someplace other than the Devonshire Grand Prix this time?"

"That wasn't me. I just told you."

"That's right, you did."

"We're shooting interiors tomorrow morning. Come to the

Radford lot at, say, ten o'clock. Just give your name to the guard at the front gate. He'll know where I am. Later, dude." And with that he hung up.

I turned out the nightstand light and dozed right off. I didn't stay asleep for long though. Shortly before midnight Lulu woke me by climbing up onto my head, trembling with fear. It was the coyotes howling. I'd forgotten about the coyotes and how they howled up in the hills in the night. I stroked her and assured her that I would never, ever let them hurt her. She curled up on my hip and promptly went to sleep, snoring contentedly. Me, I lay awake for a good long while, listening to the coyotes and wondering just exactly what I was getting myself into.

CHAPTER FOUR

The sound of that creaky side gate swinging open and shut woke me just before 6:30. It was the pool man, whistling tunelessly as he used a net to rid the pool of fallen leaves and dead insects. He looked like a young Tab Hunter. It has been my experience that all pool men in L.A. look like a young Tab Hunter. As I watched him through my bedroom window, feeling jet-lagged and bleary-eyed, I hated him on sight.

The morning air felt downright balmy. I found my swimming trunks and put them on. Made a pot of strong coffee in the coffee-maker and put down fresh mackerel for Lulu, who always wakes up hungry and does not know from jet lag. I checked my phone machine in New York while I drank my coffee.

There was no message from Merilee in Budapest.

By then Tab Hunter had left and Hector had arrived to prune the rose bushes that lined the bluestone path from the pool to the patio outside the kitchen.

"*Hola, amigo!*" he called to me cheerfully as I made my way out to the pool, blinking in the bright sunlight.

"*Hola, Hector.*"

"It is a beautiful day, is it not?"

"If you say so."

I dove in, the shock of the water jolting me a bit more awake. I swam. The ache in my shoulder had subsided in the night, and it felt good to stretch out my muscles in a nice, steady crawl. Lulu ran alongside of me as I swam, barking her head off. She does that whenever I swim laps. She's afraid that I'll drown and she won't be able to rescue me. She's the only dog I've ever known who can't swim. Sinks right to the bottom like a stone, *glug-glug-glug.*

As I swam, Maritza went bustling from the kitchen out to the pool house. Hector said something to her as she walked by him. Maritza ignored him. She wore a salmon-colored dental hygienist's uniform today and had my purloined jeans folded over her arm. She deposited them inside the pool house, then started back toward the main house. Again, Hector spoke to her. Again, she ignored him. Or tried to. This time he grabbed her by the arm and held her so she'd listen to him. Maritza shook her arm loose and spoke to him sharply before she marched off. Hector let out a big laugh before he returned to his pruning.

I swam until Maritza returned a half-hour or so later with a loaded breakfast tray.

"Good morning, Senor Hoagy," she called out to me, setting it down on an end table next to a lounge chair. "For you."

I climbed out of the pool and toweled off. "You didn't have to make me breakfast, Maritza."

"It is not a problem."

"You didn't have to resort to thievery either."

She frowned at me. "Excuse me?"

"You stole my jeans last night. Admit it."

"They had a hole. I patched it."

"Thank you very much. I appreciate it."

She'd made me an omelet stuffed with sliced avocado and melted cheese. There was bacon, wheat toast, a wedge of cantaloupe, orange juice and a carafe of coffee. Also a bowl of something that I didn't recognize.

"That is for Lulu. A cold shrimp soup with crab meat that I made last weekend. Is popular in my country. I thought she might like it. You think?"

"Oh, I think," I said as Lulu pawed eagerly at the tray. I set the bowl down on the pavement for her and she dove in nose first. "You're making yourself a huge fan, Maritza."

"Is nice to have her around," Maritza said, beaming at her.

"If you have any trouble with bunny rabbits on the property just let me know. She's a good little worker." I sampled my omelet, which was excellent. "Have Joey and Danielle left for school?"

"Yes. The senora is still here, though she is *very* upset. They spoke of her show's poor ratings on *Regis and Kathie Lee* this morning. They spoke of you also."

"What did they say about me?"

"That you are here to save her career. Are you?"

"God, I hope not." I noticed Hector watching us as he continued to prune the rose bushes. "Are you okay with him?"

"He is no worry," she assured me, starting back toward the house as Monette came striding out in a taupe-colored Armani pantsuit, her long blond hair gleaming in the morning sunlight.

"I'm off to an early morning production meeting," she informed me when she was poolside, her manner quite chilly. "I have an extremely full day ahead of me, though I am always reachable by phone should another letter from Dad arrive."

"Patrick has asked me to come see him at the studio this morning."

"What for?" she demanded.

"I'm a dude. He's a dude. We're both dudes."

"What is *that* supposed to mean?"

"I was hoping you'd know. You're the one who's married to him."

"He must want something. He always does." She treated me to her steely, unblinking gaze. "I don't want you talking to Patrick, Hoagy. You are not to speak to him. Is that clear?"

"Don't tell me whom I can and cannot speak to, Monette. I'll just pack up and go home. Is *that* clear?"

Her eyes puddled with tears instantly. She was extremely fragile underneath her tough exterior. "Of c-course . . . ," she stammered. "You're right, absolutely. Do . . . what you think is best."

"Thank you, I will. By the way, don't watch *Regis and Kathie Lee* anymore. In fact, don't watch TV at all. Not until this is over."

"This will never be over," Monette said miserably.

She hurried off toward her Land Cruiser. I heard her start it up. Heard the paparazzi roar as she drove out the gate past them. Then it was quiet again, aside from the soft *snip-snip-snip* of Hector's pruners.

I went back to the pool house to shower and shave. Maritza had expertly repaired my jeans with a piece of scrap denim that was almost exactly the same color. I wore them with a white shirt and crimson knit tie. Grabbed my flight jacket, opened the door to leave and discovered that Hector was blocking my way.

The squatly built gardener came up only to my chin, but he was as wide as the doorway. He was smiling at me. But I sensed menace behind that big smile of his.

So did Lulu. She growled at him as he stood there.

"That's a nice girl, Maritza," he said, paying Lulu no mind.

"Is she? I wouldn't know." I glanced at that Rolex Submariner on his thick, muscled wrist. "Handsome watch you've got there, Hector."

"Is a Rolex. The very best." He gazed down at it proudly, then back up at me. "Maritza is spoken for. She is private property."

"Your private property?"

Hector didn't say. Just smiled at me some more.

He smiled a lot, Hector did.

TODAY, I GOT off the San Diego Freeway at Ventura Boulevard and steered the Indian Chief toward Studio City. When I reached Coldwater I cruised past the Sportsmen's Lodge, that fading neo-kitschy relic from the Rat Pack era, and Jerry's Deli, where I once saw Gene Simmons of KISS eating lox and bagels. And, no, he was not in costume at the time. After a few blocks I passed Du-par's coffee shop, which is noted for its buttermilk pancakes and its pies. Just past there I hung a left at Radford Avenue and turned in at the Radford lot, officially known as CBS Studio Center, which had been the headquarters of the MTM empire the last time I'd been in town but no longer was because MTM no longer was. But it was still a happening place. *Seinfeld*, that sitcom starring an eerily bland New York stand-up comic named Jerry Seinfeld, was being shot there, according to a billboard on one of the giant sound stages, as was the hit series *Malibu High*, starring America's favorite TV hunk, Patrick Van Pelt, and sizzling hot Kat Zachry.

The beefy guard at the entrance kiosk gave the Roadmaster an appreciative look while I told him I was there to see Mr. Van Pelt. He checked his clipboard. "He's on stage seventeen, Mr. Hoag. Here's your pass. Make sure you park in a designated visitor parking space. Otherwise, you'll get towed."

He wasn't exaggerating. On studio lots, people take their parking spaces as seriously as they do their position in the credits.

After I'd found a visitor parking space Lulu and I moseyed past a cluster of office buildings toward the cavernous sound stages. I found an unlocked door to stage seventeen and fought my way through a pile up of cameras, lights and cables before I arrived at a horseshoe-shaped cluster of standing sets for *Malibu*

High. There was a high school corridor complete with lockers and assorted banners. There was a classroom, a principal's office and an office that belonged to Patrick's character, Chip Hinton, the school's rugged yet sensitive guidance counselor. Also sets for the kitchen, living room and bedroom of Chip's Malibu condo. Standing sets are incredibly fake-looking when you see them in person. Partly that's because you can see over and around them and are acutely aware that the doorways lead nowhere and there's absolutely nothing outside the windows. But it's also because the eye of the camera makes everything seem more real. I don't know why that's so. I don't know if anyone knows why. It's magic.

They'd been shooting a scene in the condo's kitchen. The crew was on a break. Patrick stood at the kitchen counter in a Hawaiian shirt and shorts, going over the script with the director, a weary-looking old-timer who wore a pair of reading glasses on a chain around his neck.

"Why would I say that?" Patrick demanded, stabbing at the script with his finger. "I just told her to stay away from the guy. Why would I suddenly tell her it's okay?"

"You're conflicted," the director responded.

"The fuck I am. The kids are conflicted. I never am. I'm the moral compass, understand?"

"I do understand. So do the writers. A lot of thought went into this."

"A lot of bullshit went into it."

Lulu, who has always believed she is destined to be the next Lassie or Rin Tin Tin, decided that now would be a good time to start barking at the director. I told her to stop. She ignored me.

"Who let that dog in here?" he demanded.

"She's with me," I said.

"Okay, who let *you* in here?"

"You must be Stewart Hoag." Patrick came toward me with his hand out and a huge gleaming smile on his face. "Glad to meet you, Stewart."

"Make it Hoagy."

"I am loving your sidekick. What's his name?"

"Her name is Lulu."

He bent down and gave her a pat before he turned back to the director and said, "Are those idiots going to rewrite it or do I have to do it myself?"

The director sighed defeatedly. "I'll talk to them."

"You do that. Come on, Hoagy, let's hang in my trailer." Patrick started for the stage door. I followed him. "These episode directors are strictly hacks for hire," he informed me in an extremely loud, clear voice. "And our writers suck. I end up having to write most of my own dialogue, and I'll let you in on a little secret, dude. I don't know how to write dialogue."

We headed outside into the bright sunshine and started walking. Patrick Van Pelt was an inch or two taller than me, six foot four I'd guess, a tanned, toned, forty-five-year-old slab of prime beef with shaggy blond hair that flopped down over his eyebrows, an impossibly square jaw, impossibly high cheekbones and eyes that were Technicolor blue. He'd been an All-American golden boy back in the days when he was catching touchdown passes in South Bend, and he still carried himself with the self-assured ease of one. The only thing a bit jarring about his appearance was that his face was fully made-up for the cameras—foundation, powder, eyeliner, lipstick, the works. You don't think anything of it when you see a woman in full makeup. But a man looks way too much like an embalmed corpse at an open-casket wake, surrounded by the smell of flowers and sad-faced mourners murmuring, "Doesn't he look lifelike?"

Patrick's trailer wasn't my idea of a trailer. More like a rock star's tour bus. There were maybe two dozen clustered together in a parking area like a herd of bison. He unlocked his and went up two steps to go inside. Lulu and I followed him. It had all of the air-conditioned comforts of home—a seating area with sofas and a TV, a kitchen, a built-in dining banquette. An open doorway led to a bedroom and bath. Lulu checked the whole place out, nose to the rug.

"Have a seat." Patrick gestured to the banquette, which was heaped with scripts, production schedules and videocassettes. "You hungry? Want me to order you something from Jerry's?"

"I'm all set, thanks."

"There's drinks in the fridge if you're thirsty. Oh, hey, I bet your little pal is." Patrick dug a cereal bowl out of the kitchen cupboard, filled it with water and set it down for Lulu.

She had herself a good, long drink, then curled up under the banquette at my feet while Patrick took off his Hawaiian shirt and hung it on a wardrobe rack. He was in amazing shape for a guy in his forties, I noted resentfully. Still possessed the sculpted physique of a premier athlete. Arms, shoulders and pecs that rippled with muscle. A narrow waist, washboard abs. Not so much as a hint of a gut or love handles. He was deeply tanned. Also completely hairless. The American television audience doesn't like hairy-chested men.

"How many hours a day do you work out?" I asked him.

"Not as many as I should. How about a brewski?"

"It's a little early for me."

"Really? It's never too early for me." He dug a Heineken out of the fridge, opened it and took a grateful gulp. Then he sat across from me shirtless, studying me. "Dude, what happened to your cheek?"

"I got your message, like I told you last night."

"And I told you I didn't send you any message."

I pulled the note from my jacket pocket, unfolded it and set it before him.

He examined it carefully. "Son of a bitch," he said, shaking his big, blond head. "Sure looks like it came from me. I'm right there with you, brother. But I didn't write this, I swear. That's not my signature. Here . . ." He grabbed a pen, scrawled his signature below the one on the note and turned it around for me to look at. "See?"

I saw. The two signatures looked nothing alike. "Who has access to *Malibu High* stationery?"

"Hell, anybody. Tons of people go in and out of the production office every day."

There was a knock on the trailer door. "Yo, Pats!" a man's voice called out.

"Come on in, Lou!"

The door opened and in came one of the largest humans I'd ever seen. So large he had to come in the narrow door sideways. He was at least six foot five and weighed at least three hundred pounds, and absolutely all of it was muscle. Outrageously huge body-builder muscle. The man's biceps were bigger than his head, I swear. He resembled the Incredible Hulk, except flesh colored. He was dressed for maximum display in a tank top, gym shorts and Nikes. And he was sporting the shaved head and goatee look that I'd been seeing more and more lately. In his mouth was a Tootsie Pop, a grape-flavored one by the purplish look of it. In his left hand he clutched a blue nylon zippered gym bag.

"This is my man Lou," Patrick said to me as the big guy loomed there, eyeing me suspiciously. "We were kids together back in the old neighborhood in Akron. Lou played defensive tackle for Troy State. Had a tryout with the Packers. Lou, say hey to Hoagy. He's the dude they flew in from New York to help Queenie write that book."

Lou gave me a soul brother handshake, my own hand disappearing inside his. "Real glad to know ya, bro," he said in a voice that was a sandpapery growl. "Hey, is that your pooch?"

"Nope. Never saw her before."

"Are you pulling my leg?"

"Her name's Lulu."

He knelt and patted her. "Hey, Lulu," he said gently. "Hey, girl." A lot of big guys are marshmallows when it comes to dogs. Somebody ought to write a book about it. Not me, but somebody.

"Did the plumber stop by to fix the shower?" Patrick asked him.

Lou stood back up, nodding his shaved head. "It needed a new mixing valve, Pats. After he replaced it I dropped the Corvette off with Lenny at the garage on Saticoy."

"You tell him the idle was uneven?"

"I did," Lou said, sucking on his Tootsie Pop. "He'll take care of it personally. Should be ready by the end of the afternoon. I can go pick it up."

Patrick glared at him. "Why the *fuck* would you want to do that?" he demanded angrily. I'm not talking mild peevishness here. I'm talking sudden, off-the-charts rage, as in Patrick's eyeballs were bulging out of his face, which had turned the color purple.

Lou gulped at him fearfully. "Because he asked me to."

"Do you work for fucking Lenny? No! You work for *me*!"

"And . . . you don't want me to pick it up?"

Patrick grabbed a videocassette from the pile in front of him and hurled it at Lou. It bounced off the big man's boulder of a bicep and fell to the floor. "Tell fucking Lenny to *deliver* it!"

"Right, Pats," Lou said obediently. "Sure thing."

"You're the man, Lou." Patrick drank down the last of his beer, smiling at him warmly. He seemed totally at peace again. His eyes had receded back into their sockets. The color of his face had gone from eggplant back to tan. "You bring me anything?"

Lou hesitated, shooting an uneasy glance my way.

"Hoagy's cool," Patrick assured him. "You're cool, aren't you, Hoagy? Used to be an Olympic-class wild man yourself, I hear."

"I don't blab, if that's what you mean."

"There, you see, Lou?"

Satisfied, Lou unzipped his blue nylon bag, removed two unmarked prescription pill bottles and handed them over.

Patrick smiled at him again. "I love you, brother. Grab me another brewski on your way out, will you?"

Lou fetched a Heineken from the fridge, opened it and set it in front of Patrick. Then he adjusted his Tootsie Pop in his mouth and squeezed his way out the door, closing it behind him.

"Lou kicks my ass in the gym for two hours every morning before I get here. And he deals *the* best coke on the planet." Patrick opened one of the pill bottles and shook a generous heap of cocaine out onto that letter I'd received by messenger yesterday. He found a business card among the clutter of papers in front of him and used it to make four neat, straight lines of coke. Fished a ten-dollar bill from the pocket of his shorts, rolled it tight and snorted up two of the lines. "Ahh, that's mo' better . . ." He sighed gratefully. "Care for some?"

Lulu let out a low growl. She'd been through my dark period with me and had no desire to go back.

"I'm good, thanks."

"Suit yourself." He snorted up the two remaining lines, then opened the other pill bottle and shook out two brown capsules and a yellow one. "Lou's got me on herbal and mineral supplements," he explained, swallowing them with a swig of beer. "Flaxseed oil, magnesium and I forget what else."

Me, I had a pretty good idea what else. Judging by Patrick's sculpted, flab-free physique and sudden transformation into a turbocharged rage monkey, I figured that his fitness regimen included a designer cocktail of anabolic steroids and speed. Lou had to be taking steroids himself. Nobody became as humongous as he was just by lifting. I wondered if Lou was inclined to 'roid rage, too. I sure wouldn't want to be around him if he was. As for the coke, Patrick probably thought it softened the speed's jagged edge. It didn't. It doesn't. But once you get heavy into coke, concepts such as *logical* and *real* go right out the window.

He stashed the pill bottles in a kitchen drawer, swiping at his nostrils with a paper napkin. "I'm stuck here fifteen hours a day. I don't know what I'd do without Lou, especially now that I'm on my own. I've taken a little place up on Marmont while this mess with Queenie sorts itself out. Lou's bunking in my spare bedroom. She thinks he's an uncouth boor. I said to her, 'Queenie, Lou and me grew up on the same street, played on the same Little League teams and fucked the same girls. When you look at Lou, you're looking at me.' You know what she said? She said, 'I know this, Patrick. Please don't remind me.'" He let out a laugh. "Kat invited me to move in with her in Laurel Canyon but I figured no way. The tabloid bloodsuckers would be camped outside her bungalow day and night. And her personal hygiene leaves a lot to be desired. She leaves dirty clothes all over the floor, dishes in the sink. I like things nice and tidy." He drank down more beer. "Besides, it's a package deal with her. Wherever she goes her loser of a big brother, Kyle, goes. She gives Kyle money to live on, tries to find him jobs to do. I can respect that. Family's important. I just can't stand the dude, that's all. They're from Atascadero, a nothing little town just outside of Paso Robles. Kyle did county time up there for selling weed and ludes. Stole some hunting rifles from a guy's house, too. One more fall and he'll end up in San Quentin."

"I'm surprised I haven't seen his mug shot plastered all over the tabloids. They just love it when hot young stars like Kat have ex-cons for relatives."

"The network's publicists have been doing a super job of keeping it under wraps. Plus Kyle's her half-brother. Has a different last name. His is Cook." Patrick peered across the banquette at me, his eyes narrowing shrewdly. "You're probably wondering what I wanted to see you about."

"Probably."

"Maritza, just for starters. She do that to your cheek?"

"Why would you think that?"

"Because she has a temper. Believe me, I know. I also know that she's been going in and out of the pool house every ten minutes since you showed up. Mends your clothes, makes your breakfast. I'm wondering what else she's been doing for you."

"And I've been told that she's spoken for. By you?"

Patrick stuck his jaw out at me. "It's my house. Everything there's mine."

"So Hector's keeping an eye on her for you, not himself."

"Hector's one very helpful dude."

"Does Maritza have a green card?"

"Of course not. She's an illegal. Best kind of hired help to have. They do what they're told. Do *you* do what you're told?"

"Not usually, no."

"Well, this time you're going to. Your dick stays in your pants while you're living there, got it? My house, my rules."

"You keep calling it your house. It's not your house anymore."

"You couldn't be more wrong about that. This is California, dude. Divorce is blood sport out here. I'm a warrior. Queenie isn't. Don't let that hard shell of hers fool you. She's all cream puff on the inside. I guarantee you she'll give me that *Masterpiece Theatre* freak palace just to get rid of me. And it'll fetch millions on the open market, too. Plenty of people will want to live there. Not me. The whole house gives me the creeps. The only thing in it that I want is my old leopard-skin sofa in the billiard room." A happy glow lit up his face. "You'll never guess who I once banged on that sofa."

"Wait, don't tell me. Was it Eartha Kitt?"

"Eartha Kitt? Are you fucking crazy? She's older than my mother. No, think current A-list movie star—although she was just a nobody then. Go ahead, take a guess."

"I'd rather not."

"You sure? It wasn't your wife if that's what you're worried about."

"Ex-wife, and I'm not."

"Did Merilee ever tell you that we had a fling when we were on location together in Ketchum, Idaho?"

I stared across the table at him.

Patrick erupted in laughter. "I'm just messing with you, dude. You look like an overbred WASP limp dick, but you must be a real tiger if you bagged Merilee Nash. I hear you used to bang Queenie's kid sister, Reggie, too. What sort of a person is she?"

"Why do you want to know?"

"Because they don't speak. Not one word in the entire eighteen years I've known Queenie. I've never met her. I'm genuinely curious."

"Okay, sure," I said. "She's wild, crazy, brilliant and beautiful."

Patrick considered this, nodding to himself. "That's Queenie, too, minus the wild part. But the rest of it? Hell, yeah. Plus classy. I always wanted someone classy. Or I thought I did. But classy comes at a steep price."

"Which is . . . ?"

"A man has to be able to belch and fart in his own home. Have his buds over to watch football. Kick back at the Playboy Mansion when he feels like it. I was *suffocating*," he explained, clutching his throat with both hands. "See, I was way wrong. Class and trash just plain don't belong together. And I'm trash." He gazed around at his luxurious trailer in disgust. "I'm also fed up. I hate this stupid show. Hate the TV business. Hate this whole mindless fucking traffic jam of a city. All I want to do is get my divorce and get out. Move to Maui, just me and Lou. We'll drink brewskis on the beach, play some golf, maybe open a restaurant together. Lou cooks amazing Italian food. His mom's old recipes. I'm done, dude. Seriously, I don't want to see a living soul from this town ever again."

"Not even your children?"

"I guess they could visit me if they wanted to," he conceded, thumbing his square jaw. "Although they're both major disappointments. Joey's a scrawny nerd who does nothing but mope all day. Get this, the kid's turning seventeen on Sunday and I wanted to—"

"Saturday."

He gazed at me blankly. "What's that?"

"He turns seventeen on Saturday. As in tomorrow."

"Whatever," Patrick said with a careless wave of his hand. "I want to buy him a car, okay? I asked Queenie what kind he'd like. She told me he still hasn't learned how to drive. What kind of sixteen-year-old kid in L.A. doesn't want to learn how to drive? Wheels are *freedom*." He shook his shaggy blond head in dismay. "Plus I think he may be a fag."

"Nope, don't think so."

"What makes you say that? Did you try to make a pass at him?"

Lulu let out another low growl at my feet.

"Why is she doing that?"

"Because that was genuinely disgusting, what you just said."

"I've been in this business for almost twenty years. I haven't met a writer yet who wasn't a fag deep down inside."

"That's interesting. I've had the exact same experience with actors being gay."

Patrick glowered at me for an instant before he threw back his head and laughed. "I'm going to like you, I can tell. We'll have to go out some night and chase puss together."

"Sounds delightful. Your daughter, Danielle . . ."

"Don't be getting any ideas there," he warned me. "You so much as breathe on Princess and they'll never find your body. Think Jimmy Hoffa."

"I was merely going to say that she seems a bit tightly wrapped."

"She's mommy's girl," he acknowledged. "Doesn't know how to have any fun. Neither of my kids do. I feel bad about that."

"I imagine that your separation from Monette has been tough on them."

He didn't respond to that. Just sat there gazing down at his big, brown hands. He seemed somewhere very far away. Somewhere gloomy. Until he shook himself and said, "How long are you here for?"

"That'll be up to Richard Aintree."

"Right, right. *That's* what I wanted to talk to you about." He got up and fetched another Heineken from the fridge. His third. I wondered how many six-packs he went through in a day. He opened it and took a long drink before he sat back down, wiping his mouth with the back of his hand. "Is that letter a hoax or the real deal? And don't bullshit me."

"I think it may be the real deal. His literary agent from the old days thinks so, too. It appears to have been typed on Richard's typewriter and signed by Richard. And whoever wrote it used a nickname that he had for Monette when she was a little girl."

"This would be Olive Oyl?" he asked me.

I kept my face a blank. "That's right. So you know about it?"

"Sure. Queenie mentioned it to me when we first started going out."

And yet Monette had assured me otherwise. Why? "How about Joey and Danielle? Do they know about it?"

Patrick nodded. "When Princess was eleven years old she shot up, like, eight inches in two months. You never saw such a string bean in your life. I started calling her Olive Oyl, just like Queenie's dad had called her, until Queenie told me to stop. She was afraid Princess would get a complex."

"What about Elliot Schein? Do you think he knows about it?"

"That fat schmuck? I doubt it." Patrick peered at me curiously. "Why, you think *he* could have written the letter?"

"I don't know. But he's heavily invested in her TV career, which seems to be slipping rather badly. She needs a boost. And this definitely qualifies as a boost. Have you ever seen her dad's old typewriter around the house? It's a Hermes 3000 portable from the 1950s."

Patrick shook his head. "Don't believe I have."

"Are you sure about that? Or is there some doubt in your mind?"

"No, I'm sure."

There was another knock on the trailer door—and in breezed the hottest tabloid celebrity in town. "Hey, babe," Kat Zachry exclaimed, flashing a great big naughty grin at Patrick.

He grinned right back at her. "Hey, yourself. What's up?"

"Just wanted to say hello," she said, somehow managing to make the word *hello* sound like private code for some exotic, amazing form of oral sex. She glanced at me. "Who's he?"

"That's Hoagy. He's a writer."

She treated me to a careful head-to-toe appraisal before she said, "I'm crushing on your old leather jacket. Can I have it?"

"No."

"It would look way more bitchen on me than it does on you."

"I'm sure it would."

"So can I have it?"

"No."

She stuck out her lower lip. "I think you're a poopy head."

"Get in line. *Newsweek*, the *Chicago Tribune* and *Boys' Life* have all called me that."

"Hey, you have a dog!" Kat knelt down to pet Lulu, who responded by baring her teeth at her. "Why is she doing that?"

"She's very protective of me."

Kat beamed at her. "You're a vicious little beast, aren't you? I just love vicious little . . . Whoa, her breath is *awful*."

"She has rather strange eating habits."

"What does she eat?"

"Pretty young actresses."

Kat Zachry wasn't the prettiest young actress I'd ever seen but she may have been the sexiest. The nineteen-year-old star of *Malibu High* radiated sexuality from each and every pore of her flawless, golden skin. It was right there in every glance from her big, brown bedroom eyes, in every word that came out of her pillowy lips. She was smaller than I'd realized, maybe five foot three, and very slender aside from the being-three-months-pregnant thing. She wore a sleeveless Tweetie Pie T-shirt, gym shorts and a beat-up pair of Jack Purcell tennis sneakers without socks. Her gleaming black hair was cropped in that sassy new short haircut that every teenaged girl in America was trying to imitate. Unlike Patrick, she had no makeup on. Her face was scrubbed clean, which made her look even younger than she did on camera.

"Are you writing for our show?" she asked me as she continued to eye my jacket.

"No, I'm not."

"Too bad. We could use some talent," she said, somehow managing to make the word *talent* sound like private code for some exotic, amazing form of oral sex. "Wanna hang for a while?" she asked Patrick.

"Can't. I've got another scene to do soon."

"And I've got *nothing* to do. They keep shooting around me."

"They have to. Your tummy's starting to show."

Kat stuck out her lower lip again. She did that a lot. It worked for her. "Do I look fat?"

"Not a chance. You look hot. Listen, me and Hoagy have to talk . . ."

"Okay, okay. I know when I'm not wanted."

"You're wanted," he assured her. "Come here and give me a kiss."

Kat climbed into his lap and the two of them sucked face while I sat there trying not to watch them. Happily, there was another tap at the door. A male voice called out Kat's name.

Kat got up and opened the door. "Oh, hey, Kyle," she said in a different voice than she'd just been using. Distinctly cooler. "Come on in."

Kyle came on in. "I've been looking all over for you." His own voice was a pesky whine. "They want you in wardrobe."

"Fine, okay."

He gestured at me with his chin. "Who's he?"

"His name's Hoagy. He's a writer."

"For the show?"

"He says he's not."

Kyle glared at me. "You're not a reporter, are you?"

"Why do you ask?"

"Because I don't like reporters."

"You say that as if what you like or don't like is of the slightest consequence to me."

Kat let out a giggle. "You're wicked, Hoagy. Relax, Kyle, will you? Kyle's my big brother. He looks out for me."

Kyle stood there looking shifty-eyed and resentful. A loser, Patrick had called him. I would also toss in weasel. He had *sneaky* written all over him. He was in his mid-twenties. Not large, maybe five foot eight, and decidedly pear shaped. The polo shirt and khaki pants he had on clung to him in all of the wrong places. His sandy-colored hair was thinning. He'd be bald in another few years.

"Okay, I'm out of here," Kat informed Patrick. "You going to miss me?"

He grinned at her. "Not one bit."

She stuck her tongue out at him. "Liar."

Kyle glared at me one more time as they left, Kat twitching her tail.

Patrick sighed contentedly. "As soon as I saw that juicy young piece, I had to have it. Because there is nothing, but nothing, on God's green earth like tight young pussy. Need I say more?"

"No. In fact, please don't. Kat said that Kyle looks out for her. What does that mean?"

"He's her meat puppet. You know, her flunkie," Patrick said quietly. He'd retreated back into his gloomy place again. The man was a roller-coaster ride of moods. "She wants me to marry her."

"Are you going to?"

"Do I look that stupid to you? She's strictly after my money. They're still paying her peanuts, even though she's our biggest draw, but she signed a shitty long-term contract back when she was a nobody and the producers won't renegotiate. They can't stand her. She's a headache. Good at partying, not so good at learning her lines. And now she's *pregnant*. They'd fire her if she wasn't so damned popular. The public loves her, or at least they do right now. But they'll get tired of her soon enough and move on to some new hottie. And when they do, Kat won't be able to get a job in this town. She knows it, too. She's got serious survival instincts. Figures if she latches on to me, she'll be set for life."

"Except you're not interested in being latched on to."

"Like I said, all I want to do is to get my divorce and get out. By this time next year I won't even remember what Kat Zachry looks like."

"What about her baby? Don't you care about it?"

"Why should I? It's not mine. I got a vasectomy three years ago."

I looked at him in surprise. "Why haven't you said so? You could have put this whole tabloid mess to rest weeks ago."

He didn't bother to respond. Just sat there, sipping his beer.

"Silly me. You *want* the heat turned up so Monette will cave and give you what you want."

"Don't be looking at me that way. I told you I was trash. Besides, everybody in this town lies. I'm just playing the game the way I was taught to play it."

"Who *is* the baby's father?"

Patrick shrugged his broad shoulders. "No idea. Could be any of a dozen guys. Kat likes to have a good time."

"And you don't mind?"

"I couldn't care less. Enough about her, okay?" he said with an impatient wave. "I want to talk about this book you and Queenie are doing. Is there going to be money in it?"

"Why are you asking?"

"Because if she stands to make big bucks then I'm behind you 100 percent. Community property, dude. What's hers is mine. What I don't want is our divorce getting shoved onto Queenie's back burner for months and months because you and her are all tied up writing some serious book. I hate that idea. Am I making myself clear?"

"Not yet."

"Okay, then here it is. Whatever she's paying you I'll pay double if you leave town by tomorrow morning. Easiest money you'll ever make. All you have to do is get on an airplane. How does that sound?"

"It sounds great, but it's not going to happen. I'm here to do a job."

His eyes narrowed to icy blue slits. "Quit the job."

"Or what?"

"You don't want to know the answer to 'or what?'"

"Are you threatening me?"

"I don't do threats. I just tell it like it is. Quit the job or Lou will break both of your legs so bad that you'll spend the rest of your life in a wheelchair."

"Actually, that sounded an awful lot like a threat."

Patrick drank down the last of his beer, belching hugely. "You couldn't be more wrong, dude. That wasn't a threat." He treated me to his warmest, folksiest, prime-time television smile. "It was a guarantee."

CHAPTER FIVE

I spotted a slim young woman with long black hair standing on the corner of Sunset and Bundy with her thumb out as I was roaring my way back through Brentwood. She wore a sweatshirt and jeans and had a knapsack slung over her shoulder. I noticed her partly because you don't see many people hitchhiking anymore, not like back in my own college days when hitching was considered very cool, very Kerouac. As in Jack, not Steve.

The other reason I noticed her was that her long black hair had three streaks of silver in it.

I made a quick right onto Bundy, turned around in the first driveway I came to and eased the Roadmaster over next to her.

Reggie approached me slowly, a slight smile creasing her face as she checked out my ride. Then she looked me over, her huge blue eyes glittering at me the way they used to a long, long time ago. "You've still got it, Stewie," she observed.

"My raw, animal sex appeal?"

"Your motorcycle jacket."

"Flight jacket," I said, revving the throttle.

"What happened to your cheek? Did you get thrown?"

"In a manner of speaking. When did you get into town?"

"Early this morning. Caught the red-eye."

"Are you heading for Aintree Manor?"

"That's the general idea."

"Care for a lift?"

"Will Lulu let me ride with her?"

"I don't know. That's entirely up to her."

Lulu considered it for a moment before she hopped out of her sidecar and let Reggie get in. Then she climbed into Reggie's lap and curled up there.

"You're a sweetie, aren't you?" Reggie cooed, getting her nose licked for her trouble as we idled there next to the curb on Bundy with the sun shining down on us and the cars whizzing by on Sunset. "Let's ride, *muchacho*."

"Not so fast. This is the part where I ask you what you're doing here."

"Pretty simple. I got a lift from the airport to UCLA from a very nice student whom I met on the plane. She's hoping to go into environmental law. Then I started hoofing, hoping someone would give me a lift."

"Okay, and this is the part where I say, 'I mean, what are you doing in L.A.?' If you were going to come, why didn't you just fly out with me?"

"Because I didn't know I was coming until I knew I was coming."

"What changed your mind?"

She reached down into her knapsack, pulled out an express mail pouch and handed it to me. It was addressed to her at the Root Chakra Institute in New Paltz. Had been sent from a post office in Trenton, New Jersey. First Edison, now Trenton. I opened it and removed a folded sheet of paper and a sealed letter-sized envelope. On the sealed envelope someone had scrawled the words *For Olive Oyl and Sir Reginald.*

I glanced over at her. "'Sir Reginald'?"

"Dad used to call me that when I was a kid."

"You never told me that."

"I didn't? Actually, my formal nickname was Sir Reginald Van Gleason the Third. He was one of those characters Jackie Gleason invented way back when."

"Who else knows he used to call you that?"

"Besides Dad and me? No one. Except for Monette, of course."

I unfolded the sheet of paper. It was a plain white sheet of paper. The letter to Reggie had been typed on an old Hermes 3000. It read:

Dear Sir Reginald—

Please do not open the enclosed envelope that is addressed to you and your sister. Not until you two are together in Los Angeles, and I sincerely hope that you will be very soon. It would mean everything in the world to me for my girls to be together again after so many years.

Love,
Dad

"When did you get this?"

"Yesterday afternoon." She studied me, her eyes searching my face. "What do you think?"

I stuffed the letters back in the pouch and handed it to her. "I think we're both getting moved around."

"You don't sound very happy about it."

"I'm not."

"So what do we do?"

"We keep moving."

I got back into the flow of traffic on Sunset and continued on past Kenter until I made it to Rockingham and hung a right.

"God, what a crappy neighborhood," Reggie declared, raising her voice over the Roadmaster's engine as we cruised past one camera-ready mansion after another. "I can't stand this much neatness. And I swear the color green is ten times more electric out here. It's like green used to look when we were tripping, remember?"

"I don't have to remember. I still see flashes of it on my bedroom ceiling every night when I turn off my nightstand light."

"Do you see purple, too?"

"Doesn't everyone?"

"Holy shit, there are photographers here," she gasped as we approached Aintree Manor.

"This is just the skeleton crew. Wait until Monette gets home from work tonight. Between the Pat 'n' Kat pregnancy scandal and Monette's mysterious seven-figure book deal, this has turned into a solid-gold, double-barrel tabloid wet dream. Whoa, I should call Tom Wolfe right away. I just came up with the title for his next book."

"Stewie, how long have you been here?"

"Twenty-four hours, why?"

"You sound like you're already starting to lose your mind."

"Only because I am. But thanks for noticing."

The cops had kept the driveway clear so I could pull up to the gate. I entered the access code on the keypad while the photographers hollered at us.

"Hey, Hoagy, whattaya got for us?"

"Hey, look, it's Monette's kid sis!"

"What's up, Reggie? Did you hear from da-da yet?"

"Stewie, why do they always talk baby talk?" she asked me as the gate swung open.

"It comforts them. They feel less evil that way."

I steered up the weathered-cobble drive and came to a stop at the old stone bridge over the babbling brook so that she could experience the full impact of the vast estate's colossally gaudy fakeness. "Kind of takes your breath away, doesn't it?"

"I may vomit."

"Wait until you see the inside. You will."

I pulled up next to the crouching lions and led her inside by way of the kitchen, where Maritza was making a salad. Maritza raised her eyebrows at me curiously when she saw Reggie standing there, knapsack in hand.

"Maritza, this is Regina, the senora's sister. You can call her Reggie or Sir Reginald. I call her Stinker."

Maritza smiled warmly and said, "It is nice to meet you, Senorita Regina. You are so little and pretty like a doll. The senora is so tall."

"We were always a mismatched pair," Reggie said.

"I have not prepared a room for you. The senora did not tell me you were coming."

"The senora did not know. And I wouldn't prepare that room just yet if I were you. She may not want me here."

Maritza's eyes widened. "But you are family."

"Exactly my point."

"You can always stay in the pool house with me," I assured her.

Reggie batted her eyelashes at me. "You don't waste any time, do you?"

"You know me. I've always been a fast worker."

"Really? I seem to remember you liked to take it good and slow."

"And I seem to remember that you liked that I liked to take it good and slow. You certainly didn't complain that week we were staying in that decrepit old hotel in Cadaqués."

Her eyes gleamed at me. "I loved that old hotel."

Maritza peered at us. "You two were much in love once. I can see this," she said as Lulu ambled past her to the refrigerator, sat down and stared at it. "She wants her anchovy?"

"I'm afraid so."

Maritza found a jar on a shelf in the door, pulled one out and offered it to her, almost losing a finger in the transaction.

"You must be hungry," Maritza said to Reggie. "I am making a salad with grilled chicken for Senor Hoagy's lunch. Do you eat chicken or are you vegetarian? You are so thin."

"I eat everything," Reggie said. "Just not very much of it. Will you be joining us?"

"Oh, no, I have much to do. But thank you. Would you like to see the rest of the house before lunch?"

Reggie glanced up at the exposed hand-hewn beams with those oh-so-artfully arranged bunches of dried herbs and flowers hanging from them. "I really wouldn't. Not if I'm about to eat. But thank you." She went out onto the patio, gazing with horror at all of the perfectly pruned rose bushes that lined the walkway out to the pool. "I'm being tested, Stewie. I may not survive the next twenty-four hours without totally flipping out."

Maritza brought out a pitcher of iced tea and a place setting for Reggie, then a baguette and a wheel of brie and a big bowl of salad topped with grilled chicken.

"The pool's nice. I swam this morning. Did you bring a suit?"

"Don't need one. It's not as if you haven't seen me in the buff."

"Hector hasn't."

"Who he?"

"The garden beautician. He hovers."

"I could get you one of Senorita Danielle's," Maritza offered. "She is tall like the senora, but thin like you. It will be no problem."

"That would be great, Maritza."

Maritza went back inside while we sat at the table and helped ourselves to lunch. Reggie took only a very small amount of salad and nibbled at it with scant interest. She was never much of an eater. Merilee, on the other hand, can put away an aged thirty-two-ounce porterhouse at Peter Luger and then dream about dessert.

Maritza came back with a skimpy little yellow bikini of Danielle's for Reggie to wear. Reggie thanked her and went inside to put it on while I ate. She returned a few moments later wearing the bikini and nothing else. She was riding a teeny tiny bit lower in the caboose than I remembered, but not a whole lot considering that twelve years had gone by since I'd last set eyes on said caboose. She still looked like that same nimble little ballerina she'd been when we were together.

"Why are you looking at me that way?" she demanded.

"When I saw you standing on Sunset with your thumb out, I thought you were a college kid."

"When I saw you pull over on that Roadmaster, it reminded me of that morning in Yellow Springs when you showed up way late at the inn on your Norton, looking like a wild animal. I wanted to have crazy monkey sex with you right then and there."

"It's the jacket. Must be the jacket."

She walked barefoot down the path to the pool and sat on the edge of it, paddling her feet in the water. Lulu and I joined her, Lulu watching her carefully in case she was planning to swim. I stretched out in one of the lounge chairs.

"Those were some pretty awesome times we had, weren't they?" Reggie recalled fondly. "And I don't just mean the part about how we couldn't keep our hands off each other. We had so goddamned much fun, too. I mean, we jumped out of an airplane together, remember?"

"I remember."

"So how come you haven't written about us?"

"That's a good question."

"I'm sitting here waiting for a good answer."

"All right. Because I never understood us."

"At the time, you mean? We weren't meant to understand. Just be living in the moment. But you understand us now, don't you?"

"No, I don't."

"Yes, you do."

"No, I really don't. And feel free to change the subject anytime."

"Sorry, Stewie, I can't do that. This is too important."

"Why would I want to write about us now after all of these years?"

She gazed at me penetratingly with her huge eyes. "Because you need to."

I left that one alone because she wasn't wrong. She was never wrong. That was the single most maddening thing about Regina Aintree.

"Tell me what you've figured out about us so far," she urged me. "Please?"

"Well, okay, but it's not much. Seriously, it barely qualifies as a Hallmark card. All I know is . . ." I trailed off at the sound of the soft *snip-snip-snip* of Hector's pruners. He'd appeared on the path nearby to primp the rose bushes and spy on us. "Hector, this is Monette's sister, Reggie," I called out to him. "She's come to stay for a few days. Patrick will want to know."

Hector said nothing in response. Didn't smile either, for once. Just stared at me with a stony expression on his face.

Reggie's eyes hadn't left me. "All you know is . . ."

"There's a brief slice of time in our lives, a sweet season of madness, that falls right in between who we want to be and who we end up being. That was you and me. While it lasted, it was amazing. And then it was over. That's all I know. Like I said, it's hardly anything."

"Are you shitting me? It's *everything*. Stewie—what if I told you that those were the best three years of my life? That absolutely nothing tastes as good, smells as good or feels as good as it did then?"

"It's different now," I conceded. "We were wild and crazy kids. That was a special time."

"I want you to write about how special it was."

"No, you really don't."

"Yes, I really do. I'm serious about this."

"But everyone will know that it's *you*. What if it's not flattering?"

"I don't care. Promise me that you'll write about it, okay? No matter what happens."

"Why, what's going to happen?"

She lowered her gaze. "I don't know, but I've been feeling a weird, edgy vibe ever since you walked into my meditation room. Dad feels it, too. That's why he's reached out to me. And it's why I came. Something's very wrong here. I can feel it. You can, too, or you wouldn't be here."

"I'm here because they made me a very lucrative guaranteed offer."

"Guess what? I don't believe you."

I heard the paparazzi clamoring outside the front gate. The gate opened and a car cruised up the driveway, pulling to a stop at the gravel turnaround by the crouching lions. A car door opened and closed, and none other than Boyd Samuels came striding up the path toward us in the bright sunshine, looking way too much like a cast member of *Reservoir Dogs* in his regulation HWA black suit, white shirt, black tie and Ray-Bans.

"What are *you* doing here?" I wondered as Lulu growled at him.

"Mr. Harmon Wright phoned me late last night," Boyd answered, whipping off his shades. "He's seen all of the press attention our project's getting and asked me to fly out and get personally involved. So I snagged a ride on the Universal jet, dropped my bags at the Four Seasons and here I am."

"Personally involved how?"

"When Mr. Harmon Wright makes a request like that you don't ask how. All I can tell you is that the publishing world's in a total lather over Richard Aintree. No one's talking about anything else." He gazed around at the lemon trees, very pretty, and the genuinely unreal babbling brook and, finally, at the mansion itself. "Is this place beautiful or what?"

"Or what," Reggie said, squinting at him suspiciously as she sat there on the edge of the pool.

"Boyd Samuels, say hello to Regina Aintree."

His face lit up. "This is a real honor, Miss Aintree."

"Oh, yeah? Why is that?"

"Because you're a distinguished modern American poet, not to mention a living, breathing part of our literary heritage."

She arched an eyebrow at me. "Does he always talk like that?"

"He's in the process of trying to reinvent himself."

"As what, a dickhead?"

"I prefer to think of him as a kinder, gentler asshole."

"I know all about you, Boyd Samuels," Reggie said to him with withering disapproval. "You're the single most amoral agent on the planet."

Boyd smiled at her uncertainly. "I know all about you, too. I used to read about you and the Hoagster in the gossip columns back when I was in middle school in Cherry Hill, New Jersey. Did you two really have sex on George Plimpton's pool table in the middle of a Brazilian poetry reading?"

"Can he swim?" she murmured at me.

"I don't know, I'll ask him. Boyd, can you swim?"

"Of course I can. Why?"

"Too bad," she said, sighing regretfully.

"I placed a call to Monette as soon as I got to town," he said, rubbing his hands together briskly. "She promised me she'd try to get home from today's taping as soon as possible and was kind enough to suggest I wait for her here. I don't suppose you have any news for me, do you, amigo? Because Mr. Harmon Wright is really anxious to be kept in the loop."

"Well, I did just spend a fun-filled morning with Patrick Van Pelt."

Boyd's eyes narrowed. "What for?"

"He doesn't want this project to happen, that's what for."

"Really? I'd think he'd be loving the extra media attention."

"And you'd be wrong. If Richard Aintree chooses to reappear right now, he'll shove Pat 'n' Kat off the front page. As far as Patrick's concerned that makes Richard an undesirable and potentially very expensive distraction."

"Fuck Patrick," Boyd snapped. "What's he gonna do?"

"Just for starters, someone in a black Trans Am tried to run my short-legged associate and me over in Pacoima yesterday. Naturally, Patrick denies knowing anything about it. But someone in a black Trans Am also tried to run Monette off Coldwater Canyon the night before last."

"Damn . . ." Boyd took a deep breath, letting it out slowly. "Mr. Harmon Wright will be deeply, deeply displeased if Patrick screws up our project. But you know what? I can handle this."

"How? Do you have a professional hit man on the HWA payroll now? Wait, don't tell me. I don't want to know."

"I'll convince Patrick's agent to lean on him by making it clear that our Richard Aintree project is *the* single most important thing happening in HWA's universe right now and that Mr. Harmon Wright will personally destroy the career of a certain ex–football player if he dares to mess it up. I can talk to Kat's agent, too. Remind him that we're one big happy family and we all pull in the same vertically integrated, synergistically aligned direction."

"I don't like the way he talks," Reggie said to me.

"Didn't think you would."

"I am on this, amigo," Boyd vowed excitedly. "I am girding my loins for battle as we speak." He opened his black Samsonite briefcase on a lounge chair and removed a mobile phone, then marched around to the other side of the pool with it and threw himself into the fray with Glickian zeal.

"What's with the walkie-talkie?" Reggie asked me, watching him.

"All of the big kids and their loins play with them now."

Reggie tied her hair up on top of her head with a rubber band, dove into the water and settled into a nice, easy backstroke. Lulu ran alongside her, barking and barking, while Boyd shouted obscenity-laced threats into his mobile phone.

Then the side gate opened and Joey and Danielle arrived from school with their book bags slung over their shoulders. Danielle was dressed for success in a navy blue blazer, powder blue sweater, pleated khakis and black suede slip-ons. Joey was dressed for dis-illusionment in a rumpled flannel shirt, jeans and work boots. He headed straight for the house with his eyes fastened on the ground, refusing to acknowledge me or the famous aunt whom he'd never, ever met.

Danielle did no such thing. She made her way directly to the edge of the pool and gawked at Reggie until Reggie swam over toward her and climbed out.

"I hope you don't mind that I borrowed one of your bikinis," Reggie said, toweling off.

"You're *her*," Danielle said in hushed disbelief. "You're Aunt Reggie."

"In the goose-bumped flesh," Reggie acknowledged. "And you're Danielle. Or do you prefer Dani?"

"No, I hate Dani. It's an ugly name."

"And you're not ugly at all. In fact, you look just like your mother did when she was your age."

"I've wanted to meet you for as long as I can remember. I've always wondered what you were like. But you've never . . ." Danielle broke off, her brow furrowing. "How long has it been since you and Mom have seen each other?"

"A fairly decent interval of twenty or so years."

"You mean since before I was born?"

Reggie nodded. "Since before you were born. And in answer to your next question—no, she has no idea I'm here."

"Will she be happy to see you?"

"I doubt it."

"So why are you here?"

"I'm here because I'm supposed to be here. How is your mom doing these days?"

Danielle swallowed uncomfortably. "She's kind of got a lot going on in her life right now."

"By 'a lot' do you mean your horny idiot of a dad knocking up his slutty little co-star?"

Danielle's eyes widened. "You *say* things, don't you? You're not at all like Mom."

Maritza came out to ask Danielle if she wanted anything to eat or drink. Danielle said she didn't.

"So where's my nephew?" Reggie wondered.

"Senor Joey is up in his room," Maritza informed her.

"Would you please ask him to join us?"

"He will not come down, Senorita."

"She's right," Danielle said. "He doesn't like to leave his room. His shrink calls it his cave."

"But I want to meet him."

"He will not come down, Senorita."

"Oh, he'll come down," I assured her. "Lulu, we've got a job to do. Please lead the way, Maritza." We started toward the house, leaving Reggie and Danielle alone together. Unless you count Boyd, who was still standing on the other side of the pool shouting into his phone. "I spoke to Patrick today," I told Maritza as I followed her inside toward the front hallway. "He warned me that you're 'private property.' What does that mean exactly?"

She led me up the grand curving staircase with its weirdly tacky gallery of framed magazine covers and photo spreads. "It means Senor Patrick thinks I belong to him," she answered gravely.

"Do you?"

"No, I do not."

"Maritza, has he ever forced himself on you?"

"He tries to grab me when he drinks, so I make sure I am not alone with him. I am very happy he's gone, Senor Hoagy."

The second-floor hallway was as opulently appointed as the downstairs. There were antique Persian rugs on the wide-plank oak floors, strategically placed urns, busts and side tables that were laden with fresh flowers and collections of ivory bric-a-brac and other assorted high-end dreck. There was no shortage of rooms. I counted seven doors. At the end of the hall was a set of massive mahogany double doors befitting a royal bedchamber.

"The master suite," Maritza said, following my gaze. "Would you . . . ?"

"I wouldn't say no."

There was a veddy British seating alcove with a pair of chintz-covered armchairs set before a fireplace and chintz-covered window seats built in beneath the row of windows that looked out over the rose bushes, babbling brook and a vast swath of electric green lawn. Floral-patterned curtains framed the windows. There was an old-fashioned canopied four-poster bed with frilly, white ruffled skirts, frilly, white ruffled everything. There were his and hers walk-in closets. Patrick's was completely empty except for an extensive collection of wooden hangers. Monette's closet, which was crammed to the ceiling with clothing and shoes, was bigger than my entire apartment on West Ninety-Third Street. The master bath had two antique sinks as well as a huge antique tub with clawed feet. It also had a thoroughly modern stall shower and a teak sauna. Next to the master bath there was a service stairway down to the first floor.

"That goes down to the hallway next to the kitchen," Maritza explained. "So that I may bring the senora her coffee in the morning and carry the family's laundry up and down the stairs without taking it through the main house."

I've stayed in historic manor homes in England. It's standard to find a service stairway down to the kitchen. This one, I noticed, had a door at the top of the stairs that could be closed and locked for privacy.

She led me back out into the hallway toward the second door on the right, which had a hand-lettered sign taped to it that read: STAY THE FUCK OUT!

"Senor Joey's room," Maritza informed me.

I'd expected to hear loud rock 'n' roll coming out of there, but there was only silence. When I knocked on the door, I was met with more silence.

"He cannot hear you," she explained, tapping her ear with a finger. "He wears headphones because the senora hates the *thump-thump-thump*."

"Does he lock his door?"

"He used to, but the senora hired a locksmith so he cannot."

I opened the door and in we went. The wooden shutters over Joey's windows were shut against the brilliant Southern California sunshine. It was quite dark in there, aside from a tiny desk lamp.

Stuffy, too. Smelled strongly of old sneakers, dirty socks, sweaty armpits, Right Guard and Clearasil. Joey was hunched at his desk with his headphones on, tapping away at a Macintosh on what appeared to be a homework project. Two textbooks were open on the desk next to him. As my eyes grew accustomed to the dark, I could make out a dozen or more posters pinned to his walls. A regular rogue's gallery of the tangled up in tragic—Kurt Cobain, Jim Morrison, Janis Joplin. Hanging directly over his unmade bed was that famous photograph of Charles Manson staring right at the camera with his frozen madman's glare.

"Is disgusting in here," Maritza said, glancing disapprovingly at the dirty clothing that was strewn everywhere. "But he will not let me come in and clean. The senora, she says if he wants to live in filth then let him."

Lulu was looking up at me, waiting for my go-ahead. On my nod she made her way under Joey's desk and clamped her jaws firmly around his ankle.

He yanked off his headphones with a shriek. "Ow, what the fuck is she doing? Tell her to stop!"

"I'm sorry, I can't. We don't have that kind of relationship."

"If she doesn't let go I'm going to kick her."

"I wouldn't do that if I were you."

"What do you *want*?"

"Come outside and say hello to your aunt. She's flown three thousand miles to see you."

"She doesn't want to talk to me."

"Yes, she does."

"I'm trying to finish a paper that was due two months ago, okay? If I don't do it, they won't let me graduate."

"Finish it later. Come on outside."

"Fuck off!"

Lulu sank her teeth in deeper. Not deep enough to do any damage but enough for Joey to feel as if his ankle was snared in a steel-jawed trap.

"Okay, okay, I'll come! Make her stop, will you?"

He followed us outside into the sunlight, blinking. Danielle was perched on the edge of Reggie's lounge chair, enthralled, as Reggie chattered away at her. Boyd was still shouting into his phone.

"Joey, this is your aunt Regina," I said. "She answers to Reggie."

She stuck out her hand. "Hey, Joey."

"I don't believe in shaking hands," he said coldly.

"Because you consider it an outmoded societal ritual, am I right? I can relate to that. Do you believe in having a seat?"

He stood right where he was, peering at her. "Hoagy told me I should read your work. He says you're a stone-cold genius."

"Hoagy said that?" She smiled at me impishly. "How sweet of him. But I'm no genius. Your grandmother was. Eleanor Aintree was one of the most important American poets of the twentieth century."

"What about our grandfather?" Danielle asked, her eyes gleaming at Reggie excitedly.

"Your grandfather is someone who wrote one very fine book."

"It was okay," Joey said grudgingly, frowning as he gazed across the pool. "Who is *that*?"

"Boyd Samuels, your mom's New York literary agent," I told him. "He has a more formal title but I'll spare you that."

"Every time I turn around there's another total stranger here," Joey complained. "And those yapping cretins are *always* outside the front gate with their cameras. This place is driving me nuts."

"I don't blame you one bit," Reggie said. "It's driving me nuts and I just got here. So, Joey, what are you going to do when you finish high school?"

"He wants to be a writer," Danielle informed her.

"Really? Most excellent! How about you, Danielle?"

"Yale undergrad, Harvard business school, then a job in studio development. I plan to be running my own production company by the time I'm thirty."

Reggie looked at her in horror. "You poor thing. What are your plans for this summer?"

"I have an internship lined up in Elliot Schein's office. He produces Mom's show."

"Why on earth do you want to do that?"

"Are you kidding me? It's a huge opportunity."

"It's a waste of your time. You need to experience life."

"That's what I told her," I said. "But she wasn't buying it."

"Wouldn't you rather rescue wounded elephants in Kenya?"

Danielle peered at Reggie as if she were utterly crazy. "Uh, no . . ."

"I can get you on an oceanographic research vessel that's heading to the Galapagos Islands. Wouldn't you like to do that?"

"Not really."

Reggie shook her head at her. "Young lady, you need to reassess your priorities. Find yourself a bad boy with a motorcycle, go riding off into the desert with him and don't come back until you've seen the light."

"Light?" Danielle frowned at her. "What light?"

"And you, young sir, need to ride the rails," she informed Joey. "Catch a freighter that's heading north. When you make it to San Francisco, find some cool people to hang with. Tell me, when's the last time you laughed?"

Joey took a very long moment before he said, "I don't remember."

"Both of you need to get out of this mausoleum—and I mean pronto, as in before it gets burned to the ground. Come the revolution this whole place will be nothing but charred rubble."

Joey tilted his head at her curiously. "There's going to be a revolution?"

"Oh, hell, yes. It's a millennial thing. All the signs are pointing to it. The America that we know and don't love won't exist after the year 2000. Come the year 2001 everything will change. And I, for one, say bring it on."

I heard a huge amount of shouting from the paparazzi now as the front gate swung open. Two vehicles came cruising up the driveway and parked. Two car doors opened and closed, then Monette strode briskly up the rose-lined path toward us followed by Elliot. Today, he resembled two very large marshmallows stuffed inside of bright orange Nike warm-up gear.

Boyd dashed around the pool and made straight for Monette. "How is my favorite client doing?" he exclaimed, beaming at her.

"How do you think?" she responded coolly.

"What's bright boy doing here?" Elliot demanded, glaring at Boyd.

"Mr. Harmon Wright asked me to take personal charge of the situation," Boyd informed him. "And that's all you need to know."

"Guess again, bright boy." Elliot stabbed Boyd in the chest with a pudgy index finger. "Everything that goes on in this lady's life is my business. You and me need to have a conversation."

"So we'll have a conversation," Boyd said. "Lighten up, will you? And get your fat finger out of my chest while you're at it."

"Why don't you make me?" Elliot blustered at him.

Monette paid no mind to their turf squabble. She was too busy staring at Reggie seated there poolside with Joey and Danielle. Staring at her sister as if she couldn't believe what her eyes were telling her.

"Hey, Olive, love what you've done with the place," Reggie said to Monette super casually—all except for the quaver of emotion in her voice.

"No, you don't," Monette responded hoarsely. "You hate it."

"Why do you say that?"

"Because you don't hide your feelings very well. You never have."

"Maybe that's because I don't try." Reggie got up from her lounge chair and walked slowly toward Monette, looking incredibly tiny as she stood before her sister barefoot. Monette towered a foot taller in her pumps.

The estranged sisters faced each other in charged silence.

"What are you doing here?" Monette finally asked her.

"Just passing through town. Thought I'd say hey."

Monette considered this, her lower lip clamped between her teeth. "Do you . . . have you a place to stay?"

"Relax, I won't impose on you. I know you're cramped for space."

"I have five empty bedrooms upstairs. Maritza will prepare one for you. But you still haven't told me why you're here."

"I got a letter from Dad," Reggie said. "It's addressed to both of us."

She studied Reggie guardedly. "What does it say?"

"No idea. He asked me not to open it until we were together."

"Well, where is it?"

Reggie fetched the express mail pouch from her knapsack and set it on the patio table while the rest of us gathered around her. She removed the sealed envelope and showed it to Monette. "See? It's addressed to Olive Oyl and Sir Reginald. Nobody but Dad ever called me Sir Reginald."

Monette smiled at Reggie faintly. "My God, I haven't thought of that name in years." She stared at the envelope. "Shall we . . . ?"

Reggie tore it open and unfolded the plain white sheet of typing paper that was inside. A brief letter had been typed on it. Same old Hermes 3000, it appeared:

Dear Olive Oyl and Sir Reginald—

I am so glad that you girls are together again. I want you to spend some time getting reacquainted. You two are sisters, after all. You need each other, perhaps now more than ever. I promise that I will be in touch again very soon.

Love,
Dad

Monette stood there frowning at it. "It's . . . not much, is it?"

"No, it's not," Reggie said.

Monette gulped back a sob. "This is all so *strange*."

Reggie nodded her head, swallowing. "I—I know . . ."

The Aintree sisters stood there, struggling to hold their emotions in check. They couldn't. Both let out huge sobs before they threw themselves into each other's arms.

"I've missed you so much!" Monette cried, tears streaming down her face.

"*I've* missed *you!*" Reggie cried.

"You were my best friend. I have no one. No one!"

"I know." Reggie hugged her big sister tight. "I know."

"Damn, this is one awesome Instamatic Moment," Boyd said. "I wish I had my camera. They'd plaster this on page one all across America."

"I'm so—so glad you're here," Monette sniffled, swiping at her eyes. "We'll have a party tomorrow to celebrate. It's Joey's birthday."

"I *don't* want a birthday party," Joey reminded his mother.

"It'll be fun. We'll swim. We'll cook out." Monette hesitated before she added, "And your dad wants to come. He'd like to see you. Both of you."

Joey shook his head at her. "Mom, how many times do I have to tell you? I don't want to see him. Ever."

"I feel weird about it, too," Danielle said.

"Well, he's coming," Monette informed them. "So deal with it."

"Will he bring Kat?" Danielle wondered, her voice heavy with dread.

"Oh, he'll bring her," Elliot answered. "No way those two can resist that army of tabloid lemmings camped outside the gate."

"I hate this," Joey fumed. "When do we get our lives back?"

"I don't know, sweetheart," Monette said. "I wish I could tell you. But we'll have fun, I promise. Maritza can make steak fajitas on the grill. And I'll bake you a cake. Any kind you want. How about my triple chocolate?"

"Don't bother. I'm not coming."

Monette looked at him in dismay. "Joey, you're not going to hide in your room, are you?"

Lulu let out a low warning growl.

"Why is she doing that?" Joey asked me, his voice rising in alarm.

"She doesn't intend to let you hide in your room."

"Shall we say noon?" Monette suggested. "It'll be fun."

"Mom, why do you keep saying that?" Joey demanded. "It's going to be the worst day of my entire life!" He went storming off into the house, enraged.

Monette watched him helplessly. "Talk to him, will you?" she asked Danielle.

"I'll try." Danielle started inside after him. "But he doesn't listen to me."

Maritza came out of the kitchen with a tray of guacamole, salsa and tortilla chips. Then she brought out a bucket filled with soft drinks, mineral water and long-neck bottles of Corona.

"What can I offer you?" Monette asked Boyd.

"I have to scoot," he said, glancing at his watch. "There's a mandatory team meeting at 6:00 pm every Friday at every HWA office across the globe. But I'll see you tomorrow. If I'm invited, that is."

"Of course you are," Monette assured him.

"I still want to have a word with you, bright boy," Elliot reminded him.

"Fine, whatever," Boyd sighed, retrieving his briefcase. "Follow me to my car."

The two of them started down the path toward the driveway, sniping at each other. Monette passed bottles of Corona to Reggie and to me before she opened one for herself, gazing at Reggie. "I still can't believe you're here."

"Believe it," Reggie said. "It's all part of Dad's plan."

Monette furrowed her brow. "Why is he doing this? What does he want from us?"

"Olive, my dear, I don't have the slightest fucking idea."

WE ATE OUR dinner of grilled tuna with black beans and rice out on the patio. Joey was still smoldering with anger. Refused to speak or make eye contact with anyone while he bolted down his meal. Seven minutes. He stayed at the table for seven minutes. But Danielle lingered there long after she'd finished eating, the better to soak up her mother and aunt's giggly girlhood reminiscences of slumber parties and adolescent crushes way back when they'd lived in the leafy New England town of Woodbridge outside of New Haven, back before their father became a world-famous author and their mother hurled herself off the roof of that East Village apartment building. Monette seemed genuinely thrilled to see her kid sister again. And Reggie acted as if she was happy to be there. Hell, for all I knew she was. Reggie had always been a searcher. Maybe finding herself face-to-face with her big sister for the first time since the seventies was just what she needed. Who was I to say otherwise? The two of them were still reviving giddy girlhood memories for Danielle when I excused myself and left them there.

I took Lulu for a stroll around the grounds. We paused when we reached the front gate. It was nearly ten o'clock. The paparazzi had gone home for the night, but a pair of uniformed cops remained parked there in a black-and-white cruiser anyway. Monette's well-heeled neighbors insisted upon it, I suspected.

After our walk we retired to the pool house. I stretched out on the bed and called my phone machine in New York. There were more messages from reporters who wanted to talk to me. I paid them no mind. There was still no message from Merilee in Budapest. This I did mind. We were often on separate continents for days, sometimes weeks at a time. That didn't bother me. But I didn't like it when I had no idea how to reach her. It unsettled me.

It was just past eleven when I slid under the covers and turned out the light. Lulu stretched out next to me with her head on my chest. I lay there in the darkness gazing out the open window at the lights in the windows of the big house. Gradually, the upstairs lights went out one by one. Then most of the downstairs lights went out. The last one to go out was the light in Maritza's room off the kitchen. The house was totally dark after that.

I continued to lie there watching the darkened house in the moonlight. Soon I heard the kitchen door open and close, then soft footsteps on the path that led to the pool house.

Lulu let out a low growl. I shushed her.

And then someone was tapping quietly on the bedroom window. A voice whispered, "Hoagy, are you still awake?"

I threw on my dressing gown and went to the door and opened it.

My late-night visitor wasn't Reggie. It was Monette who stood there looking nervous and big-eyed in the soft blue glow of the swimming pool's nightlights. She was wearing a matching sweat-shirt and sweatpants of what appeared to be lightweight powder blue cashmere. She had her long blond hair gathered up in a bun with a few loose strands tumbling here and there in a way that was meant to look casual but I felt quite certain wasn't. Absolutely nothing about Monette was casual. She was barefoot. "I wondered if you felt like a nightcap," she asked me hesitantly. "Perhaps out by the pool . . . ?"

"There's some single malt in the cupboard. I'll be right out."

I put on my jeans and a T-shirt and brought the bottle and two glasses out with me. Monette was stretched out on one of the lounge chairs facing the pool, her feet crossed at the ankles. I poured us both generous slugs of Scotch and took the lounge chair next to her. Lulu settled on the pavement between us with a disapproving grunt. She doesn't like to have her beauty sleep disturbed, especially by tall, attractive blondes who aren't named Merilee Nash. It was very quiet out and the cool night air was scented with the fragrance of roses and honeysuckle. I sipped my Scotch and lay there, gazing up at the three-quarter moon over-head while I waited Monette out.

"I couldn't sleep," she confessed finally. "I'm too tied up in knots about Patrick. I don't know what to say to him when he shows up here tomorrow. Honestly, I feel as if I'm about to ex-plode inside."

"Why don't you just tell him to stay away?"

"He's Joey's father. He wants to bring his son a birthday present." She gazed at me warily. "Did he say anything to you about us?"

"He said that you were class and he was trash. That he felt trapped here and he had to get out."

She thought this over, her chest rising and falling. "Anything else?"

"Just that he wants to quit the TV business and move to Maui."

"Is he still talking about that? My lord, he's been spouting that pipe dream for so many years that I've lost count. He never actually does a thing about it. The producers give him plenty of hiatus time between seasons. He could fly over there, find himself a piece of beachfront property and put his money where his mouth is. But he never does. He hasn't even been to Maui for ten years. I doubt he'd recognize it." She heaved a long sigh. "How did he seem to you?"

"He's a mess. Surely that isn't news to you."

"No, it's not. Patrick's a deeply unhappy man. His work doesn't make him happy. His family doesn't make him happy. *I* certainly don't. The only thing that seems to give him any pleasure whatsoever is running around with trampy young girls, which explains why he and I are through."

"He treated me to quite a vivid display of mood swings, including full frontal rage. Is that typical?"

"It didn't used to be. I always thought of Patrick as laid-back and easygoing. That all changed a few months ago."

"What happened?"

"He decided that he looked like a flabby old man next to all of those young hunks in the cast, so Lou upped their workouts and started feeding him megadoses of energy-boosting minerals."

"They're not energy-boosting minerals."

"I didn't think so," she said bitterly. "That fool. That vain, stupid fool. I understand from Elliot that Lou deals illegal drugs."

I nodded. "He made a delivery while I was with Patrick. In fact, I watched Patrick snort up four lines of coke and go through half a six-pack of beer at ten o'clock in the morning. I don't know if you still care about him . . ."

"He's the father of my children. I'll always care about him."

"But he's on a stairway to nowhere. I've been on it myself. I fell a long, long way before I hit the bottom. That's what will happen to Patrick. He can't keep on going the way he is."

"I'd help him if I could, but I'm the enemy as far as he's concerned. Kat will have to be the one who straightens him out."

"Is it true that he isn't the father of her baby? That he's had a vasectomy?"

"Yes, it's true. The vasectomy was his idea, not mine. Quite a few sexually active men out here have been getting them. Especially high-profile ones like Patrick who are targets for paternity suits."

"I understand why he's kept silent about it. He's loving the tabloid heat. But why haven't *you* spoken up?"

"I don't wish to play that game."

"This is no game, Monette."

She gazed out at the pool. "I'm taking the high road. I don't care how much mud he drags me through. I won't give in. I won't," she vowed defiantly. "Do you believe me?"

"I'd like to, but you haven't been totally honest with me."

"Whatever do you mean?"

"Why did you tell me that Patrick didn't know that your dad called you Olive Oyl? He did. He does."

"Because this project isn't about him," she answered brusquely.

"That's not a helpful answer."

"It's the only one you're going to get."

"That's not helpful either. Patrick did threaten to break both of my legs."

Her eyes widened in alarm. "Why would he do that?"

"He wants me to leave town. If I don't, he intends to sic Lou on me."

"Does this mean you're going to quit?"

"No chance. Nobody hands me my Olympia and tells me to leave town."

"You're a stubborn man in your own odd way, aren't you?" Monette glanced over at me for a moment, then looked back at the pool. "I noticed those scars on Reggie's wrists."

"So did I."

"When did she do that?"

"Three years ago, she said. I wasn't in the picture."

"Neither was I. I should have been. I'm her big sister. She needs me. She acts all feisty but she's not nearly as tough as she thinks she is. She's very sensitive. Mother was the same way." She took another sip of her Scotch, smiling at me faintly. "This is nice. I miss having someone to sit back and talk things over with late at night when it's quiet. May I ask you a somewhat awkward question?"

"You can ask me anything."

"Do you trust Boyd Samuels?"

"No one trusts Boyd Samuels."

"Yet Harmon Wright speaks very favorably of him. And I must admit he's done right by me so far."

"It's early. He still has plenty of time to hose you."

"Elliot thinks he's an amoral sleazeball."

"Only because he is. Why are you asking me about Boyd?"

"Because I found it very strange the way he suddenly showed up out here today. Has it occurred to you that this business with Dad could be an elaborate hoax that Boyd's cooked up to revive his own career? Or am I being paranoid?"

"You're not being paranoid. The thought's occurred to me, too. But the letters do appear to have been typed on your dad's Hermes. How would Boyd have gotten hold of it? And how would he know that your dad used to call you girls Olive Oyl and Sir Reginald?"

"Someone else would have to be in on it with him. A member of the family. Someone who knew where the typewriter's been stashed."

"Someone like who?"

"Someone like Reggie," she said bluntly.

"She and Boyd met for the first time right here this afternoon. I introduced them. They didn't know each other."

"Are you sure? How do we know they weren't faking that for your benefit? How do we know she isn't responsible for this whole crazy business? Her writing career has evaporated. She sits alone in a stone hut in the woods all day. She's suicidal. Tell me, how do we know?"

"We don't."

"So it has occurred to you that Reggie could be behind it."

"Of course it has. Same as it's occurred to me that you could be behind it." Not to mention Patrick. Not to mention one or possibly both of their extremely bright children. The old Hermes could be hidden away in this baronial pile of bricks somewhere. Elliot Schein was also in the mix. So was Alberta Pryce. They didn't call her the Silver Fox for no reason. And they didn't call me the publishing world's preeminent ghost for no reason. I trusted absolutely no one. Everyone was in play. Everyone. "I got the impression that you were happy to see your sister."

"I am. I guess I don't understand why she's here."

"Because it's what your dad wants. Or so it would seem."

Monette fell silent for a moment. "We've followed each and every one of his instructions so far. You're here, Reggie's here, we're all here. What happens if he doesn't write us again?"

"He will."

"But what if he doesn't?"

"Then I go home, Reggie goes home and your life returns to normal."

"Good lord." She tossed down the last of her Scotch. "What a truly horrifying thought."

CHAPTER SIX

It was a warm, dazzlingly bright morning and the kitchen was abuzz with activity. Maritza, who today wore a dental hygienist's uniform of pale pink, was marinating flank steaks in garlic, jalapenos, cumin and lime juice. Monette and Danielle were hard at work on Joey's birthday cake, Monette measuring and sifting the dry ingredients while Danielle melted chunks of bittersweet chocolate and butter in a double boiler. Danielle wore a white bikini under a man's unbuttoned lavender oxford-cloth shirt with sleeves that came down to her knuckles, which was a popular look among preppy teenaged girls that season. Boyfriend shirts, they called them. She was a small-breasted girl whose legs were uncommonly long and well muscled. A runner's legs. Monette wore a long-sleeved blue chambray shirt over a jade green tank top and white linen pants. There was no mistaking the cake bakers for mother and daughter. Not only because they were both tall, slender and blonde but because they wore the same exact expression on their faces. Grim.

"Is Reggie up?" I asked Monette after I'd said good morning.

"She is," Monette answered distractedly as she powered up her KitchenAid mixer. "She's . . . somewhere."

Lulu and I wandered off to find her, Lulu's nails clacketing on the oak-plank floors. We found her seated on the conservatory floor in the lotus position facing the morning sun. She was not naked, in case you were wondering. She wore a T-shirt and shorts. She was, however, sobbing.

Lulu climbed into her lap, tail thumping, and got busy licking her nose, which has been known to stem the flow of tears in no time. Or start them.

"What's wrong, Stinker?"

"Not a thing," she sniffled, patting Lulu. "When I emptied my mind of willful thoughts and let the *chi* flow through me I just started crying, that's all. I think it's being around family again. These people are my only living relatives. Other than Dad, I mean. I was thinking about that all night. Couldn't sleep."

"You should have visited me."

"I did." She squinted up at me in that way of hers. "But you already had company. You and Monette were sitting by the pool sipping brandy."

"Single malt Scotch. And you could have joined us."

"No, she wouldn't have liked that. Trust me."

Elliot Schein and Boyd Samuels were the first to arrive, in Boyd's rented black Lincoln Town Car. Elliot resembled two over-stuffed marshmallows in magenta Nike warm-up gear today. Boyd had swapped his official HWA black suit for the unofficial Hollywood pool party ensemble that had been popularized several years earlier by Grant Tinker, the Babe Paley of the power set—a pastel pink sweater thrown over his shoulders and knotted loosely at the throat, a sky blue polo shirt, cream-colored slacks and loafers. Each man clutched a mobile phone in one hand and a small gift-wrapped box for the birthday boy in the other.

"Are you two serious about each other or is this just a weekend fling?" I asked as we stood together on the patio under the grape arbor, where a washtub had been filled with ice cubes and bottles of beer, soda and mineral water.

"I'm not following you, Hoag," Elliot replied, wheezing.

"You left together last evening and now here you are, showing up together. Believe me, this is how gossip starts."

"We just came from a brunch meeting with the HWA television team," Boyd explained. "Besides, it'll be easier to cut out early this way. We can say we have another meeting to get to."

Elliot nodded his frizzy red head. "Bright boy's right. I, for one, do not relish spending a minute longer with Patrick Van Pelt than I have to." He excused himself and went inside to say hello to Monette.

Boyd stayed on the patio with me, his jaw tensing. "I don't suppose anything came by express mail from Richard Aintree this morning, did it?"

"I'm afraid not."

"Damn, this project better not go up in smoke," he muttered fretfully. "You know what'll happen to me if it does? I'll end up with a job where two, three hundred times a day I say the words 'Would you like fries with that, sir?' Seriously, amigo, I will *disappear*." Boyd peered around at the lush green hills that surrounded us. "Hey, what if Richard's already here? What if he's been here all along and *arranged* to have those express mail letters sent from New Jersey?"

"Why would he do that?"

"Because he's nutso, that's why. Richard Aintree is out of his mind. We know that for a fact. Hell, for all we know, he could be standing right outside the gate at this very minute masquerading as a tabloid photographer."

"No offense, Boyd, but this town is having a bad influence on you."

"You got that right. It's Crazy Town out here. The only way

I've ever been able to cope was to go with the flow. I've never been here *straight* before. The HWA gang went out club hopping last night and there were mountains of coke *everywhere*. It took a ton of willpower to say no. Man, I sure . . ." He broke off, breathing raggedly. "I could really go for a few lines right now."

"Do you have somebody whom you should call?"

He shifted his pastel-covered shoulders uncomfortably. "I thought I might find a meeting to go to later."

"Want me to come with you?"

"You'd do that for me?"

"Of course."

"But you don't like me."

"Doesn't matter. What matters is that you've put your life back together and you want to keep it together. Which reminds me, steer clear of Patrick and Lou when they get here."

"Why?"

"Just take my word for it."

By now Monette and Danielle had put the cake in the oven and Maritza was dumping a load of charcoal into the outdoor grill to get the fire started. Reggie and Danielle joined us under the grape arbor. And, somehow, Monette managed to persuade a highly reluctant Joey to come downstairs from his room to open the presents that Elliot and Boyd had brought him.

First he opened Elliot's, which was nestled inside a plush, hinged case. It was a black fountain pen with two gold bands. Mighty nice one, too.

"That there's a Waterman, kid," Elliot pointed out, beaming at him.

"Yes, I can see that," Joey said as he stood there miserably in his rumpled plaid flannel shirt, Nirvana T-shirt and torn jeans.

"If you're going to be a famous writer, then you got to write in style."

"That's a very thoughtful gift, Elliot," Monette said. "Isn't it, Joey?"

"Yes, it is." Joey's eyes never left the ground. "Thank you."

Boyd's gift also came nestled inside of a small, hinged case. It was a pair of sunglasses. Joey peered at them, somewhat mystified.

"Those, my young friend, are Ray-Ban Wayfarers," Boyd informed him. "The one and only James Dean himself wore a pair just like those."

"Thank you very much," Joey said woodenly.

"What else did you get for your birthday, kid?" Elliot asked.

Danielle said, "Mom and I found him this really great fringed buckskin jacket at a clothing store in Venice. It's totally Joey."

The decibel level of the paparazzi outside of the gate suddenly shot way up. There was major, major yelling. And I could hear a couple of car engines revving out there. Then the front gate swung open and the no-longer man of the house, Patrick Van Pelt, came roaring up the old cobbled drive in a shiny, bright red Jeep Wrangler that had a roll bar in lieu of a top. It also had oversized tires and an even more oversized sound system that was blasting "All She Wants to Do Is Dance," by the singularly annoying Don Henley.

Patrick pulled up beside Boyd's Town Car and jumped out wearing a Hawaiian shirt, cargo shorts and leather flip-flops, looking every inch the tanned, chiseled leading man that the American viewing public knew and loved. He flashed his bright white smile at us and waved. He appeared to be incredibly happy to be back home again. He also appeared to be incredibly bombed. He swayed more than a little as he took a gulp from the fifth of Jose Cuervo Gold tequila he was toting.

Lou Riggio, the flesh-colored Incredible Hulk, roared up the driveway behind him in a gunmetal gray mid-sixties GTO, parked it behind the Jeep and got out, looming there in a tank top, gym shorts and sneakers, a Tootsie Pop stuck in his mouth.

"Here we go . . . ," Monette murmured under her breath.

Danielle reached for her mother's hand and gripped it. "Here we go . . ."

"Hey-hey, it's a party!" Patrick called out as he started up the stone path toward us, staggering slightly. "I need me a wedge of lime, a shaker of salt and my birthday boy! Where's my boy?" He peered around. "There he is! How are you, son?"

"I'm fine, Dad," Joey answered uncomfortably.

Patrick approached Monette, who didn't blink, didn't breathe. Just glared at him. He grinned at her. "Hello, Queenie."

"How dare you show up here drunk?" she demanded angrily.

"Didn't think I could pull this off sober, did you? Hey, Princess!" he exclaimed as his gaze fell on Danielle, who seemed thoroughly mortified by her father's state of sobriety, or total lack thereof. "I swear, you're turning into a long drink of water just like your mom. Have you gotten taller on me?"

"I don't know, Dad," she said in a pained voice.

Patrick's gaze fell upon me next. "So you're still here."

"I told you that I would be."

"Big mistake, dude."

"My whole life is one big mistake. I try to stay consistent."

He frowned at me in bewilderment, as if I'd just spoken to him in a foreign tongue, before he said, "Oh, hey, you all remember Lou, don't you?"

Lou stood there in silence like a granite boulder, sucking on his grape Tootsie Pop, his shaved head gleaming in the sunlight. In his left hand he clutched that same little blue nylon zippered bag he'd had with him in Patrick's trailer.

Patrick grinned at Joey and said, "Hey, birthday boy, you see that red Wrangler in the driveway? It's all yours!" He tossed Joey the keys. Joey made no effort to catch them. They landed on the bluestone three feet away from him with a clatter. "Lou helped me pick it out, and Lou knows his wheels. It's a total rocket. Got the six-cylinder, 180-horsepower engine. Right, Lou?"

"Right, Pats," Lou confirmed in his sandpapery voice.

Joey let out a pained sigh. "I don't drive, Dad."

"Well, now you have a good reason to learn how to."

"No, you don't understand. I don't believe in cars."

"What's not to believe in? They're *real*. Go over and touch it if you don't believe me. And let me tell you something else. That Wrangler right there? That is a solid, proven chick magnet. Trust me, when you show up at school behind the wheel of that thang, you'll have to fight off the girls with a Louisville Slugger. Why, they'll be all . . ." Patrick broke off suddenly, tilting his head at me with a perplexed look on his face. "Didn't you have a kind of short, four-legged sidekick yesterday?"

"Still do."

"Where is she?"

"Guarding the keys to the Jeep."

He spotted her now, crouched on the pavement next to the keys. "Why's she doing that?"

"Force of habit. I used to lose mine a lot. Lulu was my spotter."

"Awful handy to have around," he said approvingly as he took a swig of his tequila, noticing Reggie for the first time. Couldn't help it. She was standing right in front of him, the better to peer at him. He peered back at her. "So you're the twisted sister."

She nodded. "I'm the twisted sister."

"I didn't realize you were so short."

"And I didn't realize you were a shit-faced drunk," she said, wrinkling her nose. "You smell like you started two days ago and never stopped."

He let out a laugh. "I'll tell you something, twisted sis. I don't usually go for mouthy little spinners, but in your case I'm prepared to make an exception."

"Wow, I am *so* flattered right now," Reggie responded sweetly.

Patrick took another swig of tequila, paying no attention to Elliot or Boyd. He had zero interest in either of them. "Where's my lime?" he demanded. "Where's my salt? Where's *Maritza*, damn it?"

Maritza came out the French doors from the kitchen, wiping her hands on a dish towel. "Yes, Senor Patrick?" she said in a quiet voice, her face drawn tight.

He smiled at her hugely. "How are you, hon?"

"I am fine, Senor Patrick."

"Yes, you are. Plenty fine. Get me a setup for my tequila, will you? One of those double shot glasses from my bar. A wedge of lime, shaker of salt and an ice-cold Corona. *Comprende?*"

"Yes, Senor Patrick."

"And a Corona for my man Lou," he added, eyeballing Maritza's butt as she went inside to fetch what he'd asked for. Like son, like father. Although Patrick didn't sneak furtive glances the way Joey did. He just flat out stared.

And Monette watched him stare, glowering.

"I need to make a phone call," Elliot said abruptly.

"So do I," said Boyd.

The two of them retreated to opposite ends of the swimming pool and were soon busy barking into their mobile phones.

Reggie watched them, greatly amused. "Aren't they cute, Stewie?"

"As buttons."

"You don't suppose they're talking to each other, do you?"

"I like to think they are."

Maritza returned with Patrick's double shot glass and set it on the wrought iron table for him along with a saltshaker and a bowl of lime wedges. She pulled two long-neck bottles of Corona from one of the tubs of ice, opened them and set them on the table.

Patrick didn't bother to thank her. Just splashed some Cuervo from the bottle into the glass, shook some salt onto the back of his left hand, licked it off and downed the Cuervo in one gulp. Then he squeezed the juice from a lime wedge into his mouth and took a long gulp of Corona, groaning contentedly.

Lou did thank her as he reached for his beer and took a long, thirsty drink, not bothering to remove the grape Tootsie Pop from the side of his mouth while he drank. The big man had style, I had to give him that.

"Oh, hey," Patrick said to Maritza. "Is Hector around today?"

"It is Saturday, Senor Patrick."

"He doesn't work on Saturdays?"

"Not usually. Maybe sometimes."

"Well, if he shows up, tell him I want to see him, okay?"

"Yes, Senor Patrick."

There was another commotion outside the front gate. Shouting. A huge roar of voices. Then someone out there buzzed the house.

Maritza went inside to answer it, returning to the patio to announce, "Senorita Kat has arrived."

"Now we can have us a *real* party!" Patrick whooped. "You're going to love her, Queenie. And she's been dying to see the house."

"I'll just bet she has," Monette said between gritted teeth.

A black BMW convertible with its top down came zipping up the driveway with Public Enemy's "Shut 'Em Down" blaring from its sound system, because absolutely nothing says young, privileged white TV starlet like gangsta rap. Kat Zachry's half-brother, Kyle, was behind the wheel. Kat rode shotgun. A third person was sprawled across the back seat. Kyle parked behind Lou's GTO. The three of them got out and started up the path toward us.

Kat wore an oversized number-thirty-two Magic Johnson Lakers jersey over a baggy pair of gym shorts. She looked incredibly childlike to me. She was only two years older than Joey, after all. She gave Patrick a naughty grin and a hug before she extended her hand to Joey and said, "Hey, I'm Kat. Happy birthday."

"I don't believe in shaking hands," he informed her coldly.

Patrick glared at him. "Hey, what have I told you about that goddamned mouth of yours?"

"No prob, I'll just give it a smooch." Kat kissed Joey smack on his mouth.

He immediately turned bright red.

"Queenie, allow me to introduce Miss Kat Zachry," Patrick said with exaggerated formality as he stood there, swaying more than slightly.

"Very nice to meet you, Kat," Monette said with chilly politeness.

"Nice to meet you, too," Kat said to Monette with that same naughty grin on her face. She was genuinely enjoying this incredibly awkward social encounter. "Oh, hey, everybody, this is my big brother, Kyle."

Kat's pudgy loser of a half-brother nodded to everyone but didn't bother to say anything or shake hands with anyone. Didn't budge from Kat's side at all. Just stood there, looking like a nervous weasel.

"And we brought our cousin Trish," Kat added. "Hope you don't mind."

"Of course not," Monette said with still more chilly politeness.

Cousin Trish was in her early twenties and wore a cropped, sleeveless gray sweatshirt over a white bikini. She was tall and slender with long blond hair, long legs and a tight little bottom. But she shared none of her famous cousin's fine-featured beauty. Her eyes were set too close together. Her nose was too broad. She had a thin-lipped mouth and not enough chin. Trish wasn't unattractive. She was simply ordinary-looking. Every woman on the planet seemed ordinary-looking if she happened to be standing next to Kat Zachry.

Patrick peered at her with keen interest. "Have we met before, cousin Trish? You look awful damned familiar."

"Trish had a bit in the beach party scene last week, babe," Kat reminded him. "She rode around on Kirk's shoulders until he threw her in the water."

"I came up sputtering and called him a meathead," Trish said.

Patrick nodded his shaggy blond head. "Sure, that's it."

Elliot and Boyd rejoined us, both of them acting extremely guarded now that the Pat 'n' Kat tabloid freak show was unfolding right before their eyes.

"Did you get some bitchen birthday presents?" Kat asked Joey.

"Elliot gave him a very fine Waterman fountain pen," Monette informed her. "Boyd got him a lovely pair of sunglasses. And Danielle and I found him a truly special buckskin jacket."

"That reminds me . . ." Kat turned her bedroom eyes on me. "I still want that leather jacket of yours."

"Dream on."

"And don't forget the world-class wheels his old man got him," Patrick said, splashing some more Cuervo into his bar glass.

"You are one lucky dude, Joey," Kat said as she stood there gazing up at the weathered brick enormity of Aintree Manor, tilting her pretty head this way and that, inspecting it as if she intended to move in there very soon. Possibly she did. Possibly Patrick had made her a boatload of promises. Nothing would surprise me. "I love your house," she said to Monette. "It's really classical."

"Thank you," Monette said curtly.

"Kind of old-timey for my taste," Kyle said. "Me, I like new stuff."

"Kyle, sweetie, your taste isn't something you should talk about out loud," Kat said to him. "You haven't got any."

"I know what I like," he said defensively.

"Would you care to take a tour of the downstairs?" Monette asked her.

Kat's eyes widened eagerly. "You kidding me? Come on, Trish, we're getting a tour of the mansion."

She and her leggy blonde cousin followed Monette inside through the French doors. Kyle stayed put, helping himself to a bottle of Corona.

Danielle and Joey stayed put, too. Joey had developed a healthy interest in the guacamole that Maritza had set out on the table.

And Danielle wanted a word with Reggie. "Why do we have to be nice to her?" she asked in a voice that was barely more than a whisper.

"You don't," Reggie answered. "Your mom's just trying to get through the next few minutes without going completely insane. Want to swim?"

Danielle nodded her head. The two of them started for the pool, Danielle shrugging out of the boyfriend shirt she wore over her white bikini. Reggie peeled off her T-shirt and shorts. She had on the yellow bikini that she'd borrowed from Danielle yesterday. They dove right in but didn't swim. Just hung out in the shallow end talking. Lulu stayed by my side, keeping a watchful eye on them.

"So, listen up, Trish isn't really our cousin," Kyle told Joey as he helped himself to some of the guacamole. "She's your birthday present, bro. From me and Kat to you. Knock yourself out."

Joey frowned at him. "I don't think I understand."

Kyle let out a laugh. "She's here to pop your cherry, okay?"

"I—I thought she was an actress," Joey stammered, totally flustered.

"Did you hear me say she wasn't?"

Patrick and Lou stood across the table from them listening with keen interest. So did Elliot and Boyd.

"Just go upstairs to your room, okay?" Kyle told him. "She'll join you up there in a few minutes. You can do anything you want to her. Anything you've ever dreamed of doing when you're lying in bed at night spanking your monkey. Her awesome bod is all yours. Greatest birthday present ever, right?"

Joey gaped at Kyle in horrified amazement. "That's disgusting. *You're* disgusting!"

"Hey, what did I just tell you about that mouth of yours?" Patrick snarled, moving toward Joey with his fists clenched.

Joey gulped in fright. So much fright that I had no doubt Patrick was in the habit of knocking him around. "That I—I shouldn't be rude."

"Right, that you shouldn't be rude. Do we need to have ourselves a conversation?"

"No, sir. May I please go up to my room and read now?" Joey asked, his voice quavering.

"Yeah, go on," Patrick said disgustedly as Joey fled inside. Patrick sampled the guacamole, munching on a blue corn chip thoughtfully. "I still say that boy's a faggot."

"Nope, don't think so," I said.

"Well, hell," Kyle said. "If he doesn't want to tap Trish then I may have a go. That tight little ass of hers rocks me."

"Me, too." Lou smacked his lips. "A party's a party, right?"

"A party's a party," Kyle agreed. "Help yourself."

"Hey, who are *you* to be giving him permission, dickwad!" Patrick hollered at Kyle. "This is my fucking house, not yours! If Lou wants her he can have her. And so can I!"

"Whatever you say, Patrick." Kyle held his hands out palms up, a gesture of appeasement. "You're the man."

"Damned straight," Patrick said, suddenly peering at Kyle with a mystified expression on his chiseled face. "Do I know you?"

"Kind of. I'm Kyle, Kat's brother, remember?"

"Oh, right, right. Thought you looked familiar," he said, wavering very unsteadily. He had to plant his hand on the table to keep from toppling over. "Lou, everything's starting to spin around . . ."

"No prob, Pats." Lou promptly produced a prescription bottle and razor blade from his little blue nylon bag. Opened the bottle and dumped a generous heap of coke onto the glass surface of the table. He began cutting it into lines with the razor blade.

"Hey, take that somewhere else," Elliot said to them disapprovingly.

"Mind your own fucking business, bozo," Patrick shot back.

"I *am* minding my business. I happen to manage Monette's career. This is a family affair. There are kids here."

Boyd, meanwhile, stared goggle-eyed at the four, five, six lines of coke on the table.

"All set, Pats," Lou said. "Anyone got some folding scratch?"

Kyle pulled a five-dollar bill from the pocket of his shorts. Lou took it from him, rolled it into a tight little straw and handed it to Patrick, who bent over and snorted up two lines. Boyd watched him, looking extremely uneasy.

But not as uneasy as Maritza, who'd come out onto the patio to lay a dozen ears of corn on the grill.

Patrick grinned at her. "You want some of this, hon?"

"No, Senor Patrick." She dumped the corn hurriedly onto the grill and scurried back into the kitchen.

"This is very inappropriate behavior, Patrick," Elliot said insistently.

"I just told you, fat man—butt out." He swiped at his nose, sniffling. "Help yourself, Lou. You, too, Kyle."

"Thanks, don't mind if I do," Kyle said, waiting for Lou to snort up two lines and pass him the rolled-up bill. Then he finished off the last two lines.

"I think I'll go wash up for lunch," Boyd said hoarsely. He went inside, walking very rapidly.

"Will you *please* put that damned stuff away before you-know-who comes back?" Elliot pleaded. "Because, I am telling you, she will hit the roof."

"Keep your shirt on." Patrick wiped the last traces of coke from the table with his finger and rubbed his gums with it.

Lou returned the pill bottle to his zippered bag, then handed Patrick two capsules of those so-called mineral supplements. Patrick washed them down with a gulp of tequila.

By then you-know-who had returned from her Aintree Manor house tour with Kat and Trish, who were chattering like excited schoolgirls about how *totally* amazing the house was.

"What's wrong, Elliot?" Monette demanded, noticing at once how uncomfortable he appeared.

"Not a thing," Elliot said, chuckling nervously.

She spotted Danielle and Reggie in the pool together, then glanced around, frowning. "Where's Joey?"

"Went up to his room," Patrick said. "He's turning into a god-damned hermit. Ought to do something about that, Queenie."

"Is that right?" she responded testily. "Exactly what do you suggest?"

"I want to see the house, too," Kyle said, his eyes gleaming at Trish. "Will you show me around?"

Trish looked at him with eyes that were suddenly very old and tired. "Sure, whatever."

She led him inside, Kyle staring hungrily at her tight butt in that little white bikini she had on.

Lou was staring at it, too. "Okay if I join the tour, Pats?"

"Knock yourself out, Lou. Just stay downstairs, okay? Upstairs is for family only."

Lou started inside, squeezing his way past Kat in the kitchen doorway, where she was talking quietly and purposefully to Boyd, who was listening to her and nodding his head. A moment later, she and Boyd slipped away to stroll the estate's grounds together, Kat still talking, Boyd still listening.

Elliot yanked a white linen hankie from the pocket of his magenta warm-up pants and dabbed at his forehead, which was damp with perspiration. Then he puffed out his cheeks and plopped himself down in a chair at the table.

"I have to take a humongous piss," Patrick announced to no one in particular.

"Thank you for sharing that with us," Monette said. "Please, don't let us stop you."

He let out a huge laugh. "Wouldn't think of it, Queenie," he assured her before he went staggering inside.

Monette let her breath out slowly. "I'd say we're doing fabulously well so far. Joey's hiding in his room. Patrick's bombed. His so-called friends are wandering around my home doing God knows what. It's another idyllic Saturday afternoon here on Rockingham Avenue." She pulled an opened bottle of Sancerre from one of the ice-filled tubs and poured herself a glass, taking a sip of it as Maritza came out to turn the corn on the grill. "How is lunch coming, Maritza?"

"The onions and peppers are frying on the stove," she answered quietly. "Should I put the steaks on?"

"Yes, why don't you? And thank you for your hard work and your patience. We'll get through this. Somehow."

Maritza went back inside, returned with a huge platter of marinated flank steaks and began to lay them, sizzling, on the hot grill.

Reggie and Danielle climbed out of the pool, wrapped themselves in towels and hurried up the path toward us, their wet faces shining in the bright sunlight.

"Mom, do we have time to go up and change?" Danielle asked.

"Absolutely," Monette assured her.

They dashed inside, Reggie murmuring something to Danielle under her breath and Danielle responding with a giggle.

Me, I decided to swim some laps before lunch, mostly so I could be by myself for a few minutes. I'd had just about enough of people. I took off the khaki shirt I was wearing over my swim trunks, dove in the deep end and began to swim, enjoying the cool, clean water. It made for a pleasant contrast to how soiled I felt being around Patrick, Lou and Kyle. Kat was another class act. She and "cousin" Trish. The whole lot of them made me sick. But I've discovered over the years that I always feel sick as soon as I've spent more than twenty-four hours on the left coast's so-called beautiful dreamland full of so-called beautiful people. My body, mind and soul yearn to be back in authentically filthy, noisy, smelly, freezing cold New York. Back where I belong.

I swam, Lulu running alongside me barking her head off. Over on the patio, Elliot seemed to have taken over as temporary grill master. Monette and Maritza had both gone inside the house. Elliot stood there all by himself, tongs in hand, flipping the steaks with dutiful care. Even though the man was now the head of a multimillion-dollar production empire, he'd spent the first half of his career as a shlepper of small-time comic talent. For a man like Elliot, there was no such thing as a job that was beneath him. He'd been asked to work the grill. He was working it.

I swam. Lulu barked. She barked so loud that I almost didn't hear the gunshots.

Almost.

CHAPTER SEVEN

There were two of them. They came from inside the house.

Then came silence.

I stopped swimming. Lulu stopped barking. Over on the patio, Elliot froze, tongs in hand, and stared up at the house.

The silence was broken by the hollering of the paparazzi crowded outside of the gate, their voices amped by a whole new level of hysteria. Quickly, I got out of the pool and grabbed a towel.

That's when I heard the second set of shots. Two more.

I dashed toward the house with the towel around my neck and Lulu trailing right behind me.

Elliot's eyes were wide with fright. "What the hell was that noise?"

"Gunfire. What do you think?"

"Should we call someone?"

"No need. The cops on the gate heard it. They'll phone it in."

"They won't come check it out for themselves?"

"Can't. They've got a tabloid mob out there to contain. They'll call for help. We've got a few minutes before they get up here. We'd better see what happened."

I headed into the kitchen. Elliot followed me. On the stove a cast-iron skillet of onions and peppers was cooking on a low flame. A flour tortilla was warming in a second skillet on another burner. There was a package of tortillas and a stack of white kitchen cloths on the counter next to the stove. What there wasn't was any sign of Maritza.

"She asked me to keep an eye on the steaks while she finished up in here," Elliot said to me. "I wonder where she went."

I turned off the flames under the pans and hurried toward the grand front rooms, hearing voices upstairs. Lulu dashed her way up the curving stairway. I followed her.

Reggie and Danielle were standing together in the upstairs hall, both wearing terrified expressions on their faces as they stared down the hall at the big double doors to the master suite, which were closed. Lulu headed straight for the double doors and sat, staring at them.

"Where's Monette?" I asked them as Elliot came waddling up behind me, still clutching the grill tongs. "What's happened?"

"We d-don't know." Reggie's voice was quaking with fear. She'd changed from her wet bikini into an old Grateful Dead T-shirt and shorts. I put my arm around her. She nestled against me, trembling.

Lulu continued to sit and stare at the doors to the master suite.

"Did you knock?"

Reggie shook her head.

"Monette . . . ?" Elliot called out. "Everything okay, hon?"

There was no response.

Danielle hadn't said a word. Just stood there in wide-eyed fear.

"Did you hear anything?" I asked her.

She blinked at me. "Like what?"

"An argument, raised voices?"

She shook her head. "I was in my shower rinsing off the chlorine from the pool." She wore a pair of blue jeans now with her untucked lavender boyfriend shirt. Her hair was wet. "I was drying off when I heard the shots."

"And what about Joey? Where's he?"

"In his room, I guess. That's where he always is."

I heard rapid footsteps on the stairs. It was Maritza, who was puffing a bit and looking more than a bit shaken.

"Where have you been?" I asked her.

"In the kitchen, Senor Hoagy," she replied, her brown eyes avoiding mine. "The peppers and onions. I was stirring them."

She hadn't been in the kitchen stirring the peppers and onions. I'd just come from the kitchen. But I didn't dispute her outright lie. Nor did I say anything about the fact that thirty minutes ago Maritza had been wearing a pale pink dental hygienist's outfit and now wore a powder blue one. What I did say was, "If you were in the kitchen why didn't you use the service stairs?"

"I tried, but the door to the senora's suite is locked," she explained, snatching the grill tongs from Elliot. "You told me you would keep turning the steaks. They are burned now. No good to eat."

"I don't think anyone will be eating lunch," I said to her.

Now I heard more footsteps on the stairs. They belonged to Lou, Kyle and Joey's seventeenth-birthday present, Trish.

"I heard shots," Lou growled. "What's going on?"

"That's what we're trying to figure out. Where have you been?"

"Hanging out in the room with the pool table in it."

"That would be the billiard room. You were shooting pool?"

"Why is that any of your business?" Kyle demanded. "And where's Kat?"

"No idea," I said, noticing how flushed and sweaty all three of them were. They all gave off the same musky animal smell, too. They'd been having themselves a three-way, which is to say that Trish had been doing both men at once, and the doing hadn't been gentle. She had blotchy red finger marks around her throat, fresh abrasions on her knees and her white bikini was on a bit crooked.

I wondered if they'd been making use of the Eartha Kitt sofa. The romantic in me wanted to think they had.

"What's Pats up to?" asked Lou, who—just this once—wasn't clutching his blue nylon zipper bag full of drugs. Must have stashed it somewhere in that room with the pool table in it. "Where is he?"

I could hear the LAPD sirens way off in the distance now. The first responders were on their way. Lulu was still parked in front of those double doors to the master suite, staring right at them.

"Stay here," I said to the others, starting down the hallway toward the suite. I knocked.

"Who is it?" Monette responded in a calm, clear voice.

"It's Hoagy, Monette. Are you all right?"

"Perfectly fine, thank you."

"May I come in?"

"Are you alone?"

"Lulu's with me. No one else."

"You and Lulu may come in."

I opened the door and in we went. It smelled faintly of gunpowder in there. The windows were wide open, a breeze billowing the white lace curtains.

"Please close the door," Monette said to me.

I closed it, my eyes flicking around as I took in the scene before me. Monette was standing, gun in hand, over the cooling sack of dead meat that until very recently had been one of network television's biggest stars, not to mention her husband. Patrick lay on his back on the floor next to the bed in his Hawaiian shirt and shorts, bleeding out onto the stylishly worn Persian rug underneath him. He had two bullet holes in his chest, one in his right shoulder and one in his left side. His eyes were wide open. Surprised. He looked very surprised.

The master suite, which had been primped and fluffed enough

for a magazine shoot the last time I'd seen it, was a total mess. There were desk and dressing table drawers flung open, items of clothing and jewelry tossed about. And then there was the blood spatter that was all over the ruffled white canopy bed, white linen bedspread and plump white pillows, not to mention the wall behind the bed.

There was also blood all over Monette. Her nose was bleeding profusely into her chambray shirt, which she'd stripped off and held to her nose like a wadded towel. The blood had dripped down her chin onto her tank top and white linen pants. She had long, bloody gouges on her bare forearms—fingernail gouges by the look of them—and red finger marks around her upper arms.

The gun she was holding was a stainless-steel Beretta 9mm with a black textured grip.

"Would you please put that gun down, Monette?"

"Yes, of course," she responded calmly. Eerily so. Possibly she was in shock. "Shall I hand it to you?"

"Just put it down on the floor."

She set it down on the rug next to her feet while Lulu nosed around in search of the four shell casings on the floor. She found them with no difficulty.

"Would you like to tell me what happened?"

"Patrick attacked me like a crazy man," she answered in that same calm voice. "He grabbed me, punched me. He was completely deranged. So I took my Beretta from my nightstand and shot him. I had to. He was going to kill me."

"How did you two end up alone in here together?"

"I came up here to powder my nose and when—"

"Is that your way of saying use the bathroom?"

"It is. And when I walked in I found him ransacking those drawers like a lunatic. He insisted he was looking for a valuable Rolex Submariner that he'd misplaced. I said, 'Do you mean like the one you gave to Hector?' He became outraged and said, 'Are you telling me that he stole my Rolex?' I said, 'No, I'm telling you that you gave it to him. He's very proud of it.' Patrick said, 'He's lying. I never gave him that watch.' And I said, 'Patrick, you don't remember half the things you do anymore. You're bombed every waking moment. How dare you show up drunk for your son's birthday party? How dare you bring your little tramp of a girlfriend? How dare you?' That's when he lost it and punched me in the nose *really* hard. I've never been hit in the nose before. It hurts like hell."

"Yes, it does. Bleeds a lot, too. Here, let me . . ."

She lowered the wadded, bloody shirt from her nose. It was oozing blood from both nostrils and was starting to swell up.

"We'll get some ice on that soon. But for now . . ." I took the bloody shirt into the bathroom and set it in one of the sinks, glancing at it for a moment and not liking what I was seeing. I brought Monette a towel. "Here, press this against it," I said before I took a quick look around the suite. Monette's immense walk-in closet was orderly and neat. Patrick hadn't gone in there, apparently. The door that led to the service stairs was closed. Maritza had told me it was locked. I checked it and discovered it was unlocked—which might or might not mean something. I didn't know. I didn't know anything yet. "How many times did you shoot him?" I asked her as I heard the police sirens growing nearer.

"Twice," she answered, holding the towel to her nose. "The first time, that is. I hit him in his shoulder and side, I believe. He fell back against the bed and slumped slowly to the floor. 'You shot me, Queenie,' he said, staring at me in utter disbelief. I said, 'You're damned right I did, you horrible bastard. Do you have any idea what kind of hell you've put me through? Do you even care?' His response was to laugh at me. I thought he might apologize. Say something decent and human. Instead, he laughed and told me what a rotten bed partner I was. Went so far as to inform me that he'd had better sex with total strangers in the parking lot of Jerry's. He *wanted* me to shoot him, I swear. So I did. Twice more, right in the chest. And I'm not the least bit sorry."

"I'd advise you not to say anything more until Elliot can hire you an attorney. Just keep quiet when the police get here."

"But I have nothing to hide."

"Nonetheless, you'll be better off if you keep quiet."

She tilted her head at me curiously. "Why am I getting the impression that you've been through this sort of thing before?"

"Because I have. Take a seat in one of those armchairs by the fireplace. Keep holding that towel to your nose, okay?" I went back out into the corridor with Lulu, closing the door behind me.

Everyone was waiting out there expectantly. Everyone except for Kat and Boyd, who still hadn't turned up. And Joey, whose bedroom door remained closed.

"What's happened?" Danielle demanded tearfully, clutching Reggie's hand tightly in her own.

"I'm sorry to say your father is dead. Your mother shot him."

Maritza let out a gasp. Danielle and Reggie exchanged a look of utter horror.

"Is . . . Monette okay?" Reggie asked me, her voice faltering.

"She got beat up but she's okay."

"I don't fucking *believe* this!" roared Lou, who picked up a glass vase filled with roses from a hall table and hurled it against the wall, sending shards of broken glass flying everywhere. "I'll kill that bitch!"

"You're not killing anyone," I said to him. "Get a hold of your-self."

"I want to see Mom," Danielle said.

"I know you do, but that's a crime scene in there. The police will want everyone to stay out." I heard the LAPD sirens drawing nearer on Sunset. They'd just about reached the foot of Rocking-ham by the sound of them. "Elliot, she's going to need a good criminal defense attorney."

He nodded his frizzy head. "I'll get her the best."

Lulu was busy sniffing her way from the master suite directly to Joey's closed door, the one that had the hand-lettered STAY THE FUCK OUT sign taped to it. When she arrived there she sat, looking at me.

"Does Joey have any idea what's happened?" I asked Danielle.

She let out a sob. "He always yells and screams at me if I bother him."

I knocked on Joey's door. When he didn't answer I opened it and went in, Lulu darting in ahead of me as I shut it behind us. It was dark in there aside from his small desk lamp and the light coming from the screen of his Macintosh, where Joey was seated tapping away at the keyboard. He had his headphones on.

I thumped him on the shoulder.

He jumped, startled. "What do *you* want?" he demanded, re-moving his headphones.

I opened the wooden shutters over his windows, sending sun-light streaming into the darkened room. Joey blinked at me like the cave dweller he was. Or make that the cave dweller he wanted me to think he was. Because there was definitely something not right about Joey. He was wearing different clothes than he'd been wearing a half-hour ago out on the patio. Different flannel shirt, different T-shirt, newer, darker blue jeans. The cuffs of his flannel shirt looked damp. So did its collar and his long, stringy hair that tumbled over it.

Lulu went under the desk and sniffed at Joey's beat-up black-and-white Chuck Taylor All Stars, snuffling and snorting.

"Your father's dead, Joey. I'm sorry. Your mother shot him."

"What are you talking about?" he cried out. "When?"

"Just now, in their bedroom. You didn't hear the shots?"

He shook his head. "My headphones block out everything. That's kind of the whole point."

"Don't you want to know if your mother's okay?"

"I'm assuming she is or you would have said otherwise."

"Fair point. Come with me, Joey. Your sister needs you."

He gulped. "What am *I* supposed to do?"

"Be her big brother. Comfort her."

"Okay. I can do that, I guess."

Everyone was still standing out in the hallway. Except for Lou, who'd vanished. And Boyd and Kat, who still hadn't appeared.

Danielle rushed to Joey and flung herself at him, sobbing. "Daddy's *dead*, Joey! What are we going to do?"

The kid wasn't exactly what I'd call a boa constrictor in the hugs department. He stood there stiffly, patting her gingerly on the back. They were quite a study in contrast. She was so golden, athletic and beautiful. He was so pale, pimply and gawky. It was hard to believe that they'd been produced by the same two humans.

"It'll be okay . . . ," he said as the police sirens pulled up outside the gate on Rockingham. Two cars, it sounded like. "Should we . . . go talk to Mom?"

"Hoagy said not to yet."

"And God knows the Hoagster's always right," Boyd joked as he and Kat came up the stairs at long last. Boyd wore a cheerful grin on his face. Kat wore no expression at all on hers. Bored. She looked bored. "We've been looking everywhere for you folks. Why are you all up here? And what's with the sirens?"

A buzzer went off in the kitchen. The police at the gate wanted in. Maritza went downstairs to buzz them in.

"Where have the two of you been?" I asked Boyd.

"Why, what's going on?"

"Monette just shot and killed Patrick. Didn't you hear the shots?"

"We thought they came from up in the hills. Somebody trying to take out a coyote or—or . . ." Boyd looked at me in disbelief. "Monette *killed* him? For real?"

"Doesn't get more real," I said as big Lou came charging back up the stairs. I didn't bother to ask him where he'd been. I had a pretty good idea where.

"I have to phone Mr. Harmon Wright right away." Boyd's voice was heavy with dread. "He *hates* finding out this kind of news from CNN."

I could hear the police cars pull up in the pea gravel turnaround outside. Car doors opened and closed. Footsteps approached the house. The doorbell rang. Maritza went to let them in.

Kat started toward the door of the master suite.

"You'd better stay out of there," Elliot cautioned her.

She ignored him. She was Kat Zachry. Nobody told Kat Zachry what to do. She opened the door, took two steps inside and stopped, staring at the body of her lover dead on the floor.

I pulled her out of there, shutting the door. "You don't want Danielle and Joey to see their father in that condition, do you?"

"I've never seen a dead person before," she said to me, stunned.

"Did you care about him at all?" I asked her, hearing the husky voices of the cops downstairs. "Or was it strictly a career move?"

She gazed up at me with those big, brown bedroom eyes of hers and said, "Fuck off."

Then she found Kyle and stood there with him, glaring at me. He put an arm around her protectively. Trish stood next to them in her bikini with her red, splotchy neck and red scraped knees, possibly wondering why she hadn't chosen to spend the afternoon scrubbing the stubborn mold from the grout between her bathroom tiles. It would have been a major improvement over this.

Two burly young cops in uniform came barging up the stairs and, from that moment on, the official process unfolded in its own painstaking, step-by-step way. One of them herded us downstairs and took down our basic identification and contact information while the other called in Patrick's death and Monette's injuries. The pair of cops who'd arrived in the second car remained outside in the driveway to make sure that none of the paparazzi jumped the wall and tried to get in the house. An EMT crew arrived soon to attend to Monette's bloodied nose and arms. A pair of homicide detectives showed up soon after that. Then came two vans full of crime scene personnel—the technicians who would, just for starters, take a million and one Polaroid photos of Patrick's body, Monette's wounds, the murder weapon, the shell casings on the floor and the blood that was spattered everywhere. And then came the county medical examiner's man to examine Patrick's body and move it so that more Polaroids could be taken of the blood-soaked rug underneath him.

While all of this went on upstairs in the master suite, we waited downstairs to be questioned by the homicide detectives.

Danielle and Joey sat huddled close together in the conservatory with Reggie, who spoke to her grief-stricken niece and nephew in a soft, soothing voice. Maritza sat near them with her hands folded in her lap and a frightened look on her face as she watched the authorities clomp up and down the stairs.

Kat, Kyle and Trish sat together on one of the chintz sofas in the living room in impatient silence. Trish now wore her cropped sweatshirt over her bikini. Lou sat in an armchair by the fireplace sucking on a grape Tootsie Pop and perspiring like crazy. He was barely keeping it together. His breathing was rapid and shallow, and his massive hands were gripping the arms of the chair so tightly that I half-expected him to rip them from the body of the chair, let loose with a roar and go crashing out the nearest window.

Boyd and Elliot paced. The living room. The hallway. The dining room. Back to the living room. They'd made the calls they needed to make. Now all that was left was to ponder the dollars and cents ramifications of what had just happened. And pace.

Me, I grabbed Boyd by the back of his polo shirt and yanked him into the billiard room. "Where were you and Kat?" I asked him in a low, quiet voice. "And please don't tell me you two were getting it on."

"No way," he protested. "She's got a kid inside of her. What kind of a sleazy perv do you think I . . . ? Never mind, don't answer that. We were out back behind the pool house, okay?"

"Doing what?"

"Climbing in through the window. Well, *I* was climbing in. Kat couldn't risk it herself, being pregnant and all."

"Why on earth were you climbing in my window?"

"She wanted to borrow your leather motorcycle jacket and—"

"Flight jacket."

"And she told me you'd said it would be okay, but that you must have forgotten—because when we tried your door it was locked."

"Did you honestly believe that bullshit story?"

Boyd's eyes widened. "She was trying to steal it?"

"No, she's not that dumb. She convinced *you* to do it."

"Well, I didn't. Couldn't find the damned thing."

"Of course you couldn't. I hid it." Tucked it safely away in one of the Roadmaster's saddlebags. "What I can't believe is she talked you into breaking and entering."

"It was strictly business," he said defensively. "She said if I helped her she'd let me represent her book."

"Book? What book?"

"What difference does it make? We'll cook something up. Kat's *money*. And her upside is huge, or at least it was until an hour ago. Help me out here, amigo. You're the one who knows everything there is to know about showbiz murders. Will this be good for her career or bad?"

At our feet Lulu let out a low growl.

"Why is she doing that?" he asked me.

"Because she knows that if you don't get away from me right now I'm going to slug you."

"All I meant was—"

"*Far* away."

"Okay, okay . . ." He went back out into the hall and resumed his pacing.

I didn't feel like talking to anyone else so I stayed in the billiard room and shot some pool. Lulu was planning to curl up on the Eartha Kitt sofa until she sniffed at it with a basset hound's version of puritanical disdain and opted for a leather armchair instead. It wasn't bad there in the clubby silence of the billiard room. The antique table was a beauty. The cue stick that I'd chosen from the rack on the wall was balanced just right. The balls went exactly where I wanted them to go. I found it comforting to listen to the timeless clink of ball against ball as the crime scene professionals tromped their way up and down the curving stairway, speaking in loud voices.

I didn't hear the last of them arrive. Didn't even know he was there until I saw him standing in the doorway of the billiard room watching me shoot pool with a boyish grin on his face. I knew him from the last time I'd been in town. Different star. Different murder.

Lieutenant Emil Lamp was the department's go-to celebrity homicide ace. And as unlikely-looking an ace as I'd ever come across. He was a fresh-scrubbed, bright-eyed, eager little guy with neat blond hair, alert blue eyes and wholesome apple cheeks. He bore an eerie resemblance to Howdy Doody, to be perfectly honest. He wore a tan suit made out of something no-iron, a yellow button-down shirt, a striped tie and a pair of nubucks with red rubber soles. Lamp specialized in high-profile showbiz killings because he and his nubucks happened to be uncommonly good at not stepping on famous, sensitive toes. He was polite, tactful and way, way sharp.

"Cheese and crackers, Hoagy!" he exclaimed. "What in the holy heck are *you* doing here?"

"I was just asking myself that very same question, Lieutenant."

He considered this for a moment before he said, "Shall we make it Chuy's?"

"Chuy's, by all means."

CHAPTER EIGHT

Chuy's was a little neighborhood place on Sawtelle and National where Chuy's ancient mother made the soft corn tortillas by hand over an open hearth and served them to you fresh off the griddle—hot, fragrant and golden around the edges. It was a Saturday night but we got there at 5:30 so it wasn't crowded yet. In another hour people would be lined up outside on the sidewalk, waiting for a table. Chuy's didn't take reservations.

Emil Lamp and I both ordered the chiles rellenos, which were the best I've ever had anywhere. I sipped a Dos Equis, feeling the comfortable weight of Lulu dozing on my left foot. Lamp had a Coke, sucking on the ice cubes as he sat across the table from me with a small notepad and a ballpoint pen at his elbow. The jacket of his suit was off, his shirtsleeves rolled up. He wore a bracelet of turquoise and silver on his right wrist. On his left a bulky digital watch with a black plastic band.

"It's good to see you again, Hoagy," he said brightly.

He was so chirpy that he made me feel tired and old. Mostly old. "Good to see you, too, Lieutenant."

"How is Miss Nash?"

"Still circling Budapest, to the best of my knowledge."

"What's she doing there?"

"Shooting a film with Nick Nolte."

"Oh, him."

"And how is life treating you?"

"Super. Mom's met a real nice fellow named Ron who teaches ceramics in Playa Del Ray. They're having a blast together."

"And you? Are you dating girls yet?"

"Hoagy, I'm not the innocent that you make me out to be."

"So you've made it all the way to second base with some lucky girl?"

"I never kiss and tell."

"So there *has* been kissing."

He let out a laugh before his face fell and he said, "I sure wish we'd run into each other under happier circumstances."

"As do I, Lieutenant."

Monette Aintree had been arrested for the murder of her husband and taken downtown to be booked, fingerprinted and have her hands swabbed for gunshot residue. It being a Saturday, she couldn't be arraigned until Monday morning, but in California they allow bail if a suspect's arraignment appearance will be more than twenty-four hours away. Her criminal defense attorney, a high-priced Century City dick swinger whose name—I kid you not—was Seymour Glass, had secured her release for a $1 million bond. She'd been sprung by the time I left Aintree Manor to meet Lamp at Chuy's, and she was currently at the Beverly Hills office of her personal physician, who'd met her there to examine her bloodied nose and arms and prescribe any medication she might need.

When I came riding out the front gate on the Roadmaster to meet Lamp, I discovered that the media mob had quadrupled in size. Now there were camera crews from all three network news operations out there, not to mention CNN, *Entertainment Tonight* and *Inside Edition*. There were newspaper reporters, wire service reporters, radio reporters. There were so many people out there that they filled the entire street, their cars and vans parked up and down Rockingham as far as the eye could see. News helicopters even circled overhead. Several additional cops were on duty to try to contain the madness but no one can do that when a Hollywood star has been murdered.

Elliot had made a brave, futile attempt at media damage control. The pudgy producer ventured outside the gate to read a brief statement, which was carried live on CNN, in which he called the shooting death of Patrick Van Pelt "a horrible family tragedy" but maintained that Monette had acted out of self-defense and that he was confident she would be exonerated. He asked that the media please allow the family to grieve in peace.

Joey and Danielle remained secluded inside the house with Reggie and Maritza. The others who'd been there at the time of the shooting had been questioned and allowed to leave—although we'd all been advised that further questioning would likely take place on Monday, which was the LAPD's tactful way of saying don't leave town.

"What do you think Monette will be charged with?" I asked Lamp.

"That's for the DA to decide, but I'd say manslaughter," he replied, sucking on an ice cube. "She'll plead self-defense and I'm guessing she'll be found innocent. The victim did beat her up pretty badly. But an acquittal's not a slam dunk. The DA can build something out of her firing that second round of shots into his chest. She could have stopped after she wounded him with the first two. The man was down. A plausible case can be made that he was no longer a physical threat to her."

"A plausible case can also be made that she was bleeding profusely and terrified for her life."

"Which is exactly what her lawyer will say. Hoagy, how much time elapsed between those two sets of shots?"

I tugged at my ear, mulling it over. I'd been swimming laps when I heard the first two shots. I had enough time to swim to the edge of the pool, get out, grab a towel and make my way to the patio before I heard the second set of shots. "I'd guess two minutes at least. It could have been three."

"And have we spoken to everyone?"

"What do you mean by *everyone*?"

"Is there anybody else who might have been on the grounds at the time of the shooting? Anybody we don't know about?"

"There's Hector, the gardener. He's been spying on the place for Patrick. In return, Patrick gave him the Rolex Submariner that Monette told me Patrick was tossing the bedroom for when she encountered him. Patrick was so heavy into drugs that he forgot he gave it to Hector, apparently."

"Back up one second, please." Lamp jotted this down in his small notepad. "Spying on the place as in . . . ?"

"Letting Patrick know if Monette was taking up with another man. Also keeping an eye on Maritza for him. Patrick had the hots for her. So does Hector."

"She involved with either of them?"

"Not to my knowledge."

"Was Hector around the property today?"

"Patrick asked Maritza that very same question. She told him no."

"Did you believe her? Are we sure he wasn't there?"

"Lieutenant, I'm not sure of anything." I sampled some of Chuy's salsa with a tortilla chip, munching on it. "If Hector entered the property today by the service gate, the paparazzi out front would have seen him, wouldn't they?"

"Maybe not. People don't notice what they're not looking for, in my experience."

"There's also a pool man. I saw him come in through the service gate early yesterday morning. I don't know if he showed up today."

"He and Hector must know the access code to the security system. I'll contact the home security company. They can tell me if the service gate keypad was used today."

"They can do that?"

He nodded. "The newest keypads have a memory. And, believe me, the system at that place is as up-to-date as they come." He glanced through his notepad for a moment before he sampled some salsa himself. "Tell me about Lou Riggio, the victim's trainer or assistant or whatever the holy heck he is."

"Enabler is more like it. Lou totes around a blue nylon ditty bag stocked with Patrick's coke supply. As soon as he learned that Patrick was dead and your people were en route he disappeared downstairs. I guarantee you he was hiding that bag in his GTO. If you'd searched his car, you would have found it."

"We had no probable cause to search his car," Lamp countered with a shake of his head. "That's why Lou put it there. The man knows the ins and outs. He moves a lot of coke and pot on the Radford lot. Our narcotics people have him in their sights. They've just been waiting to land on him hard enough that he'll be forced to give up his supplier—or spend the rest of the nineties in San Quentin."

I signaled our waiter for another beer. "Does Lou have priors?"

"A pair of assault and battery charges back when he played at Troy State. He beat up some frat boy in a bar after a game one night and urinated on him. A year later he went off on a clerk at a 7-Eleven and put him in the hospital with a ruptured spleen. Got off with community service both times since he was a great big football hero." Lamp paused, leafing through his notepad. "Elliot Schein claims he saw Lou and Patrick snorting coke together shortly before Monette encountered Patrick in the master bedroom."

"I did, too. Your medical examiner will find coke galore in Patrick's system. I'm guessing you can also throw in a designer cocktail of anabolic steroids and speed, not to mention a whole lot of Cuervo Gold. He arrived for the party shit-faced. Patrick's nice-guy image was a sham. The real Patrick Van Pelt was a drugged-out rage monster. Extremely volatile. He was also not my idea of reputable."

"Can you give me a for instance?"

"I can, but this isn't for the media. Deal?"

"Deal."

"Patrick informed me that he had a vasectomy three years ago. Your medical examiner will no doubt confirm that."

Lamp looked across the table at me in surprise. "You're telling me he isn't the father of Kat Zachry's baby?"

"Exactly."

"Who is the father?"

"He said it could have been any of a dozen guys. He didn't know and didn't care. He was just trying to stampede Monette into a more lucrative divorce settlement."

"I see . . ." Lamp frowned. "And Kat was, what, just playing along for the hell of it?"

"She's an actress who wants the media's attention and doesn't care how she gets it. Out here they call that star quality."

"That half-brother of hers, Kyle Cook, has a sheet up in Paso Robles."

"I know."

"Did you know that Elliot Schein has a sheet, too?"

"That I didn't know. Do tell."

"He served eighteen months in Rahway, New Jersey, for aggravated assault in 1965 back when he was a struggling talent manager. It seems he tried to strangle an old-time borscht belt comic named Sam Fingerhut to death over cheesecake and coffee at a diner in Paramus, New Jersey."

"Things like that are liable to happen if you go to Paramus. That's why you'll never find me there. Interesting that you should mention New Jersey."

Lamp peered at me curiously. "Why is that?"

"Because both of the letters that Monette and Reggie received from their long-lost father, Richard, originated from there. First Edison, then Trenton."

"I loved his book when I was a kid," Lamp recalled fondly. "Heck, I must have read it a half-dozen times."

"As did I, Lieutenant."

"May I ask how you got involved in Monette Aintree's project?"

"Richard asked for me, by name."

"Why would he do that?"

Our waiter brought me my second Dos Equis.

I took a sip. "All sorts of reasons. For starters, I have tremendous literary cachet. That and thirty-five cents will buy you a cup of coffee. Alberta Pryce, his literary agent from way back when, happens to be my literary agent. I also have a preexisting family connection. Reggie and I used to be an item."

Lamp's eyes twinkled at me. "Regina Aintree is a very attractive little package."

"Yes, she is."

"Was this before you met Miss Nash?"

"Long before."

He peered at me. "All sorts of reasons, you said. Are there any others?"

"Yes, there's one more."

"What is it?"

"It's personal."

"To do with Regina?"

"Like I said, it's personal."

Lamp's eyes narrowed slightly. "I understand she's been living in New Paltz, New York. Did you fly out here together?"

"No. I did visit her up there before I left, but she told me she didn't want to have anything to do with the project."

"What changed her mind?"

"She got a letter from him herself. Decided to fly out yesterday."

"What airline did she fly?"

"I have no idea, sorry."

"That's okay. I can check it out."

"Why would you do that?"

"It's what I do, Hoagy. I check things out."

Our chiles rellenos arrived on giant plates surrounded by rice and refried beans and accompanied by a basket of warm, soft corn tortillas. We dove in. The food at Chuy's was even more delicious than I remembered.

"Reggie and Monette have a complicated, acrimonious history," I said as I ate. "Hadn't seen each other for twenty years. Reggie had never even met Joey and Danielle."

"Joey's had some problems," he informed me, reaching for a tortilla. "He set a couple of fires back when he was twelve. One was in the boys' room at his school. The other in a Dumpster out behind Vicente Foods."

"Doesn't surprise me a bit. He's an angry loner. Guys like us tend to act out at that age."

Lamp's eyes widened. "Don't tell me that you . . ."

"I didn't set fires. Shoplifting was my thing. Candy bars, comic books, magazines. You name it, I stole it."

"Ever get caught?"

"Never. I was a master thief. To this day part of me still thinks I should have chosen a life of crime. Stealing was a hell of a lot more fun than writing. I take it Joey did get caught."

Lamp nodded his head. "His parents agreed to put him in counseling, and he hasn't been in any trouble since then. Talk to me about Boyd Samuels. You've crossed paths with him before, haven't you? I seem to recall reading about it."

"I have. You did. He's a major-league scam artist. Don't believe a single word he tells you."

"And yet you're back in business with him."

"Couldn't be avoided. You can't work in publishing anymore without scraping people like Boyd off the bottom of your shoe. Do you mind if we don't talk about him anymore? I was enjoying my dinner."

"No problem." Lamp worked on his own dinner, leafing through his notepad. "Lou Riggio is claiming that he, Kyle Cook and this actress friend of Kat's, Trish Brainard, were in the billiard room together when the shooting happened."

I nodded. "Having themselves a real good time on the Eartha Kitt sofa."

"Sorry, the Eartha Kitt . . . ?"

"The leopard-skin divan. Your crime scene technicians will find semen stains on it. Lulu certainly did."

Lamp made a note of this, crinkling his nose. "Trish has a SAG card. A couple of bit roles in TV shows here and there including *Malibu High*, which is how she came to be acquainted with Kat. She's twenty-two, comes from Yorba Linda. No priors, but no regular source of income either. Shares an apartment on Zelzah Avenue in Northridge with another young actress named Lila Lunt who has a slew of credits in films with titles like *Splendor in the Ass* and *Babette's Feet*. But we couldn't find any porn credits for Trish. What's her deal?"

"Nothing very out of the ordinary. Kat and Kyle paid her to be at that party—which is to say Kat paid her since Kyle has no actual job. Trish was Joey's seventeenth-birthday present. They introduced her to everyone as their cousin from back home. Cute touch, don't you think? Gave it a quaintly *Petticoat Junction* feel."

"You're telling me they hired Trish to have sex with that kid?"

"I am. As soon as Joey made it clear that he wasn't interested, Kyle and Lou decided to help themselves. Trish's time—and body—had been paid for, after all. Don't expect me to sit here in judgment of her, Lieutenant, because I won't. Young actresses like Trish are expected to perform sexual favors for powerful men at parties for free. That's how they get jobs. Or, to put it another way, if they don't perform favors they don't get jobs. So if Trish can get paid for it, why not?" I said as Lamp looked across the table at me in total dismay. "I'm not telling you anything you don't already know, am I? Granted, you look like someone who climbs into bed at night with a plate of Fig Newtons and a glass of warm milk. But you do know how the business works, don't you?"

"I know how it works," he said with quiet disapproval. "I'm the one who has to clean up the wreckage, and if you ask me, it stinks the way men in that business take advantage of vulnerable young girls."

"I knew there was a reason I liked you, Lieutenant."

Our waiter came and cleared our plates away. The Saturday night crowd had started to arrive. The place was filling up fast. We ordered coffee.

"You went into the master bedroom suite after the shooting, correct?"

I nodded. "Monette was still standing there holding the gun."

"What did she say to you?"

"That she'd come upstairs to powder her nose, which is Miss Porter's speak for pee, and found Patrick flinging drawers open like a crazy man in search of his Rolex Submariner. She reminded him that he'd given it to Hector. He accused Hector of stealing it. She accused Patrick of being a drunken mess as well as an all-around disgrace of a human being. He attacked her. She grabbed her Beretta from the nightstand and fired off two shots, wounding him. She carries a Beretta in the glove compartment of her Land Cruiser, too, by the way."

"She has permits for both weapons. An extremely high percentage of the wealthy people in this city are armed. And then . . . ?"

"They exchanged more ugly words. And she shot him again. Fatally this time."

Our coffee arrived. I sipped mine as Lamp leafed through his notepad.

"You were in the pool when you heard the first shots. Where were the others?"

"Elliot was on the patio tending to the steaks on the grill. When he and I got upstairs we found Reggie and Danielle cowering in the hallway. They said they'd been in their rooms changing out of their wet bathing suits when they heard the shots. Joey was holed up in his room with his headphones on. Didn't hear a thing, he claims. You already know about Lou, Kyle and Trish."

"What about the housekeeper, Maritza?"

"She told me she was in the kitchen," I said, volunteering nothing more, such as that I'd seen no sign of her in the kitchen.

"And how about Kat Zachry and Boyd Samuels?"

"Boyd told me they were busy trying to break into the pool house."

"Why in the holy heck would they want to do that?"

"They were trying to steal this old leather flight jacket that I'm wearing. Kat saw it on me yesterday and decided I should give it to her. I refused."

"Kat claims that she and Samuels had taken a stroll to discuss a book project."

"Which is true, very loosely speaking. She offered Boyd a chance to peddle a tell-all book for her if he agreed to help her steal my jacket."

"Tell me about your book, Hoagy. Is there any connection between the Richard Aintree project and what happened at the house on Rockingham Avenue today? Or is that a stupid question?"

"It's not a stupid question. I've asked it myself several times. I do know that Patrick was against the idea. He told me so yesterday. He wanted Monette focused on their divorce, period. I also know that someone tried to scare me away the moment I got to town. There was a note from Patrick typed on *Malibu High* stationery waiting for me when I arrived. He asked me to meet him at a location shoot in Pacoima. When I got there the place was deserted—until someone in a black Trans Am pulled into the parking lot, floored it and tried to run me and my short-legged partner over."

"Is that how you got that scrape on your cheek?"

"It is."

"Do you still have the note?"

I pulled the folded note from my jacket pocket and handed it to him. "Patrick swore to me up, down and sideways that he didn't write it."

Lamp glanced at it before he tucked it into the breast pocket of his jacket. "Did you believe him?"

"Wait, there's more. Monette told me that the night before I got here someone tried to run her off Coldwater up near Mulholland. Guess what he was driving? A black Trans Am."

"Did she report it?"

I shook my head. "She was afraid of the negative publicity."

"Well, I can sure find out if anyone associated with this case drives a black Trans Am. You never know where a little piece of information like that might lead us."

"But you're already there, aren't you, Lieutenant?"

Lamp sipped his coffee. "I don't know what you mean, Hoagy."

"Monette has already confessed. I found her with the murder weapon in her hand, blood streaming from her nose and bloody gouges up and down her arms. It seems like an open-and-shut case."

"Not to me it doesn't," Lamp said with a shake of his head. "It's too organized. I may not be the sharpest knife in the drawer but I know an organized homicide when I see one. Domestic violence, in my experience, is always highly *dis*organized. This isn't. It's tied up nice and neat. The whole scene feels staged to me. I'm not buying it. I'm especially not buying that two- or three-minute time lapse between shots. Something happened during those two or three minutes. Something besides her standing there exchanging choice words with the victim. Nope, I'm not buying it. And you aren't either, Hoagy."

"What makes you say that?"

"Because you *are* the sharpest knife in the drawer. So let's not kid ourselves. We both know that Monette Aintree's version of what happened in that bedroom today isn't what really happened. Do you know what did?"

"No, I genuinely don't."

"Okay, then what do you know that you're not telling me?"

"What makes you think that I know something, Lieutenant?"

His alert blue eyes locked onto mine. "Because I know you."

I weighed my answer carefully. There was plenty that was bothering me. Maritza bothered me. She'd changed into a different uniform by the time she came upstairs after the shooting and had lied to me about the door to the service stairs being locked. Why? Joey bothered me. He'd changed clothes, too. Yet Lulu had still smelled gunshot residue on the boy's sneakers. Why? I didn't know. Until I did, I was keeping my mouth shut. But I couldn't get up from the table without giving Lamp something. So I said, "Monette's long-sleeved chambray shirt."

He studied me curiously. "What about it?"

"She was wearing it when Patrick attacked her. Told me she took it off to soak up the blood that was streaming from her nose. It wasn't doing a particularly effective job so I grabbed a towel for her from the bathroom. When I put the shirt in the sink I noticed something odd about it."

"Which was . . . ?"

"The cuffs were buttoned at the wrist. That tells me Monette wasn't wearing her sleeves rolled up when Patrick attacked her. She had deep, bloody gouge marks up and down both of her forearms, yet there were no corresponding bloody marks on her shirt-sleeves. Wouldn't you think there would be?"

"You said she'd gone upstairs to use the bathroom. Maybe she'd taken the shirt off."

"Stripped down to her tank top, you mean? Maybe. But if she was going to fetch something to soak up the blood pouring from her nose wouldn't she have chosen a towel? Why the shirt?"

Lamp stuck out his lower lip thoughtfully. "You were out on the patio with Patrick shortly before the shooting, correct?"

"Correct."

"Is there any doubt in your mind that he was capable of becoming enraged enough to punch the lady in the nose?"

"No doubt at all. But your medical examiner will be able to tell that for certain, won't he? The knuckles on one of Patrick's hands will be bruised or reddened, I would think."

"Not necessarily. In fact, the preliminary exam showed that neither fist was bruised. The human nose is soft tissue, Hoagy. It's not like hitting someone on the jaw, which is hard bone. And it doesn't take much of a blow to produce a lot of blood. The ME did say it looks as if the victim had somebody's blood and tissue under his fingernails."

"Which you'll be able to identify as Monette's blood and tissue."

Lamp frowned at me. "Will we?"

"Won't you? I keep hearing all about this magic DNA wand of yours."

"This DNA business has been blown totally out of proportion by bad TV cop shows. The reality of PCR—polymerase chain reaction—is that it'll enable our lab people to identify the blood type that's present under Patrick's fingernails. But they can't individualize it to a specific person. Not yet anyhow. That's strictly make-believe. Let's say they find a blood sample under his nails that's the same blood type as Monette's, okay? If it's Type O then that represents 45 percent of the population, which is to say practically half of the people who were there at the time of the shooting. If it's Type A then that's another 42 percent. A prosecutor can't walk into a criminal court with that and call it evidence, understand?"

"I understand." I drank down the last of my coffee. "How long will it take for them to determine the blood type?"

"For a super high-profile case like this one, the whole lab will be called in tonight. They'll have results by tomorrow."

"Tomorrow is Sunday."

"Doesn't matter. They'll be on the job."

"And so will you, I imagine."

"Count on it." He gestured to the waiter for our check before he studied me carefully from across the table. "It's good to see you again, Hoagy. I enjoy your company. I sure do hope I don't have to land on you hard this time."

"Why would you need to do that?"

"For holding out on me," he said quietly. "Possibly even lying to me."

"We're both interested in the same thing, Lieutenant."

"No, we're not."

"You're right, we're not. But you have my word that Lulu and I will do everything we can to point you in the right direction. Besides, no matter what happens, you'll still come out ahead."

"How so?" he asked me as the waiter brought us our check.

I grabbed it. "Because I'm paying for dinner."

BACK AT AINTREE Manor, Monette was seated in the library with Elliot watching the live cable news coverage of Patrick's murder, which had officially crossed over into surreal, as in what they were watching as I stood there with them was *me* pulling up at the front gate on the Roadmaster a few seconds earlier. *Me* not responding to any of the questions that were being shouted at me by the mob of reporters out there. *Me.*

Monette and Elliot were sipping Sancerre as Monette held an ice pack to her nose. She wore a pale blue silk kimono with wide sleeves, the better to allow those bloody fingernail gouges on her forearms to breathe. The gouges were shiny with ointment. There were two prescription pill bottles on the end table next to her.

Monette lowered the ice pack from her face and hit the mute button on the TV remote. "I'm glad you're back, Hoagy," she said, continuing to strike me as eerily calm considering that she'd pumped four shots into her husband that afternoon. "I feel better with you here."

"That's kind of you to say," I responded as Elliot glared at me resentfully. "How is your nose?"

"Not broken, happily. It's just a quote-unquote contusion, although I swear I sound as if I'm wearing a clothespin on it."

She sounded slightly nasal, though not that bad considering how swollen it was. "My doctor gave me an antibiotic ointment for my arms and warned me that I'll probably end up with visible scarring, which will mean plastic surgery if I ever want to wear short sleeves on air again. Assuming, that is, that I still have an on-air career after this mess is over," she added offhandedly. "You've missed dinner. Maritza can rustle something up for you if you're hungry."

"I'm all set, thanks. How is the rest of the family doing?"

"Joey's in his room being Joey. When I suggested that he might want to talk this out with his therapist he told me to kindly leave him the fuck alone. So I am. Danielle and Reggie are in Danielle's bedroom, watching a videocassette of *Dirty Dancing* together and pigging out on ice cream. Reggie's idea. She is being so wonderful." Monette arched an eyebrow at me. "Do you mind if I ask where you've been?"

"I was having dinner with Lieutenant Lamp. We're old pals."

"Oh, that's just great," Elliot grumbled.

"Be nice, Elliot," she scolded him. To me she said, "Did he talk to you about the case?"

"No, he's very tight-lipped."

"I trust that you were also . . ."

"Tight-lipped? Of course. Besides, I don't actually know anything."

"You know everything there is to know," Elliot said, stabbing at the air with a chubby index finger. "You know that Patrick tried to kill this brave lady and that she fought back. End of story."

"I wish it were that simple," Monette said, staring at the muted image of the dozens of TV cameramen who were mobbed outside of Kat Zachry's Laurel Canyon bungalow where, according to the crawl at the bottom of the screen, the pregnant young star was "in seclusion with her closest advisers."

"You ought to turn that off, Monette. It'll just make you crazy."

I got no argument from her. She reached for the remote and flicked the TV off.

"So you and the detective who's in charge of this case are friends," Elliot said to me accusingly.

"Exactly where are you going with this?" I asked him.

"Please don't take offense, Hoagy," Monette said. "Elliot just wants to make sure that we can rely on your discretion. Isn't that right, Elliot?"

Elliot didn't say yes or no. Just glowered at me. He didn't like having me around. He especially didn't like the ease with which Monette spoke to me.

"I'm a celebrity ghost. Keeping my mouth shut is what I do for a living. I don't blab to the police. I don't blab to the press. However, if you don't trust me, I'll collect my things and check in to a hotel."

Monette's pale blue eyes widened with alarm. "Please don't do that. You're absolutely right. I apologize. *We* apologize. Isn't that right, Elliot?"

Again, Elliot didn't say yes or no. Just kept on glowering at me.

Maritza entered the library, looking very uneasy. She and Monette couldn't quite manage to make direct eye contact, I noticed. "Would you like for me to make up your bed for you now, Senora?"

"My own bedroom is an official crime scene," Monette explained to me. "I'm now in the room next door to Reggie's. Yes, please, Maritza. The powder blue sheets and pillowcases, please."

"*Si, Senora.*"

"In fact, why don't I give you a hand? It'll give me something to do."

"And I'll be taking off," Elliot said, wheezing as he hoisted his magenta marshmallow self up off the sofa. "Sleep tight, hon.

Call me anytime for any reason. Nobody on this earth matters to me as much as you do. I'll be back first thing in the morning, okay?"

Monette smiled at him wearily. "Thank you, Elliot. You're a rock." Then she went up the grand, curving stairway with Maritza.

"Walk me out, would you?" he asked me gruffly.

Lulu and I went out the front door with him onto the porch. From where we stood, I could see the lights of the TV cameras that were clustered outside the wall on Rockingham. Reporters were still filing stories for late news broadcasts. Elliot's Range Rover was parked in the pea gravel turnaround next to Monette's Land Cruiser. I found it exceedingly strange that so many wealthy people in L.A. had taken to driving four-wheel-drive off-road vehicles instead of luxury cars. Considering that they lived in a place where there was no such thing as an unpaved road, I mean. Or snow. Joey's rugged new no-top Jeep Wrangler remained parked there, too, waiting for the birthday boy to take it boulder climbing somewhere. I had a feeling it would be waiting there for a long, long time.

Elliot pulled the front door shut behind us and immediately poked me in the chest with his finger. "Listen, schmuck, I care about that lady in there."

I looked down at his finger. "Care to remove that?"

"I'll remove it when I feel like it."

Lulu let out a low growl. She didn't particularly care for the tone of his voice.

Elliot immediately backed away from me. But he wasn't done talking. No chance. "I've known guys like you my whole life. You're a charmer. Charmed your way right into the bed of an A-list movie star, didn't you? A class act like Merilee Nash wouldn't spread those legs of hers unless you had some pretty slick moves.

You think I didn't notice the way Monette lit up when you walked in? That lady's frightened, vulnerable and very alone right now. You stay away from her, hear me? You want to shtup the crazy sister, go right ahead. You can shtup the hell out of her for all I care. But keep your hands off Monette."

"I don't work for you, Elliot, so don't tell me what I can or cannot do with my hands. Speaking of hands, I understand you spent some quality time in Rahway for wrapping yours around a client's throat back in the sixties."

"I guess your cop friend isn't so tight-lipped after all." He raised his chin at me. "I used to have trouble controlling my temper. So what?"

"Does Monette know about it?"

"Of course she knows. I have no secrets from her."

"How about the tabloids? Because that would make for a mighty juicy sidebar right about now."

Elliot began to breathe more rapidly, his chest heaving. I wondered if he was about to have a heart attack right there on the porch, and if he did whether I'd attempt to perform CPR. His breath smelled like aged muenster cheese. "You . . . going to feed that to somebody?" he gasped. "That what you're saying?"

"No, I'm not. Not if you stop crowding me."

"I'm not somebody who you want to mess with," he warned me. "I know people. Powerful people who owe me favors. Understand?" Then he waddled toward his Range Rover and got in, started it up and sped his way toward the front gate.

Monette was waiting for me at the top of the stairs when I went back inside. "What were you and Elliot talking about?"

"He just wants to make sure you're okay."

"Dear Elliot. Sometimes I think that he's my Jewish mother from a former life. After Maritza and I make the bed, I'm going to stretch out and try to relax. It's early. Why don't you join me for a few minutes? You can bring the Sancerre up with you. It's in the fridge."

"I'll be right up."

First, I headed toward the kitchen with Lulu. If Maritza was upstairs with Monette, that meant now was our chance. The kitchen lights had been dimmed. There was a faint smell of garlic and chili powder in the air. We went through the doorway off the kitchen that led to the laundry room, service stairs and Maritza's room. The door to Maritza's room was open. Her nightstand lamp was on. It was a small bedroom, very tidy. The door to the laundry room was closed. I opened it and we slipped inside. I flicked on the overhead light, closing the door softly behind us.

The washer and dryer were huge top loaders. Biggest I'd ever seen in a private home. I opened them. Both were empty.

There was a white wicker basket next to the washer that had a full nylon laundry bag stuffed inside of it. Lulu made straight for the bag and started sniffing at it. I dumped its contents out onto the floor. The crime scene investigators hadn't searched through it yet, as far as I knew. Why would they? Monette had already confessed to shooting Patrick. They had Monette. They had the murder weapon. They had everything they needed. True, Emil Lamp had voiced his doubts to me about Monette's version of what happened. But he hadn't ordered a top-to-bottom search of the entire mansion. Not yet anyhow.

Lulu sniffed and snorted her way through a heap of soiled kitchen towels and linen napkins, bath towels, hand towels. She found the salmon-colored dental hygienist's uniform that Maritza had been wearing yesterday. But not the pale pink one she had on earlier today—the one she'd changed out of after Patrick got shot. There was no sign of the clothing that Joey had been wearing prior to the shooting either. Lulu didn't get so much as a whiff of gunshot residue on anything in the bag. She would have let me know if she had. Instead, she simply backed away from it and gazed up at me in silence.

Damn.

I crammed everything back in the laundry bag, returned it to the wicker basket and got the hell out of there. Next I headed for the kitchen trash bin, which was built in under the sink and disguised as a pullout drawer. I was moving fast but not fast enough—I'd only made it as far as the refrigerator when Maritza strode into the kitchen from the main hallway, silent in her white Nikes.

"I can help you with something, Senor Hoagy?" she asked, flicking on the overhead lights.

"I don't suppose you have any licorice ice cream tucked away in the freezer, do you?"

She frowned at me. "Did you say *licorice* ice cream? There is such a thing?"

"There is, and it's hard to find, let me tell you. Actually, I was looking for the bottle of Sancerre Monette and Elliot were drinking. She suggested I bring it upstairs."

"It is in the refrigerator in the billiard room. There are clean glasses behind the bar. I will get it for you if you wish."

"No need, I'll get it," I said, noticing how much strain was etched on her pretty young face. Her dark brown eyes shone at me like wet stones. "Is everything okay with you, Maritza?"

"It has been a hard day."

"Yes, it has. Is there anything you wish to tell me?"

She peered up at me uncertainly. "Tell you?"

"The bedroom door at the top of the service stairs wasn't locked at the time of the shooting. You weren't honest with me about that, Maritza. You also changed into a different uniform."

"The police . . . they know this?" she whispered, trembling with fright.

"Not yet. And they don't have to. Not as far as I'm concerned."

"I see . . ." Her face went totally blank. "You want sex from me, is that it?"

"No, I don't want sex from you, Maritza. I want the truth. If you help me, I can help you."

"I am concerned only for the senora."

"I admire your loyalty, but you have to look out for yourself. If you don't you'll get sent back to Guatemala."

"You cannot help me, Senor Hoagy," she said with quiet resignation in her voice. "No one can. I have nothing more to say. I am sorry."

"So am I, Maritza."

She stayed put in the kitchen. Fetched canisters of flour and sugar from a cupboard over the counter, eggs and butter out of the refrigerator. She intended to bake something, it appeared, meaning I'd have zero chance to search that kitchen garbage bin any time soon. So I went into the billiard room, grabbed the open bottle of Sancerre out of the fridge, found two glasses and made my way upstairs with Lulu.

Yellow police tape was stretched across the double doors to the master suite. Joey's door was closed. So was Danielle's, though I could hear the sounds of *Dirty Dancing*, the movie that she and Reggie were watching on TV together.

Monette had chosen a modest room for herself, one that was no more than three times the size of my apartment. It had a four-poster king-sized bed with a huge old steamer trunk parked at the foot of it that was covered with stickers from long-gone cruise ship lines and European luxury hotels. It had an early twentieth-century walnut desk with a high-back leather swivel chair. The matching wardrobe cupboard and chest of drawers were at least a century older than the desk and appeared to be made of cherry. The shutters over the windows were closed. The nightstand lamp was on, casting the room in a warm, soft glow. Monette lay propped up on the bed in her kimono with a blanket thrown over her legs. She was still holding an ice pack to her nose.

Lulu climbed from the steamer trunk up onto the foot of the bed, pausing for permission before she proceeded any farther.

"Would you like a four-footed nursemaid?"

"A four-footed . . . ?" Monette frowned at me before she noticed Lulu there. "Oh, certainly. By all means."

Lulu settled herself on Monette's hip and plopped her head down on Monette's stomach.

Monette petted her. "You're a very sweet girl, aren't you?"

I poured each of us some wine, handed her one glass and sat down with the other in a chintz-covered armchair that was positioned next to the bed. It amazed me how quickly I was getting tired of chintz. After a mere two days in Aintree Manor I felt quite certain that I never wanted to see it again for as long as I lived. "How are you really, Monette?"

"How am I really?" she repeated wearily. "They hustled me out of here like a criminal. Drove me downtown, dragged me into police headquarters, fingerprinted me, questioned me. Everyone was incredibly polite. And yet I still felt as if I'd suddenly become someone else. I've worked terribly hard to build a life for myself. Today, I realized it can all be taken away from you in an instant." She set the ice pack aside and sipped her wine. "Joey didn't say one word to me when I got home. Danielle couldn't stop crying. Reggie has been incredibly supportive and strong. She's really come through for me."

"She's your sister. That's what sisters do."

"I know, but I wasn't expecting it. Not after all of these years. I'm glad she's here. And I'm glad *you're* here," she added, coloring slightly.

"I won't be for long if we don't hear from your father again."

"I've been lying here wondering if this dreadful mess will scare him off."

"It might."

"I hope and pray it doesn't. If Dad disappears back into the fog, then all I have to look forward to is *this*—the agony of an endless, horrible trial in which they'll paint me as a bitter old hag who murdered her famously likeable husband for taking up with a younger woman. How pathetic and humiliating is that?"

"Plenty pathetic and humiliating. But your attorney won't let them get away with spinning it like that. He'll retaliate."

Monette furrowed her brow at me. "How?"

"By leaking to the news media just exactly what kind of a man your famously likeable husband really was—especially while he was using illegal drugs. And the medical examiner *will* find illegal drugs in his system."

"He came at me like a madman," she said, her pale blue eyes gleaming at me in the lamplight. "I had to stop him. I'm not sorry. But I am sorry that Joey and Danielle no longer have a father. And I did love him once, before I saw the ugliness that was inside him." She took another sip of her wine, glancing at me nervously. "Would you do me a small favor?"

"If I can."

"Would you sit here on the edge of the bed and hold my hand?"

I moved to the edge of the bed and took her hand, which was cold from the ice pack. Also strong. Monette had one hell of a grip.

"Hoagy, do you think they'll send me to jail?"

"No. Your attorney will plead self-defense and you'll get off."

"What about afterward? Assuming I get off, that is. Will I still have any kind of a career? And what about Danielle and Joey? Will they ever be able to lead normal lives again?"

"You'd know that better than I would. You went through the page-one wringer yourself when you were young."

"And I barely survived," she recalled, her hand still squeezing mine tightly. "I felt so alone. I feel the same way now. Alone."

"You're not alone. You have Reggie."

"That's true, I do, thanks to those letters from Dad." She fell silent for a moment. "Assuming they really are from Dad."

"You think they're not?"

"I don't know what to think anymore. I'm so tired. I just . . ." She gazed at me searchingly. "Can I trust you, Hoagy? Really trust you?"

"Of course you can. Why don't you just go ahead and do it?"

"Do what?"

"Tell me what really happened in that bedroom today."

She let go of my hand. "I told you what really happened."

"And I didn't believe a single word that you said. If you confide in me I may be able to help you. But if you don't then I can't."

Her eyes avoided mine, examining the ceiling and the closed shutters before they settled on Lulu, who lay there staring up at her.

"Lulu has my complete confidence. Anything that you want to say to me you can say in front of her."

Monette's eyes met mine again, staring at me long and hard before she said, "You know what happened."

"Do I?"

"Yes, you do. Please tell me that you believe me."

"What I believe," I said, "is that you did what you had to do."

She sorted through that in silence for a moment before she said, "I think I'll get some sleep now. Or at least try to."

"Good idea." I bent over and kissed her on the forehead. "Good night."

She reacted in surprise. "How did you know I wanted you to do that?"

"I just did."

"Will you still be around in the morning?"

"I'll still be around."

"I haven't driven you away?"

"You haven't driven me away."

"You're a dear. Good night. And good night to you, too, Lulu," she said as Lulu made her way down off the bed by way of the steamer trunk.

It was just after 9:30, according to Grandfather's Benrus. Danielle and Reggie were still in Danielle's room together watching *Dirty Dancing*. Joey's room was still silent. Downstairs in the kitchen, Maritza was shoving pans of blueberry muffins into the oven for tomorrow morning's breakfast. She didn't say good-night to me as I passed by her on my way out the French doors to the patio. Wouldn't so much as look at me.

Lulu and I strolled the grounds in the cool night air before we retired to the pool house, where I headed straight for the telephone in the bedroom to call my phone machine in New York City. I had a slew of new phone messages from reporters and gossip columnists, not to mention cash offers from three, count 'em three, different tabloid editors for the inside dope on Patrick's killing. The highest offer was for more money than I'd been guaranteed for the Richard Aintree project, which in the supremely glam world of ghostwriting is what passes for upward mobility. I didn't return any of the calls.

There was still no message from Merilee in Budapest.

By now it was after 1:00 am in New York City, but I happened to know that the Silver Fox was partial to reading manuscripts deep into the wee hours, propped up in bed chain-smoking Newports and drinking snifters of Courvoisier.

"I was just thinking about you, dear boy," she said when she heard my voice on the phone. "Tell me, how are you?"

"How do you think I am, Alberta? I came out here to help Monette Aintree make literary history. Instead, I'm smack dab in the middle of Hollywood tabloid hell."

"I do apologize, but it's not as if I saw this coming. No one did."

"Boyd Samuels did—I guarantee it."

"How on earth could he do that? I realize Boyd's a tad oleaginous, but even he couldn't have known that Monette would shoot Patrick to death in the middle of their son's birthday party."

"I'm telling you, somehow, some way, he's mixed up in this. It was awfully damned strange the way he suddenly showed up out here yesterday. Monette was certainly surprised to see him. And he and Kat Zachry were oh-so chummy today. Went off by themselves, huddled, schemed, tried to steal my flight jacket."

"Tried to steal your *what*?"

"I wonder how long he and Kat have been cooking up scams together. It wouldn't surprise me one bit if he put her up to seducing Patrick and destroying his marriage. It made for one hell of a career move on her part. That girl's hotter than hot right now. And Monette didn't, by the way."

"Monette didn't what?"

"Shoot Patrick to death."

"Of course she did. She was found standing over his body with the murder weapon in her hand. By *you*."

"I know."

"And she's confessed to doing it."

"I know. But she didn't kill him."

"Who did?"

"I don't know yet. But the detective who's been assigned to the case is no idiot. Neither am I, which is why I want out. I want to come home, Alberta. This isn't what I signed up for."

"I know it isn't, dear boy, but it's *huge*. Why, there isn't a writer in New York who wouldn't jump at the chance to be in your shoes right now."

"Glad to hear it. Anyone who wears a size 11B is welcome to them. I know exactly what you're going to say now. You're going to say that all of this publicity will turn our book into pure gold. But here's the problem, Alberta. No one gives a damn about Richard Aintree's return from oblivion anymore. All they care about is Monette's arraignment on Monday morning. CNN will probably carry the whole damned arraignment proceeding like it's a live courtroom drama. Besides, you and I both know that Richard will never show up here now. Not in the middle of this zoo. It's never going to happen. The project's dead."

"We don't know that."

"Yes, we do. Seriously, can you get me out?"

"Seriously? I can give you some advice. Get some sleep."

"Does that mean no?"

"It means that this will look a lot better in the morning. Really."

"No, it won't. Really."

"Good night, dear boy."

I turned out the lights, stripped and got under the covers. Lay there in the dark with Lulu sprawled across my chest and watched the lights in the big house go out one by one. First the upstairs lights, then all of the downstairs lights except for the ones in the kitchen and Maritza's room. Then those went out, too, and there was only the moonlight and the faint blue glow of the swimming pool's nightlights. I lay there, my wheels spinning.

The French door to the kitchen clicked open and shut so softly that I almost didn't hear it. But I heard it. I also heard the quiet footsteps on the bluestone path that were heading directly toward the pool house. Lulu let out a low growl of warning. I shushed her, got out of bed in the dark and went to the bedroom window for a look.

It wasn't Monette paying me another late-night visit.

It was Maritza who I spotted out there in the dim lights of the pool. And she hadn't come sneaking out of the darkened house to pay me a social call. She was toting a black plastic trash bag over toward that fenced enclosure by the service gate where the trash barrels were kept. When she got there, she eased open the gate to the enclosure, deposited the trash bag soundlessly in a barrel, closed the gate and hurried back to the house, closing the kitchen door softly behind her.

Silence.

I waited several minutes before I put on my silk target-dot dressing gown, opened the pool house door and made my way in barefoot silence to the trash enclosure. I retrieved the trash bag and carried it back to the pool house. Closed the living room shutters, flicked on a light and got busy. The trash bag had been closed with a twist tie. I untwisted it and dumped the contents of the bag out on the kitchen floor. Monette had a garbage disposal for food scraps so I wasn't too concerned about anything wet or disgusting being stuffed in there. What came tumbling out was junk mail, plastic food wrappers, used paper towels . . .

And a wadded-up pale blue bath towel.

I spread the bath towel open on the floor. Lulu immediately busied herself snuffling and snorting at the things that were balled up inside of it. There was a rumpled white T-shirt that even my human nose could tell smelled of something oily and metallic. There was the pale pink dental hygienist's uniform that Maritza had been wearing before the shooting—which had smears of blood all over it. When Lulu was done sniffing at it she moved on to the flannel shirt, Nirvana T-shirt and jeans that Joey had been wearing before the shooting. The boy's clothes were smeared with blood just like Maritza's were. Unlike Maritza's, Joey's carried the scent of gunshot residue on them. Lulu let me know this with a low whoop.

I sat back on my heels, my mind racing. After the shooting, Lulu had followed the residue scent to Joey's room and found it on his sneakers. Joey had neglected to change out of those, although he had bothered to wash his hands and face. The collar and cuffs of his shirt had been damp. Why had he done that? To wash off more blood? Did this clothing prove that he'd been in the master suite at the time of the shooting? He sure as hell hadn't been in his room with his headphones on. What did it mean that there was blood on Maritza's uniform but *no* gunshot residue? Why had she lied to me about the door to the service stairs being locked? What had really happened in that master bedroom suite today? A staged homicide, Lamp had called it. Staged how? What was I missing?

As I sat there, wondering, I reached for the black trash bag and discovered that I hadn't completely emptied it. There was still one more item in the bottom of the bag—a rolled-up pale blue hand towel. I unrolled it and found two more bloodied articles of clothing that I hadn't been expecting to find. I stared at them for a long moment, my pulse quickening, before I gathered up both towels full of clothing and stashed them in my empty suitcase in the bedroom closet. Then I stuffed the trash back into the bag, tiptoed out into the darkness and returned it to the trash barrel.

I was starting my way back to the pool house when a voice whispered, "What in the heck are you doing?"

Reggie. She was standing outside my door in a T-shirt and shorts, barefoot.

"Tossing the dried mackerel remains from Lulu's bowl. It isn't a pleasant smell. What's going on, Stinker?"

"Couldn't sleep. Too much strange shit happened today. Thought I'd bum a nightcap off you. You alone?"

"Why, you think I've got Monette sprawled languorously across my bed?"

"It's polite to ask. I do try to be polite."

"Do shut up and come in."

She shut up and came in, glancing around at the furnishings while I poured each of us a shot of single malt. "Monette's accustomed to getting what she wants," she warned me. "And she wants you. Big sis has a major crush on you."

"No, she doesn't."

"Yes, she does. She got all fluttery while you were gone for dinner. Kept wondering where you were and when you were coming back. And you should have seen her fuss over which color kimono to wear."

"We're not getting involved," I said, handing Reggie her Scotch.

"Why not? She's a widow now." Her huge eyes twinkled at me wickedly. "As in available."

I drank down my Scotch in one gulp. "Well, I'm not. I never get involved with a celebrity employer. It's unprofessional."

She drank down her Scotch in one gulp, studying me curiously. "You sure about that?"

"Positive."

"In that case can I snuggle with you for a while? My bed seemed awfully big and lonely. Not to mention cold. My feet are like ice."

"I seem to recall your feet are always like ice."

"Will you warm them up for me for old time's sake? I won't get frisky, I promise. I really just . . ." Reggie lowered her gaze uncomfortably. "I don't feel like being alone right now."

I stood there looking at those thin white scars on the insides of her wrists. "For old time's sake? Sure."

I turned out the living room light before we went into the

darkened bedroom, where Lulu had already claimed more than half of the bed.

"Shove over, Your Earness," Reggie commanded Lulu as she dove under the covers in her T-shirt and shorts. "You've got company."

Lulu didn't budge. Not until I told her to. Even then she moved a grand total of six inches, grunting at me with supreme disapproval.

I took off my dressing gown and slid under the covers. Reggie's feet found mine right away.

"Good God, they feel like two blocks of frozen hamburger."

"They'll warm up soon." She turned onto her side so that she faced me in the moonlight. "Hold me, will you?"

I put my arm around her and she settled against me with her head resting on my chest. I stroked her long, beautiful hair, recalling the scent and feel of her like it was yesterday. "How was *Dirty Dancing*?"

"Corny and old-fashioned, like out of the not-so-fabulous fifties. I thought we'd outgrown such silly fables."

"Never. Silly fables make people happy. How is Danielle doing?"

"How do you think? The poor kid's whole world is falling apart around her." Reggie fell silent for a moment before she said, "Monette's amazing. She's so strong, not like me. I feel incredibly shaky right now."

"Monette thinks you're the one who's being strong, actually."

Reggie lifted her head up and gazed at me. Our faces were very close. Close enough that I could feel her breath on mine. "Well, she's wrong," she said softly before she lowered her head back down onto my chest, snuggling closer.

"What about Joey? How is he doing?"

"Stewie, why are you asking me so many questions?"

"A lot of strange shit happened today, like you said."

"No, that's not why. The gerbil wheel between your ears is

going around and around. You've got something on your mind. What is it?"

"If I ask you something, will you give me an honest answer?"

"Of course I will, silly wabbit."

"What happened in that bedroom today?"

She raised her head again, gazing at me. "You know what happened. You saw it for yourself."

"Did I?"

"Just leave it alone, Stewie. As a favor to me. Will you do that for me?"

"I don't know what I saw."

"Yes, you do," she said insistently. "You do."

"Okay, I do."

"Say it like you mean it. Say it or I'll tickle you."

"That won't work anymore. I used to be ticklish years and years ago, but I'm not anymore."

"Oh, really? We'll just see about that . . ." Her nimble fingers went probing for the sensitive flesh beneath my ribs.

"Okay, okay . . ." I grabbed her hands and held them. "I *do*."

"Thank you." She lowered her head back down on my chest once again and put her arm around me, hugging me tight.

I lay there, stroking her hair. The Aintree sisters had circled the wagons. Whatever had happened in that bedroom was strictly a family affair. I was an outsider, and a potentially dangerous one at that—a friend of the homicide lieutenant who was in charge of the case. Was Reggie visiting me to find out what I knew? Had Monette put her up to this?

"Stinker, about your dad . . ."

"What about him?"

"I'm thinking he'll be scared off by all of this. That he won't show up now. How about you?"

The coyotes began to howl. Lulu shifted around uneasily on the bed.

"I heard them last night." Reggie's voice was barely more than a whisper. "I thought I was dreaming." She breathed in and out for a moment before she said, "I don't believe those letters are real. I think he's dead."

"What makes you think that?"

"Just a feeling I have."

"So who's been writing them?"

"Monette, who else?"

The same Monette who'd suggested to me last night by the pool that it was Reggie who was writing them—in cahoots with Boyd Samuels. "Why would Monette do that?"

"That's obvious."

"Trust me, nothing is obvious to me right now."

"Monette's an inventor of stories. It's what she does when she's in crisis mode. She made up that story about Dad sexually abusing her to deal with the pain of losing Mom. And she's made up this story about Dad magically reappearing after twenty-plus years in the wilderness to cope with the pain of losing Patrick to Kat. It's about her. It's always about her."

"And yet you flew out here. Why?"

"I told you why. Because I thought I'd be needed. And I was right. Not that I had the slightest idea Monette was going to shoot the cheating bastard. I can guarantee you she wasn't planning to. If she had been then she wouldn't have bothered with those fake letters, would she? She doesn't need them now. She's *got* her story." Reggie fell silent, exhaling slowly. "Can we talk about something else now?"

"Such as . . . ?"

"Why did you dump me?"

"You really want to talk about that?"

"Yeah, I really do."

"Okay," I said, stroking her hair. "I had to."

"What does that mean?"

"It means that I was having so much fun with you that I could barely even remember what my novel was supposed to be about. And then, poof, off you'd go to Havana or Senegal, and instead of writing I'd just pine away for you, wondering when I'd get to see you again. I knew I'd never write my book if we stayed together. I had to end it."

"Why didn't you just *tell* me that? Why did you shut me out? You wouldn't see me. You wouldn't even talk to me on the phone."

"That was my size-huge ego. You were Regina Aintree. *The* Regina Aintree. I was just an angry young nobody who'd published a couple of short stories. I was so desperate to prove to you that I was a serious writer. It was the single most important thing in the world to me. Nothing else mattered."

"I hated you."

"I know."

She lay there in silence for a moment. "You really wrote it because of me?"

"Of course. That's why I dedicated it to you."

"I did it for you, too. Getting involved in all of those political causes, I mean. I wanted you to think I was incredibly daring and independent and fascinating. But do you know what I really wanted? I wanted my family back. My mother had killed herself. My father had disappeared. My big sister had sold out and written that horrible book about him. My whole life had been torn away from me. A few months before you broke up with me, I was sitting on stage at a women's poetry symposium in Gabon, waiting to read one of my poems, and it hit me right between the eyes that where I really, truly wanted to be was settled down with you at some nice little college in New England raising kids in a sweet old cottage, puttering in my garden and making my own jam the way Mom used to."

"You never told me that."

"I couldn't. I was afraid you'd be disappointed if you found out how conventional *the* Regina Aintree truly was. I wanted you to think I was gutsy. I'm not. Monette's the gutsy one. Look at what she's accomplished. Her own TV show, a retail empire, two kids. I could never have had kids. I'd have forgotten them somewhere or dropped them on their heads. I'm the fraidy cat of the century. I wake up scared every morning and I stay scared all day long. The only time in my whole life when I ever felt truly calm inside was when I was with you. Want to know something? This feels nice, Stewie. Like old times," she murmured as Lulu lay there next to us, mouth-breathing. "Although it smelled a whole lot less like low tide at Rockaway Beach in those days."

"If I kick her out of the room, she'll start barking."

Reggie rolled a bit more over onto her side, her inner thigh resting on top of my legs. Slowly, I became more and more aware that she was no longer an old friend with frozen feet who'd come in out of the night to snuggle. She was a soft, pliant, very alive woman who was stretching and arching herself against me.

"What are you doing?" I asked her.

"What do you think I'm doing? I've been desperate to jump you ever since I got here. I tried to visit you last night but Monette had already claimed you."

"We had a drink by the pool and talked. That's all."

"I know. I watched you from my window."

"I'm not going to get caught in between the two of you, am I?"

"You are so clueless. You're already caught and you don't even know it. But you're mine. You belong to me. And I'm going to make this as easy as possible. You don't have to tell me you still love me. You don't even have to move. All you have to do is let me ravage you."

"You've become an awfully canny little negotiator, Stinker."

"Besides, if you're going to write a novel about us—and I'm positive that you are—then you're going to need this scene. It'll be wonderfully poignant. The two of us together in your bed like this after all of these years. Unless you'd rather do it the other way around."

"With me on top instead of you?"

Her lips broke into a smile. "No, with us in my bed instead of yours. I can go back to my room if you'd like. You can tiptoe inside and tell me how desperate you've been to jump me. It would be more traditional that way."

"We're not traditional and never have been. Besides, you've got neighbors—Danielle on one side, Monette on the other. There's liable to be some moaning."

"I can keep quiet."

"But I can't. And I'm perfectly content to stay right here."

She touched my face with her fingers before her lips gently brushed mine. "Good, so am I."

"It's never going to happen, you know."

"What isn't?"

"The sweet old cottage. The garden. The jam. Especially the jam."

"I know."

"I'm still in love with Merilee."

"I know."

"And you're okay with that?"

"Why don't you just kiss me and find out for yourself?"

So I did. Gently at first, and then not so gently.

By then Lulu had decided to get a drink of water from her bowl in the kitchen. She's always been very discreet.

It wasn't 1977 anymore. We weren't two wild kids crazy with passion for each other in her third-floor room of the Chelsea Hotel. We were a pair of battle-scarred middle-aged people who were ensconced in the pool house of her sister's multimillion-dollar Brentwood estate. Steamy it wasn't. It was affectionate, tender and just a tiny bit wistful. A warm embrace between two old friends that just happened to include reentry. It was also a profound acknowledgment that we were breaking the spell we'd held over each other for so many years. I was letting go. She was letting go. We both knew it and so we both took our time, savoring it.

And when, at long last, she collapsed on top of me, her kaleidoscope eyes twirling and glittering in the moonlight just like they had on that warm summer night in Yellow Springs a million years ago, she whispered, "Hello, Stewie."

And I whispered, "Hello, Stinker."

Even though we both knew it wasn't hello. It was goodbye.

CHAPTER NINE

Wﾠe checked with the people who installed the home security system here," Lamp informed me as he drove us out the main gate, past the media horde, in his stylishly dented white LAPD Chevy Caprice sedan. "The keypad on the service gate does indeed have a memory. It was accessed early yesterday morning."

"How early?"

"At 6:47 am. We talked to Hector Villanueva at his home in Pico Rivera. He swears up, down and sideways that he hasn't been here since Friday. A neighbor across the street says Hector's truck hasn't left his driveway all weekend."

"Did you check with the young Tab Hunter?"

"If by that you mean the pool man, Gavin Cliff, we did."

"Is Gavin Cliff his real name?"

"Why wouldn't it be?"

"Sounds bogus to me. Highly bogus."

"He confirmed that he was here early yesterday morning."

"Was that the only time the service gate was accessed yesterday?"

"The only time," Lamp confirmed, his hands gripping the steering wheel tightly as he made a left onto Sunset and started in the direction of Bel Air and the Hills of Beverly. Today he wore an olive-colored suit made of something no-iron, a white shirt, striped tie and the same pair of nubucks with red rubber soles that he'd worn yesterday. Unless, that is, he owned two identical pairs and rotated them for proper foot hygiene. "Did Gavin show up this morning?"

"I didn't see him, but I wouldn't expect to. It's Sunday."

A bright, sunny Sunday, and not yet 9:30. I'd been stropping Grandfather's razor when Lamp had shown up at the pool house to ask me if I wanted to take a ride. So we were taking a ride. I didn't know if he was taking me to church or to Du-par's for a stack of their buttermilk pancakes. I just knew that he seemed a lot more awake than I was. I'd barely managed two hours of sleep after Reggie tiptoed discreetly back to her room at 5:00 am. I had a dull headache and the strong taste of library paste in my mouth even though I'd downed two glasses of fresh-squeezed orange juice and a pot of strong coffee. I wore the glen plaid tropical worsted wool suit from Strickland & Sons with a pale green shirt to match my complexion, a blue-and-white polka-dot bow tie and my Panama fedora low over my eyes to shield them from the bright sun. Lulu rode on the seat between Lamp and me, her tail thumping happily. She loves to ride in police cars.

"It may interest you to know," Lamp said, "that one of the guests who was at Joey's birthday party yesterday is the registered owner of a black 1988 Pontiac Trans Am just like the one that tried to run you over."

"And shove Monette off Coldwater Canyon, don't forget."

"I haven't."

"Well, who is it, Lieutenant?"

"Kat Zachry's half-brother, Kyle."

I mulled this over as we cruised our way past the Bel Air Gate at Sunset and Bellagio. Lulu climbed into my lap, planted her back paws firmly in my groin and stuck her large, wet black nose out my open window, her ears flapping in the breeze. "Kyle is Kat's flunkie," I said. "He has access to the production offices. Could have typed that fake note from Patrick to me on *Malibu High* stationery and had a studio messenger deliver it to Aintree Manor. But why?"

"I thought we'd drop by and ask him. Kat rents him an apartment north of Fountain on Sweetzer. She hasn't left her place in Laurel Canyon since yesterday. Kyle was there with her until he went home late last evening. My people tell me she's hunkered down there this morning with a network publicist, her agent and the honcho producer of *Malibu High*. Boyd Samuels showed up there, too. Don't ask me why."

"Don't have to. I can tell you why. Because he smells money."

Whitney still reigned supreme on the Sunset Strip's mammoth billboards. And Marky Mark and Kate Moss were still almost, kind of getting it on. But the Strip was eerily quiet on a Sunday morning. Ours was the only car on the road. The sidewalks were empty, clubs and restaurants shuttered. It felt like a ghost town.

"We have some preliminary autopsy results on Patrick," Lamp informed me. "The blood spatter patterns on the wall and bedspread seem to indicate that he was seated on the bed when Monette hit him with the first two shots. The blood smears on the bedspread indicate that he slid from the bed down onto the floor, where she fired the kill shots straight down through his heart. He bled out right there. All of which backs up her version of what happened. He had a blood alcohol level of 0.23, nearly three times the legal limit to operate a motor vehicle in the state of California. The man was seriously drunk. We don't know what else was in his system—toxicology will take at least a week—but you saw him snorting coke out on the patio with Lou and Kyle shortly before he went upstairs, didn't you?"

"I saw Lou slip him some pills, too. I also wouldn't be surprised if Patrick smoked a doobie on his way to the party. The man was a serious druggie."

Lamp shook his neat blond head. "Based on his blood alcohol level alone, I'm surprised that Monette didn't find him passed out cold on the bed."

"Maybe she did. Maybe she's lying to us."

He glanced over at me, frowning. "Where are you going with this?"

"Nowhere. I'm just trying to deal with my disappointment."

"Over . . . ?"

"I was hoping that you were taking me out for buttermilk pancakes."

"Sorry, I'm afraid not. We already ate."

"'We' being . . . ?"

"Belinda and me. She's the lady I'm currently seeing. Really terrific person. She teaches kindergarten in Huntington Beach, makes jewelry." He showed me the turquoise and silver bracelet on his wrist. "Like it?"

"I do, but I'm reeling a bit. Does your mom know that you date girls?"

"You're such a rib tickler, Hoagy. Trust me, I'm not the innocent lamb that you make me out to be."

"Then kindly explain something to me. How is it that you're not all grumpy, cynical and sour?"

"Because I don't let the job get to me. When I clock out I put it out of my mind and I enjoy being alive. Sometimes that's not easy, but it's what I do."

"Lieutenant, I admire you." We rode along the slumbering Strip in silence for a moment, Lulu with her nose stuck out the window. "Did you find out anything from the Beretta?"

"What we expected to find. Four shots fired. One set of fingerprints. Monette's. The barrel and trigger were clean otherwise."

"How clean?"

"Meaning . . . ?"

"Had the gun been wiped clean before she used it?"

"Actually, it did appear to have been wiped clean."

"With . . . ?"

"Who knows? A rag or cloth of some kind."

"Does that tell you anything?"

"Yeah. It tells us that she likes to keep her gun clean." He glanced over at me. "Our lab people did turn up something a bit unexpected this morning. Blood and tissue from *two* different blood types under Patrick's fingernails—Type O and Type A."

"I don't suppose you know what Monette's blood type is, do you?"

"We do. She let us take a sample while she was in custody. Could have refused in the absence of a court order, but she didn't, even though her lawyer advised her to."

"And . . . ?"

"Monette is Type O."

"Meaning the Type O blood and tissue under his nails are hers."

"Presumably. She does have those gouge marks on her arms."

"So where did the Type A come from?"

"We don't know. One possibility is Patrick himself. He was Type A."

"His own blood and tissue ended up under his nails? Does that typically happen?"

"Blood? Absolutely. If he was clutching at the wound in his side, for instance. But tissue? That's a big fat no. I've encountered heroin addicts gouging themselves when they're going through extreme withdrawal, but not gunshot victims. Never. Besides, the ME found no fingernail gouges anywhere on Patrick's body."

"So what do you make of that?"

"He gouged someone else is what I make of it. Someone with Type A blood."

"Meaning that someone else was in the room when he was shot?"

"Not necessarily. He could have gotten into an altercation with somebody before he went upstairs. You didn't happen to notice blood under his nails when he was snorting that coke out on the patio, did you?"

"No, I didn't."

"And he went up to the master bedroom suite shortly after that?"

"Correct." I glanced at him as we rode along. "What are you thinking?"

"That we've got something concrete to work with now. I can get a court order to compel everyone who was in that house yesterday, including you, to submit to a thorough physical exam as well as give us blood and hair samples."

"Why hair?"

"Our people discovered several different hair samples on the bedspread, which may prove valuable if we find a hair that belongs to an individual who had no credible reason for being in that bedroom." Lamp fell silent for a moment. "I'm also thinking that something happened in there yesterday that we still don't know about. I don't believe Monette is telling us the whole story. Do you?"

"Not even maybe."

"How about you, Hoagy? Are you telling me the whole story?"

"I'm just out here earning a paycheck, Lieutenant. Or trying to."

"You didn't exactly answer my question."

"I gave you the best answer I can."

He peered over at me, his blue eyes narrowing, before he looked back at the road before us.

We were passing Tower Records and Spago on our left. Sweetzer ran into Sunset around the bend from there just past the ornate white art deco Sunset Tower Hotel. Lamp eased off the gas and made a right turn, taking it slow as Sweetzer made a steep drop down from Sunset, tumbling its way past apartment houses that ranged from new and nice to old and nice to just plain not so nice. Kyle Cook's building, Sweetzer Court, ranked in the not-so-nice category, although it had probably been splendid twenty or thirty years ago. It was one of those pink two-story Spanish-style stucco places built around a central courtyard. But no one had been taking care of Sweetzer Court for a long time. It needed a decent paint job, unless you consider stained, discolored and peeling a decent paint job. There were red roof tiles missing, more than a few cracked windowpanes and the landscaping had been seriously neglected. The bamboo in the beds out front grew wildly to the rooftop. The jacarandas and oleanders needed to be pruned way back. The lawn, if you want to call it that, was mostly hard bare earth with patches of weeds growing wherever they felt like.

There was a black Trans Am parked out front.

Lamp parked behind it, checking its license plate number against the one he'd jotted down in his notepad. "That's Kyle's car, all right. Does it look like the one that tried to run you down in Pacoima?"

Lulu answered for both of us with an emphatic woof.

"He appears to be home. Apartment 2C. Let's go have a talk with him, shall we?"

We followed a brick path into the courtyard, which had the remains of a dead concrete fountain in its center. A couple of cheap, woven plastic lounge chairs were set around it. The bare ground around them was strewn with empty, greasy pizza boxes and empty, greasy Jack in the Box wrappers and beer cans and cigarette butts. As we strode toward the front door I found the place was summoning up images of the San Bernardino Arms, the faded apartment house where Tod Hackett mooned hopelessly over Faye Greener in *The Day of the Locust*, the Nathanael West novel that will teach you pretty much everything you'll ever need to know about Hollywood. Although you'll be much happier not knowing it, if you want my honest opinion.

Inside the front door there were mailboxes for eight apartments and a downstairs unit that probably belonged to the manager—if Sweetzer Court still had one, which I seriously doubted. The entry hall smelled of cat urine. Or at least I think it was cat urine. So did Lulu, who turned up her nose disdainfully.

The rubber treads on the stairway up to the second floor were worn through. As we climbed I heard the menacing din from somewhere up there of "Welcome to the Jungle" by Guns N' Roses, a song that had achieved iconic status as the unofficial anthem of bad-boy frat parties, minor league hockey games and skeevy biker bars from sea to shining sea. Axl Rose's off-key wailing and Slash's majestically inept guitar licks were not exactly welcome blasting from somebody's apartment at 10:00 on a Sunday morning. As we started down the hallway toward apartment 2C the music got even louder.

A longhaired young guy who was wearing what I swear were *Star Trek* PJs was pounding on Kyle's door and yelling, "If you don't turn that the fuck down I'm calling the police! You hear me, bro?"

"I'm the police," Lamp said to him over the blaring music.

"Well, *do* something, will you?"

"Please go back in your apartment, sir."

He returned to his apartment across the hall, slamming the door shut.

Lamp knocked on Kyle's door, even though Captain Kirk had just been pounding on it to no avail. He removed a clean hand-

kerchief from the back pocket of his trousers and tried the doorknob. The door was unlocked. Lamp pushed it open. It swung
open about eighteen inches before it hit something and stopped.
Something was blocking the door.

Make that someone.

One whiff and Lulu was already slinking back toward the
stairs with her tail between her legs. She'd had just about enough
death for one weekend, thank you very much. I ordered her to
come back. She came back, grumbling, and in the three of us
went, Lamp using his handkerchief on the doorknob to close the
door behind us.

Kyle Cook was lying on his back just inside the door of his
studio apartment in a T-shirt and boxer shorts with his unseeing
bloodshot eyes bugging out of his head.

Lamp crossed the room to a battered boom box on Kyle's nightstand and flicked off the music. Blessed silence. Then he returned
to Kyle's body, studying it carefully. "See all of that hemorrhaging
in his eyes?"

"Pretty hard to miss it."

"That's a good indication he was strangled."

"Yeah, I surmised that from those red finger marks that go all
the way around his throat."

Lamp bent down and touched Kyle's arm. "He's still warm.
Hasn't been dead for more than a half-hour. Whoever did this has
much bigger hands than I do, see?" He positioned his in the air
around Kyle's throat for comparison before he glanced up at me,
frowning. "Did you just say *surmised*? I've never heard anyone use
that word in ordinary conversation before."

"There's a first time for everything, Lieutenant. And, just for
the record, this is not my idea of ordinary conversation."

"The knuckles of his right hand are red and swollen, see?"
Lamp said, examining it closely. "That means he threw a punch at

his killer and connected with hard bone. Whoever we're looking for will have a bruise somewhere on his face."

"'His' face. You're positive it's a man?"

"She'd have to be a strong woman with a mighty big pair of hands."

"Monette has big hands."

"Where are you going with this, Hoagy?"

"Nowhere in particular."

I gazed around at the apartment, which wasn't much. Just one small room with worn carpeting, a Pullman-style kitchen and very little in the way of furniture. His bed was nothing more than a convertible sofa, currently open. The pillows and sheets were rumpled. There was a nightstand with two drawers. The bottom drawer was pulled open wide and appeared to be empty. Several moving company cartons were stacked in the corner of the room. One of the boxes served as a hamper to hold his dirty laundry. There were no pictures on the walls. No curtains or shutters over the windows, which looked out over an alley that was lined with decoratively colored Dumpsters.

Lamp took a peek inside the small refrigerator. It was empty except for a carton of orange juice and a six-pack of Coors. Then he gave the bathroom a quick once-over before he said, "Not exactly living large, was he?"

"He probably spent most of his time on the Radford lot or at Kat's place. Just came here to crash when she wanted him gone." My eyes fell on Kyle's boom box. "Why the loud music? Woke up the neighbors."

"But also drowned out the sounds of their voices. If punches were thrown then they must have argued. I wonder what they were arguing about."

"I have a pretty good idea. And so do you."

"You're right, I do. But I value your input. You have an atypical mind."

"Thank you, I think. I'm guessing that someone didn't want Kyle talking to you because Kyle could finger him, or her, as the person who hired him to throw that scare into Monette and me with his Trans Am."

Lamp nodded his head. "Agreed. So who are we looking at for this?"

"Offhand, I can think of two possibilities. One is Kat . . ."

"Kat's been home all morning. She's got a media mob watching her house and we've got officers watching the media mob. She hasn't set foot outside of her door. Besides, she's tiny. No way those were her hands wrapped around Kyle's throat. Who else?"

"Lou Riggio. Possibly Lou hired Kyle to scare us on Patrick's behalf. Possibly Patrick told him to do it. Patrick swore to me that he didn't, but I assumed he was lying to me."

"Why did you assume that?"

"Because everyone lies to me. It's what they do. That's why they pay me the big bucks. It's possible, I suppose, that it was all Lou's own idea. I don't know. I do know that he has big, strong hands."

Lulu had moved over to Kyle's body, where she began sniffing at the floor near his right shoulder, snuffling and snorting as she dug her large wet black nose under his T-shirt. Or tried to. He wasn't exactly budging. Thwarted, she sat back on her haunches and let out a frustrated moan.

"Why's she doing that?"

"Thinks she's found something underneath him. Shall we roll him over?"

"Can't. The coroner goes bananas if we disturb a body."

"Well, then how about we just give his shoulder a bit of a tilt?"

"Hoagy, you're a bad influence."

"Thank you, Lieutenant. I try."

"Here, let me . . ." Lamp knelt and grabbed the former Kyle Cook by his hip and shoulder and rolled him a bit.

Lulu wasn't wrong, not that I for one second thought that she was. Attached to the underside of Kyle's right shoulder was a wet, sticky Tootsie Pop. Grape by the looks of it.

"Big Lou loves grape Tootsie Pops."

"Not real bright of him to leave it behind." Lamp didn't touch it. Just released his hold on Kyle and settled him back as we'd found him.

"Could be he's freaking out. His meal ticket got killed yesterday. Plus he takes vast quantities of steroids. He also played defensive tackle in college, don't forget."

"What does that mean?"

"It means he got hit in the head a lot," I said as Lulu began to bark at Lamp. And bark.

He frowned at her. "Why is she doing that?"

"She wants you to give her an anchovy as a reward."

"I don't carry anchovies on me. I work for the LAPD, not SeaWorld."

I thanked her for a job well done and told her I owed her an anchovy. I also told her to knock it off.

Lamp went over to that open nightstand drawer and knelt before it, sniffing at it. "We don't want to touch this drawer until they dust it for prints, but stick your nose in there and tell me what you think."

I stuck my nose in there and told him what I thought. "It smells like weed."

He sniffed at it again. "And not just a joint or two either. It smells like he had a whole stash of bricks in here—which Lou made sure he grabbed on his way out the door. I wonder if Kyle was dealing for Lou on the sly."

"Makes perfect sense."

"Why do you say that?"

"Your drug people think Lou moves a lot of dope on the Radford lot, right?"

"Right . . ."

"He'd need someone plausible to go in and out of the trailers of the *Malibu High* cast members for him. He'd stick out himself, being a middle-aged, muscle-bound pinhead. Kyle wouldn't. Kyle had no source of income other than handouts from Kat. We know he did some small-time dealing up in Atascadero. Besides, we know that he and Lou were buds."

"We do?"

"They got into a sweaty three-way with Trish on the Eartha Kitt sofa yesterday, remember? Men who aren't buds wouldn't do that. They'd take turns."

Lamp looked at me in dismay. "How on earth would you know that?"

"I'm sorry to disillusion you, Lieutenant, but I had some pretty wild times back in my cocaine eighties."

"I have to call this in." He glanced around. "Except I don't see a telephone. He didn't even have a phone." His gaze fell upon Kyle there on the floor. Kyle with his bulging, bloodshot eyes. "Not much of a life, was it?"

"That all depends upon your definition of living. Yesterday afternoon he was at a Brentwood mansion snorting coke with a TV star. He probably thought he was living the dream."

"You're right, he probably did. Me, I want to die in my own bed with my wife of fifty-plus years holding my hand and my children and grandchildren surrounding me. How about you?"

"I haven't got a fraction of your courage. I don't want to die at all."

"I'd better phone this in from my car."

We let ourselves out, Lamp closing the door behind us. As we started back toward the stairs, Lulu came to a sudden halt and went in the other direction, her nose to the floor.

"What's she doing now?" Lamp asked me.

"Following the killer's scent. I'll meet you at your car."

Lulu led me to the other end of the hallway, where a set of stairs went down to the Dumpsters in the alley out back. She followed the scent out to a spot ten feet from the alley door, where she snuffled and sat, her tail thumping.

"Good girl, Lulu. Now I owe you two anchovies."

We made our way around to the front of the building. Lamp was still calling it in from the front seat of his Caprice. He rang off as Lulu and I got in.

"He parked in back by the Dumpsters," I informed Lamp. "One of Kyle's neighbors may have seen him take off."

"Thanks, that's good to know. I'll have some men canvass them." He gripped the steering wheel in silence for a moment before he said, "Lou's holding down the fort at Patrick's cottage on Marmont for the time being. I just checked with our men who are on security detail outside."

I looked at him curiously. "And . . . ?"

"The big guy went out at 8:45 this morning in his GTO. He returned about forty minutes ago."

"Did they notice if he had a fresh bruise on his face?"

"They didn't get close enough to see him. He pulled into the attached garage and went straight in the house."

"What happens now, Lieutenant?"

"I stop by and personally notify Kyle's next of kin, Kat, that her half-brother has been murdered. That's what happens. But it also so happens that Patrick's place is on the way to her house, so I suggest we swing by and have a quick little chat with Lou first." He glanced over at me. "Unless you have a problem with that."

"No problem at all."

WE MADE OUR way back up to Sunset Boulevard, hung a right and then took a quick left onto Marmont Lane, where the majestic old Chateau Marmont is nestled in a hillside above the Strip. The Chateau Marmont is the hotel where John Belushi died of a speedball injection in bungalow three ten years back, thereby flushing away one of the five or six most promising careers in the history of show business. Marmont Lane twisted its way past the hotel, became Marmont Avenue and then climbed way high up into the hills past a collection of modern, post-modern and post-post-modern houses that clung to tiny fingernail parings of land for dear life.

The late Patrick Van Pelt's rental cottage had no front yard to speak of. Just an ivy-covered wall and a closed garage door flush up against the sidewalk. The gate in the ivy-covered wall was of solid wood for maximum privacy. What little I could see of the cottage gave me the impression it had been designed by an architect who'd been heavily influenced by *The Jetsons*.

The narrow street was crowded with dozens of grief-stricken fans who were dutifully leaving flowers, cards, candles and other mementos outside of Patrick's wall to honor this great star who had meant so much to them. Celebrity mourners. I've never understood people who feel the need to congregate and sob over the death of someone whom they've never actually met. I used to be married to a celebrated movie star. I'm a former celebrity myself. Take it from me, celebrities are not who their fans think they are. Patrick certainly wasn't. The man was a twenty-four-karat shitbird. But these people didn't know the real Patrick. They only knew the kindly, heroic Patrick whom they'd seen on the small screen. What they were grieving over was a myth, not a man.

There were two LAPD black-and-whites parked outside of the front gate along with a gaggle of TV news crews who were there to talk to the tearful mourners and grab footage of the makeshift shrine they were erecting.

Lamp found a place to park and exchanged a few words with one of the cops in uniform before he buzzed the house from the intercom at the front gate.

After a moment a voice answered, "For the last time . . ." It was Lou's sandpapery voice. "Will you media people *please* leave me the hell alone?"

"This is Detective Lieutenant Lamp, Mr. Riggio," Lamp said into the intercom. "I'd like to have a word with you, if you don't mind."

"Oh, sure thing, Lieutenant. Sorry about that. I'll buzz you in."

Lamp pushed the front gate open when it buzzed. The cop he'd spoken with started up the path toward the front door of the house, his meaty right hand resting comfortably on his holstered weapon. Lamp turned to me and said, "You'd better wait here. There's no telling what we're about to walk into."

I was just about to tell him what a bad idea that was when I heard the electric garage door open and a car's engine start up with a roar. Then Lou's vintage gunmetal gray GTO came zooming out of the garage in reverse, sending mourners and cameramen scattering. As he hit the brakes I caught a glimpse of the big man hunched over the wheel—lips pulled back from his teeth in a tight grimace, eyes wide with fright—before he put it in gear and went tearing down the hill.

Lamp made a dash for his Caprice. Lulu and I sprinted along with him and jumped in as he started it up and pulled away. Off we went down Marmont, twisting and turning our way past the

Chateau just in time to see Lou hang a screechy right turn on Sunset.

Lamp came to a complete stop at the corner and said, "Okay, this is where you get out. I can't endanger your safety in a high-speed chase."

"Lieutenant, I'm the first major new literary voice of the 1980s. Do you honestly think I'm going to die on Sunset Boulevard riding shotgun in an unmarked police car?" Lulu let out a low moan from the seat between us. "Along with my short-legged companion? Get moving, will you? He's getting away."

"Fine, have it your way." Lamp made a right turn, floored it and went after him. "But, I swear, if you get killed, I am going to kill you."

The Sunday morning traffic on the Strip was still practically nonexistent, which was a good thing because Lou was barreling along at seventy miles per hour right down the center of the boulevard and zigzagging his way over the yellow line into what would have been oncoming traffic if there'd been any oncoming traffic. I wasn't sure whether he was coked out of his gourd or simply flipping out at the prospect of spending the rest of his life in jail. All I know is that he was a full-blown accident ready to happen.

Lamp sped up to within four car lengths of Lou, flashing his lights to no avail, and called in to report that he was in the midst of a high-speed pursuit of a gray 1965 GTO heading west on Sunset toward La Cienega. He provided the license plate number and the name of its driver in a crisp, clear voice. He was very cool under the circumstances. Professional. Emil Lamp was a professional.

As we shot past Doheny into Beverly Hills and the huge billboards changed over to palm trees, I heard the distant sirens of the black-and-whites that were responding to Lamp's call. Lou was still tearing along at seventy, Lamp remaining a steady four lengths behind him. The Beverly Hills Hotel loomed up ahead in the distance—and the big man was showing absolutely no inter-est in slowing down despite the oh-so-obvious peril that lay just beyond it.

I felt my stomach muscles tighten. "Please tell me he's going to slow down."

"He's not going to slow down."

"He has to."

"He's not going to."

"But he's almost at North Whittier. This is no place to play."

"Playing? Who's playing?"

"Lieutenant, I have a terrible feeling that Lou's going to find out for himself that everyone was right."

"Hoagy, what in the holy heck are you talking about?"

Lou was closing in on the sharp right bend at North Whittier now, the one that had been made legendary by Jan Berry and Dean Torrence. I held my breath as he tore his way toward it go-ing way too fast. And realized it way too late. He panicked. Tried to swerve left instead of right. Went into an out-of-control skid across the intersection and crashed head-on at full speed into a parked Mercedes on North Whittier.

The crash was so loud that Lulu dove to the floor at my feet, shaking.

The horn on Lou's GTO started blaring. And kept right on blaring right up until both it and the Mercedes exploded into flames. Lamp pulled over to the side of the road a safe distance away and called it in. Then we sat there in stunned silence, Lulu continuing to shake. I reached down and stroked her.

The big red trucks from the Beverly Hills Fire Department got there in a matter of moments to put out the flames. There was nothing left of Lou Riggio beyond his charred remains. Fortu-nately, there hadn't been anyone in the Mercedes, which, it was later reported, belonged to a member of the writing staff of

Married with Children who'd been having brunch at his agent's house across the street at the time of the crash.

In death, Lou Riggio achieved a level of pop cultural infamy that had eluded him in life. He'd been a decent but undistinguished lineman at Troy State, a body builder, personal trainer and low-level supplier of illegal drugs to various show business personalities. As near as the LAPD could determine, he'd also murdered Kyle Cook. But none of that was what made Lou famous enough that his name would still mean something to people twenty years in the future. No, on that bright, sunny Sunday morning on Sunset Boulevard, Lou Riggio achieved a rare and lasting place in American folklore not for what he did but for what he didn't do.

He didn't come back from Dead Man's Curve.

"I *DON'T WANT* to see Kyle's body!" Kat hollered at Lamp as she sat there with a small cluster of advisers in the living room of her bungalow on Stanley Hills Drive in Laurel Canyon. "And don't give me any of your cop bullshit about how I have to because I am *really* not in the mood right now!"

"There's a process here, Miss Zachry," he pointed out politely. "It's the law, and the law has to be followed."

"I don't give a shit about your law! And I don't want to talk about this anymore! Are you hearing me?"

"Quite well. There's nothing wrong with my ears."

Kat's bungalow was a furnished rental by the look of it. The décor was early Ramada Inn. Patrick had told me that Kat was a total slob who left dirty clothes and dishes everywhere, yet when we'd fought our way through the mob of cameramen and reporters out front and made it inside, we found that the place was neat and tidy. I had zero doubt that it was someone other than Kat who'd done the tidying. My money was on the network's publicist, a beleaguered-looking young woman with Baba Wawa hair whose name was Rhonda. Kat's HWA agent, a pint-sized young ferret named Joey Bamber, was there. So was the executive producer of *Malibu High,* a tanned, pencil-thin woman in her forties named Marjorie Braman, who wore a denim shirt, tan suede pants and red cowboy boots. And so was Boyd Samuels, who stood over by a front window talking on his mobile phone.

Lulu took a quick lap around the place, nose to the floor, before she settled by the front door with a wary look on her face. She doesn't care for explosions. Never has.

Kat hadn't exactly seemed shocked or grief stricken. Her only response to the news that her half-brother had been strangled to death was petulant annoyance that Lamp was bothering her about it. She flat out didn't seem to care. She hadn't exactly been blown away by the sight of Patrick lying dead in a pool of blood on the bedroom floor at Aintree Manor either. If anything or anyone touched Kat Zachry I hadn't seen it so far. I was beginning to wonder if she had a heart of stone. I was beginning to wonder a lot of things about her.

She was nibbling on some limp-looking takeout fries from McDonald's and sipping a Coke through a straw as she sat there on the sofa in her Magic Johnson jersey and gym shorts, her bare feet up on the coffee table. Considering that she was three months pregnant, my feeling was that she'd have been better off with a stack of golden brown buttermilk pancakes and a glass of milk, but don't go by me. I'd been obsessing about buttermilk pancakes all morning, and being around two dead men in the past hour simply made me crave them even more. My stomach's a bit funny that way.

"You still haven't given me a straight answer, Marjorie," Kat said to her executive producer. Apparently, she was finished talking to Lamp about Kyle's murder. "What happens now?"

"What happens now," Marjorie responded quietly, "is that *Malibu High* will go on hiatus for two weeks so that our writers can construct an off-ramp for Patrick that is tasteful and respectful. The network would like to see his death handled in as dignified a manner as possible."

Kat peered at her dubiously. "Like how?"

"One idea they were spitballing this morning was that Chip Hinton decides to go surfing during a powerful storm even though the Coast Guard has advised everyone in Malibu to stay out of the water. But Chip wants to catch that one last big wave while he's still young enough to ride it."

Kat continued to peer at her. "And . . . ?"

"And he drowns. His body will be found washed up on the rocks."

"He was *shot*! You think our audience doesn't fucking know that?"

"*Patrick* was shot," Marjorie countered, keeping her voice soft. She did not wish to rile her nineteen-year-old star. "The network doesn't want Chip's departure from *Malibu High* to draw any attention to what actually happened to Patrick on Rockingham Avenue. They're quite firm about that, Kat." She mustered a warm, supportive smile. "Don't worry about this, okay? The writers will work morning, noon and night until they get it right. They'll come up with something brilliant."

Lamp cleared his throat. "Miss Zachry . . . ?"

Kat looked at him in surprise, as if she'd forgotten he was there. "What do you want now?"

"The same thing I wanted before. I need for you to formally identify your brother's body. It's an official legal process. You have to do this."

Kat rolled her big brown eyes at him. "Do I have to do it today?"

"No, tomorrow will be fine."

"Fine, whatever." She chewed on another limp French fry. "Where is he?"

"Right now he's being transported to the county coroner's office."

She stopped chewing. "You mean he's, like, stuffed inside a big plastic bag? Ewww . . ."

"I'll have someone from the coroner's office contact you in the morning. Is there anyone whom I should be contacting up in Atascadero?"

"Like who?"

"Any other relatives?"

"None that I want to talk to. They'll just try to hit me up for money."

"Were you and Kyle close?" Lamp asked her.

"Not really. We didn't grow up in the same house together or anything like that. And he was six years older than me."

"Still, you must find this very upsetting."

Kat glared at him. "Dude, I'll do what you want. I'll identify him. I'll see that he gets a proper burial. But don't tell me how I must be feeling, okay? When I moved down here, he tagged along to keep an eye on me. Things were going kind of sour for him up there. He needed a change of scenery. When I got the *Malibu High* gig, I asked him to help me deal with stuff. Answer my fan mail, run errands. I needed the help and he was family. But once a screwup, always a screwup, right?"

Lamp frowned at her. "I'm not sure I understand what you mean."

"If he didn't feel like doing something, it didn't get done, okay?"

"Would you happen to know anything about a business relationship between Kyle and Lou Riggio?"

"Business relationship?" Kat looked at him incredulously. "You're kidding me, right? They were a couple of dum-dums."

"So Kyle never said anything to you about doing a job for Lou?"

"What kind of a job?"

"One that required Kyle to tail certain individuals in his Trans Am."

"I have no idea what that even means."

"How about drugs? Was Kyle dealing for Lou?"

"Kat, I wouldn't answer that if I were you," her agent, Joey, interjected. "Not without a lawyer here."

"Right." She crossed her arms in front of her chest. "What Joey just said."

Boyd's mobile phone rang. He answered it and talked into it for a moment before gesturing wildly at me to follow him into an adjoining bedroom, which was as tidy and impersonally furnished as the living room. Lulu followed us in there. She's very protective of me if I'm alone in a room with Boyd.

"It's Mr. Harmon Wright," he informed me in a hushed, reverent voice. "He's calling from *London*."

"What does he want from *London*?"

"To find out what's up with our Richard Aintree project."

"It's been temporarily kicked to the curb due to a slight death in the family, in case Mr. Harmon Wright hasn't noticed."

Boyd murmured something a bit more tactfully worded into the phone, then listened before he said to me, "He considers Patrick's death a minor tabloid distraction."

"The minor tabloids may beg to differ."

"He still wants to know where things stand."

"We haven't heard from Richard. Not since Reggie showed up here with the letter he sent her in New Paltz. We're waiting for him to reach out again. He likes to use express mail. The U.S.

Postal Service delivers that on Sunday. Maybe we'll hear from him today."

"So you'd say the ball's in his court?"

"I would, although I try to avoid using that expression whenever possible."

Boyd reported into the phone and then listened, his eyes widening before he said to me, "Mr. Wright wants to know if there's any possibility that it was Richard who shot Patrick."

"I don't see how. The man's not even on the same coast as far as we know."

"Wait, hold on . . ." Mr. Harmon Wright had more to say to him. Boyd listened, nodding, before he said to me, "He wishes to make it clear that he's not happy with how this is unfolding. He expected more results from you."

"We're getting plenty of results. They're just not the ones we anticipated. But tell him I'll be delighted to leave on the first plane for JFK if he wants to bring in someone else."

Boyd gulped at me. "Do you really, truly want me to tell Mr. Harmon Wright that?"

"Boyd, I really, truly don't care what you tell him."

"Mr. Wright, Hoagy said that he'd be happy to . . . Hello, Mr. Wright . . . ?" Boyd exhaled slowly. "He hung up on me. That's not a good sign." He went over to a front window and peered through the bamboo shade at the media mob that was gathered out on the street. "God, has this project turned to shit or what? I hate it when this happens."

"Do you?"

He looked at me curiously. "What does *that* mean?"

"It means that whenever I get involved with you, the body count suddenly starts to pile up faster than I can say Terence Trent D'Arby. It means I should have told Alberta that there was no way I was getting caught up in another one of your toxic scams. If it had been anyone but Alberta, I would have. I am telling you right now, Boyd. If I find out you're mixed up in this, I will bury you."

"Hoagy, I had no idea anything like this would happen, I swear."

"Is that right? You sure zoomed in on Kat awfully damned fast."

"That wasn't my idea. Mr. Harmon Wright *ordered* me to. He has high hopes for her. Keeps telling me how much she reminds him of a young Natalie Wood. And, between us, he is *not* unhappy that her sleazy brother is out of the picture." Boyd glanced through the open doorway at Kat sitting there with Lamp and the others. "The police think Lou Riggio killed him?"

"They do. Was Kyle dealing dope for him?"

"How would I know?"

I glared at him in response.

He ducked his head, nodding. "Kyle wanted to make some money of his own so he wouldn't have to keep sponging off Kat, so Lou put him to work dealing to the kids in the cast along with their assorted friends and hangers-on. They really like to party. Half of them are still wrecked when they show up for makeup in the morning—*if* they show up. The production's a total mess. Over budget, late, the works. I'm hearing that the network wants to fire Marjorie Braman and bring in an old-time ball buster to restore order. It wouldn't surprise me one bit if they fire everyone in the cast, too. Everyone except for Kat, that is."

"And you're saying Harmon Wright knows all about this?"

"Of course. He told me to be his eyes and ears out here. Why, where are you going with this?"

"Nowhere. Just making conversation."

"Amigo, you are never just making conversation."

Lamp was on his feet and coming across the living room toward us, pointing at his wristwatch. "I have to get going, Hoagy. You mind?"

"Not at all," I said, following him back toward the sofa.

"Thank you for speaking with me at this difficult time," Lamp said to Kat. "We'll be in touch first thing tomorrow morning in regards to the formal identification. And I'm sorry for your loss."

"Whatever," Kat said with a dismissive wave of her hand.

Lamp and I went out the front door with Lulu on our heels. The media mobsters descended on us at once, shouting questions:

"Hey, Lieutenant, what's the mood like in there?"

"What's she doing?"

"What's she wearing?"

"Is she crying?"

"What can you tell us?"

"What's she wearing?"

"I have no statement to make at this time," Lamp replied crisply.

"Aw, come on. Give us a break . . ."

"How about you, Hoagy?"

"Yeah, give us a break, Hoagy. You're one of us, remember?"

Just when I thought this day couldn't get any shittier. "I have no statement to make either," I said.

And then Lamp turned to me and said, "I suggest we amscray."

"Excellent idea. Hold on, did you just speak to me in pig latin?"

He didn't respond—in English or pig latin. Just started elbowing his way through the reporters and camera crews to his car. Lulu and I took off after him, Lulu baring her teeth and growling as we fought our way toward the Caprice and got in. Lamp started it up immediately and pulled away from the mob.

After he'd driven two blocks, he pulled over to the side of the road, shut off his engine and stared straight ahead in taut silence, his jaw muscles clenching and unclenching.

"Care to talk about it, Lieutenant?"

"Not really," he said tightly.

"Then would you care to listen?"

"To what?"

"What would you say if I told you that I know how you can get this whole case buttoned up in time to take Belinda out for a nice steak dinner tonight?"

"I'd say that you've been smoking some of Lou Riggio's weed. Besides, Belinda's a vegetarian. She eats tofu. Tastes like wet Styrofoam."

"Does this mean you don't want to hear what I have to say?"

"I'm listening."

"You mentioned that you'll be wanting blood and hair samples from each and every person who was at Joey's birthday party. Each and every person who's still alive, that is."

"We need to check everyone for fingernail gouges, too. So?"

"So can you assemble them back at Aintree Manor this afternoon? Grab some technicians from the medical examiner's office and take care of it there?"

"Why in the holy heck would I want to do that?"

"Because I think it might prove to be very useful."

"Hoagy, have you been holding out on me?"

"Not exactly. I've simply been working my side of the street while you work yours."

Lamp studied me long and hard from across the seat. "You know what happened, don't you?"

"I believe I may."

"But you're not sure?"

"That's correct."

"You think you *will* be sure if I get everyone together at the house?"

"Yes, I believe I will."

He stared straight out the window again. "Fine. Consider it done."

"Thank you, Lieutenant. I appreciate it."

"But I need to ask you something, Hoagy."

"Of course. What is it?"

"Am I going to regret this?"

Now it was my turn to stare straight ahead out the window. "Lieutenant, I can assure you that we're both going to regret this."

CHAPTER TEN

As I walked in the front door of Aintree Manor my ears were assaulted by Beethoven's thundering piano sonata *Pathetique*. This was no recording. Danielle was playing the intensely dramatic piece on the Steinway in the conservatory. I stood there in the front hallway, watching her and listening. *Pathetique* is no breeze to master. It demands both tremendous strength and delicacy, not to mention a deep wellspring of emotion. Technically, Danielle played it quite skillfully for a girl of fifteen who was not a stone-cold prodigy. It was obvious that she took the piano very seriously. But it was also obvious that she was not gifted. Her approach to the music was workmanlike and passionless. There was nothing transcendent or moving about it. No elation. No heartbreak. Just dogged determination. As I watched her pound the keys, seated there in her gray Brentwood School hooded sweatshirt and sweatpants, her long blond hair tied back in a ponytail, face a mask of focused concentration, I realized that for Danielle playing the piano was no different than running laps around the track or studying for a chemistry exam. Simply another accomplishment to be crossed off her daily checklist of accomplishments that stretched day after day, week after week, all of the way off into the year 2006, when she intended to independently produce her first utterly joyless feature film.

I found Monette and Elliot in the library wallowing in the live cable news coverage of the fiery death of the late Patrick Van Pelt's personal assistant, Lou Riggio, on Sunset Boulevard's fabled Dead Man's Curve. The crash, according to a breathless correspondent on the scene, had occurred during a high-speed chase with members of the LAPD less than an hour after an investigator had discovered Kyle Cook, Kat Zachry's half-brother, strangled to death in his Sweetzer Avenue apartment. Speculation was rampant about a link between Kyle's murder and Patrick's shooting death yesterday on Rockingham Avenue. The words *possible retribution killing* were even tossed out by a second breathless correspondent who was on the scene outside of Kyle's apartment building— which qualified as one hell of a leap for a reporter to make without so much as a shred of evidence. A year ago such wild speculation would have shocked me. It didn't anymore. Outright conjecture, also known as the "some say" source, now qualified as legitimate cable news reporting.

"Jesus Christ, Hoag," Elliot cried out, flicking the TV's volume to mute. In the conservatory, Danielle continued to pummel Beethoven into submission. "What the hell's going on?"

"Not much. Just a typical Sunday morning in paradise."

"Don't crack wise with me." Today, he resembled two marshmallows stuffed inside a Nike warm-up suit of Kelly green. "I've got one very upset lady here."

Monette didn't seem particularly upset to me. She appeared calm and composed, seated there in a short-sleeved knit top and linen pants. The railroad tracks of fingernail gouges on her forearms looked red but as clean and healthy as could be expected.

"A small bit of panic on Lou's part, it appears," I said.

"Panic?" Her swollen nose still made her voice sound a bit nasal.

"It seems that Kyle owned a black Trans Am."

She blinked at me. "Do you mean like . . . ?"

"Like the one that tried to shove you off Coldwater and go bumpety-bump over me in that parking lot in Pacoima."

"What's he talking about?" Elliot demanded. "What happened on Coldwater?"

"I'll explain it to you later, Elliot. Please go on, Hoagy."

"When Lieutenant Lamp and I arrived at Kyle's apartment to talk to him about it, we found Kyle dead on the floor. He'd been strangled by someone with big hands." I looked at Elliot's, which were pudgy, freckled and small. "My short-legged friend here found some physical evidence that Lou may have been involved. When we went to Patrick's house to talk to Lou about it, he freaked and took off in his GTO like a crazy person. You just saw for yourself in living color what happened after that."

Monette studied me intently with her steely blue eyes. "Why would Lou kill Kyle?"

"To shut him up before the police got to him. I'm guessing it was Lou who hired Kyle to throw that little scare into us."

"Do you think Lou came up with such an idea on his own?" she wondered. "Or did Patrick put him up to it?"

"I'm afraid we'll never know the answer to that. But I'd say Lou was more of a follower than a leader."

"I agree. The big ape did exactly what Patrick told him to do, no more, no less." She shook her head in disgust. "It was Patrick's idea. Had to be."

"What's Lieutenant Lamp planning to do about this mess?" Elliot interjected. "That's what I want to know."

"For starters, you'll want to stick around this afternoon. He intends to take care of some follow-up."

"What kind of follow-up?"

"Blood and hair samples from everyone who was here yester-day. Minus the three men who are no longer alive, of course."

"Why would he want that?" he asked.

"Routine procedure, he told me. He's rounding up Kat and Boyd and bringing them here so the technicians can take care of all of us in one fell swoop."

Monette stiffened. "He's bringing *her* here?"

"Also Trish Brainard."

"I can't say it thrills me to have either of those young women in my house again."

"I can't say that I blame you."

"He can't make us do it," Elliot said.

She frowned at him. "Do what, Elliot?"

"Give them our blood and hair samples."

"They already have a sample of my blood," Monette pointed out. "But I don't believe they took any of my hairs."

"We can say no," he insisted. "Refuse to do it."

"You can," I said. "But he can get a court order forcing you to comply."

"Let him try." Elliot grabbed his mobile phone. "Monette, I'm calling your lawyer."

"Please don't, Elliot."

He looked at her in surprise. "Why not?"

"Because Hoagy's right. The lieutenant will ask a judge to force everyone to comply, the media will hear about it and that's exactly the sort of publicity I don't need right now. This isn't just about legal proceedings. I'm being tried in the court of public opinion, and it's vital that the public sees me as being totally candid and cooperative. If I come across as even the least bit slippery, then my career in television will be history. So will my brand. I've got to think about how I'm going to support my children in the future.

That is, assuming I have a future." She took a deep breath, letting it out slowly. "Besides, what the lieutenant is requesting sounds fairly harmless. It's not as if they're planning to strip all of us naked, are they?"

"I don't believe so, no," I said.

"Then I think we should do as he wishes."

Reluctantly, Elliot put his phone back down and ran a hand over his round, freckled face. "How well do you know this guy Lamp?" he asked me.

"What do you want to know about him?"

"What's his deal is what I want to know about him."

"He's honest and he's smart. If he's asking for blood and hair samples then he has his reasons."

"What reasons? He already knows what happened here yesterday. We all know."

"Do we?"

"Yes, you do," Monette said. "I made a full and complete confession while I was in custody. There's nothing he doesn't know. Not one single thing."

I stood there gazing at her. "If that's the case then there's nothing to be concerned about."

She gazed back at me, her eyes narrowing. "Nothing at all."

Lulu chose this moment to thud her head into my shin.

"I've just been reminded of something I promised to do, if you'll excuse me."

"You're excused," Elliot said, flicking the TV's volume back on.

Lulu led me into the kitchen and sat directly in front of the refrigerator until I'd opened it and given her both of the anchovies that she'd earned.

Joey was slumped at the big trestle table reading a dog-eared paperback book. Reggie was helping Maritza prepare lunch, which appeared to be sandwiches of leftover grilled pork tenderloin with coleslaw and potato salad. Reggie grinned at me devilishly, but Maritza seemed even more upset than she had last evening. So shaky that she dropped a glass jar of homemade mayonnaise when she pulled it out of the refrigerator. The jar exploded all over the kitchen floor, sending Lulu scurrying under the table.

"Oh, I am so sorry!" she cried out, aghast.

"Not to worry." Reggie grabbed a sponge from the sink. "I'll clean it up."

"No, no. You will cut yourself." Maritza fetched a sponge mop from the closet. "Let me."

"We'll make it a team effort, okay?" Reggie offered.

"And I'll handle the sharp knife." I got busy cutting the fragrant, spicy tenderloin into thin slices. "Are you okay, Maritza?"

"I am not okay, Senor Hoagy," she confessed. "I am scared. Today is my day off and I do not wish to go anywhere. There are all of those TV cameras out there. I feel safer here."

"I know how you feel. You're better off staying here. We all are."

"We are?" Reggie stuck out her lower lip. "Lulu and I were hoping you'd take us for a ride to the beach on your awesome bike. We could have a picnic."

"I'd love to, but the paparazzi will tail us the whole way down there. The contents of our sandwiches will be front-page news tomorrow." I switched to a serrated knife and started in on a big, round loaf of sourdough. "Besides, we've been asked to stick around. Lieutenant Lamp has some technicians coming by to take samples."

Joey looked up from his book, scowling. "Samples of what?"

"Our blood and hair."

He considered this for a moment before he shrugged and went back to his reading. In the conservatory, Danielle segued from her dogged rendition of *Pathetique* to a dogged rendition of Scott Joplin's "Maple Leaf Rag."

"What's that you're reading, Joey?"

"It's, um, *Journey to the Center of the Earth* by Jules Verne." He colored slightly. "It was my favorite book when I was a little kid. When I woke up this morning I felt like rereading it. Don't know why."

"It's comfort food for the soul, that's why. I've read that book ten times."

"You have not. You're jerking my chain."

"Am I? Okay, butthead, you asked for it: 'Descend into the crater of Sneffells Yokul, over which the shadow of Scartaris falls before the calends of July, bold traveller, and you will reach the center of the earth. I have done this. Arne Saknussemm.' I guess you're feeling just a tiny bit ashamed of yourself right now, aren't you?"

"I'm impressed semi-large," he admitted grudgingly.

"These sandwich fixings are good to go," I said to him. "Help yourself."

Joey got up and made a sandwich piled high with sliced pork and coleslaw. Set it on a plate, poured a glass of milk and headed back upstairs to his room with his favorite childhood book tucked under his arm.

I made a sandwich for myself, cut it in half and found a cold bottle of Corona in the refrigerator before I headed out onto the patio. Lulu joined me out there as I sat down at the table. So did Reggie, who had that same devilish grin on her face.

I took a bite of my sandwich. "You're not eating?"

"I'm not hungry," she said, grabbing the other half sandwich from my plate and taking a bite of it.

I glared at her. "I cannot believe you still do that."

She took another bite. "Do what?"

"Say that you're not hungry and then proceed to steal half of my lunch. Haven't you figured out by now that men *hate* that? We don't share our food and we don't try on each other's shoes—or any other article of clothing, for that matter."

"Forgive me for saying this, Stewie, but you are acting really peculiar right now." Her huge eyes searched my face. "Are you feeling weird about last night?"

"No, not at all."

"Good, because I had an amazing time."

"So did I. That was far and away the best sex I've had in the nineties. It was also the only sex I've had in the nineties."

Reggie tilted her head at me curiously. "So you and Merilee don't . . . ?"

"No, we don't."

"That seems like a real shame."

"Yes, it does, doesn't it?"

"You know, you could finish your sandwich in the pool house just as well as here," she said, looking at me through her eyelashes.

"True."

"And I could join you out there."

"Also true."

She drew back, squinting at me. "And yet that's not going to happen, is it?"

"What makes you say that?"

"Because I'm getting a very weird vibe off you right now."

"Weird as in . . . ?"

"Guarded. You seem very guarded. What's going on, Stewie?"

Maritza came charging out the French doors from the kitchen. "The lieutenant is back," she announced with a tremble in her voice.

I heard the riotous shouting from the media mob at the front gate. Vehicles pulling in, the gate clanking shut. Then I saw Lamp pull up behind my Roadmaster in his Caprice and get out. Kat and Boyd were with him. Then a black-and-white pulled up and out stepped a tall, tanned cop in uniform accompanied by Trish

Brainard. An L.A. County coroner's van arrived, too, and a pair of technicians in dark blue windbreakers got out.

Reggie tensed up as she watched all of them approach the front door. "It looks like they mean business. I guess we'd better join them."

"I'll catch up with you in a minute."

She looked at me, puzzled. "Why, where are you going?"

"I left something in the pool house. Just have to grab it."

It being the suitcase that was in the bedroom closet. Or, more precisely, the contents that I'd stuffed inside of the suitcase.

When I made my way inside the house with it, I encountered the tall, tanned cop leading a peevish Joey downstairs from his room. The cop escorted him into the library, which was where everyone seemed to have congregated—including the medical examiner's lab rats, who looked as if they weren't allowed out in public very often. They were extremely pale. Stood with their backs to the wall and their eyes fastened on the floor. At their feet were two large briefcases that appeared to have been constructed out of recycled aluminum beer cans.

Joey slouched his way over to one of the two matching leather sofas and flopped down next to Monette. Danielle sat on the other side of Monette in her hooded gray sweats, eyeing Lamp warily. Everyone in the room was eyeing Lamp warily. Reggie and Elliot, who were seated in the leather armchairs. Kat, Trish and Boyd, who sat on the other sofa. Maritza, who stood stiffly next to the desk with her arms crossed in front of her chest.

I moseyed over by the fireplace, where I set the suitcase down on the floor and leaned against the mantel. Lulu stretched out next to the suitcase. Monette looked at it, frowning, before she studied me with that steely gaze of hers.

"I *don't* see why you're making me do this," Kat fumed, seated there in her Magic Johnson jersey and gym shorts.

"I'm sorry for the inconvenience, Miss Zachry. But it's a routine forensics procedure," Lamp responded.

"If it's so routine then why couldn't we do it at my house?"

"I thought you'd appreciate getting out of there for a little while."

"Not to come *here*! Patrick was murdered here yesterday, remember?" She glared at Monette. "By *her*."

Monette's face tightened but she remained silent.

"What am I doing here?" asked Trish, who wore a flimsy yellow camisole, tight blue jeans and pink ballet slippers. Her long blond hair was gathered in a ponytail. "I mean, this feels like a harassment thing, you know?"

"It's routine procedure," Lamp said patiently.

"This must be a tremendously weird day for you, Trish," I said.

"Really?" She stared at me blankly. "Why?"

"The two guys who you boinked in the billiard room yesterday both suffered violent deaths this morning. That isn't the sort of thing that happens every day." I tugged at my ear. "Or is it?"

She shook her head at me in confusion. "*Who's* dead?"

"Kyle and Lou."

"Was Kyle the little one?"

"Yes."

"He was kind of dopey but okay. I wasn't into the big guy at all. He was rough. I don't like rough." Trish frowned at me. "Did you just say they're both dead now?"

"Yes, I did."

"Whoa, how sick is that?"

"Very, if dead is your idea of sick."

"I just mean it's, like, strange."

"I agree. It, like, is."

"You know, you're being really nasty to me right now."

"Sorry, Trish. I don't mean to be. After all, none of this is your fault. Well, it is, but it isn't, if you know what I mean."

"No, I *don't* know what you mean."

"I don't either," Boyd spoke up. "And I sure don't appreciate the way I was dragged here against my will. Lieutenant, I've placed a call to Mr. Harmon Wright about this. And when your superiors hear about this little farce, you'll be lucky to get a job guarding the cash register at a Pep Boys in Newhall."

"I understand that everyone's feeling a bit put out," Lamp said placatingly. "But I assure you there's absolutely nothing to be worried about."

"You're wrong, Lieutenant. There's a great deal to be worried about."

He looked at me in surprise. "What are you talking about, Hoagy?"

"I don't like being lied to. That's what I'm talking about."

"I haven't lied to you."

"I wasn't talking about you."

"Then whom are you talking about?"

"Every single member of this family," I said as Reggie shot a sharp look at me. "And Maritza as well. Which isn't to let Kat and Boyd off the hook. Or you, Elliot."

"Me?" Elliot let out a nervous chuckle. "What did I do?"

"Nothing. Not a damned thing. That was your contribution to this ugly little scenario. You stood out there on the patio turning those steaks, and you heard it and you didn't do a damned thing. That makes you complicit as far as I'm concerned." I turned to Kat and said, "You're complicit, too, because you're the one who brought Trish here. You were also a willing participant in an utterly fake tabloid scandal. You've known all along that the baby you're carrying isn't Patrick's. Yet you didn't care. You loved the attention. Loved tearing Monette's house down. Loved every glorious moment of it, you toxic little brat."

"Hey, you can't talk to me that way!" Kat protested.

"And yet here I am talking to you that way."

"What did I do?" Boyd demanded.

"You set the Richard Aintree project in motion. Made sure it got huge media saturation, which not only messed with Patrick's tabloid scheme to stampede Monette into a multimillion-dollar divorce settlement but totally screwed with his head. Made him so crazy that he told Lou to have Kyle put a scare into Monette on Coldwater Canyon and another one into me the moment I got here. So crazy that his intake of alcohol and drugs spiked way over the red line. Patrick was already bombed on Cuervo Gold when he showed up here for Joey's party. What was his blood alcohol level, Lieutenant? Three times the legal limit?"

"That's correct," Lamp answered.

"He did start getting high a lot more," Kat admitted in a rather meek little voice. "He never used to drink or snort in the morning. Not right there in his trailer. He always told me that a professional didn't do things like that. But that changed. *He* changed. He'd get super angry for no reason. And I swear he couldn't remember half the things he said or did."

I looked at Monette, who sat between Danielle and Joey on the sofa, staring at me coldly. "Which explains why you found him upstairs in the master bedroom suite rummaging around like Lon Chaney Jr. on a bad hair day, looking for the Rolex that he'd given to Hector."

Monette nodded her head ever so slightly.

"Which brings us to the shooting. Or shootings, I should say. Specifically, to that two- to three-minute gap between the first two shots that wounded Patrick and the last two shots that killed him. It should be clear to you by now, Lieutenant, that virtually everything we've been told about that particular gap in time was a carefully crafted lie."

"I've had concerns." Lamp glanced down at the floor by my feet. "Hoagy . . . ?"

"Yes, Lieutenant?"

"What's in the suitcase?"

"This suitcase? Not much, just a few odds and ends that I've picked up along the way thanks to my short-legged friend." Lulu gazed up at me, her tail thumping. She appreciates it when I don't Bogart all of the credit. "I was just about to get to it. Actually, it would be a lot easier to explain if we all moved upstairs to the master suite. Do you mind, Lieutenant?"

"No, I don't mind."

"Well, *I* mind," Monette said angrily. "I don't wish to go back into that room. And I don't appreciate being called a liar."

"I think he called me a liar, too." Reggie squinted at me. "Did you?"

"I'm afraid so, Stinker. You may also be guilty of obstruction of justice. Not that I'm a lawyer. Or even play one on television."

"Um, okay, I don't understand what's going on right now," Trish said.

"I don't either," Elliot said. "Lieutenant, I thought you people wanted blood and hair samples from us. What is this?"

"What this is," Lamp replied, "is that we're all going upstairs."

"I'm not going anywhere," Elliot said stubbornly.

"Mr. Schein, I really don't think that's the right approach for a man with your criminal record to be taking, do you?" Lamp said.

And so we all went up the grand staircase to the master suite. Lamp removed the yellow crime scene tape that was over the double doors and led us inside. The crime scene remained as the investigators had left it yesterday. The outline of Patrick's body was still marked on the floor, as were the locations of the shell casings. The bedspread had been removed for lab analysis. The only noticeable difference from yesterday was that someone had closed the windows. It smelled sour in there.

Lamp opened the windows to let in some fresh air. Monette stood in the middle of the room with her children, stone-faced. Reggie stood next to them, her eyes blazing at me. Maritza found a place for herself over by the fireplace, as did Elliot. Kat, Boyd and Trish moved over by the windows. The tall, tanned cop in uniform and pale crime lab technicians hovered by the door.

"I'd like to know what you meant before, Hoag," Elliot blustered at me. "You said I heard something from the patio. What did I hear?"

"The screams." I set the suitcase down on the bed. Lulu remained by my side, the better to guard it. "You must have heard them. Those windows overlooking the patio were wide open and you were right there turning the steaks on the grill. I was swimming laps and Lulu, my designated lifeguard, was barking her head off—so I didn't hear them. Kat and Boyd were in the process of breaking into the pool house. They didn't hear them. Lou, Kyle and Trish were making all sorts of noise of their own on the Eartha Kitt sofa, and they didn't hear them. But everyone else who was in the house at the time did. *You* heard them, didn't you, Joey? Just this once, you weren't wearing your headphones. And it's a good thing that you weren't. Also a bad thing that you weren't, considering what happened after that."

Joey gulped, his Adam's apple bobbing. "I don't know what you mean."

"Sure you do."

"Don't say anything, Joey," Monette ordered him. "Lieutenant, I've changed my mind. I want my lawyer, Seymour Glass, to be present before anyone in this room is allowed to say one more word. May I phone him, please?"

"Of course," Lamp said. "Go right ahead."

"One more word about what?" I asked Monette. "You've already confessed to Patrick's murder. Your lawyer will build such a strong case for self-defense that no jury will convict you. It's a slam dunk that you'll get off. You have nothing to worry about. All I'm doing is moving some pieces around."

"Pieces?" She gazed at me suspiciously. "What pieces?"

"Pieces like the fact that Joey has a mad schoolboy crush on Maritza."

"I—I do not," he sputtered, reddening.

Maritza lowered her eyes to the rug, swallowing uneasily.

"It's nothing to be ashamed of, Joey. Maritza's a very attractive young woman. In fact, your dad had a major crush on her himself. He even gave Hector that Rolex to pay him for keeping an eye on her. The one Patrick was rummaging around for in here." I glanced over at Maritza, who'd begun to tremble with fright. "Patrick told me to stay away from you, Maritza. He called you his 'private property.' I asked you this once before. I'm going to ask you again. Did he ever attack you?"

Maritza shot a worried look over at Monette, breathing in and out raggedly. "If he—he found me alone, he would speak of things he wished to do to me. Filthy things. Then he would laugh. After that, I tried to never be alone with him. Senor Patrick was not a good man. Hector, he is also no good. He talks of wanting sex with me—but he is married, just as Senor Patrick was married. I do not go with married men," she stated firmly, her gaze landing on Kat.

"What are you looking at *me* for?" Kat demanded. "Who are you to look at me that way?"

Maritza immediately lowered her eyes.

"Given Patrick's infatuation with you, Maritza, my initial thought was that it was *you* whom he attacked in here yesterday. It made perfect sense. You did disappear, after all. Told me you were in the kitchen stirring the onions and peppers. You weren't. You lied to me about that. You lied to me about the service stairway being locked. You'd also changed into a different uniform by the time you came upstairs after the shooting. It all added up. Except it didn't. Just for starters, both of your uniforms were short sleeved, just like the one you're wearing now, and you have no scratch marks or bruises on your arms. But there's an even more compelling reason why my initial thought was totally wrong."

Lamp said, "Which is . . . ?"

"The simple, obvious fact that it's not what happened." I looked over at Trish and said, "Am I right?"

Her eyes widened. "Why are you asking me? I don't know anything."

"Sure, you do, Trish. You're the key figure in this scenario."

"I am?"

"You wore a white bikini to Joey's birthday party yesterday, didn't you?"

Trish shook her head at me in confusion. "So . . . ?"

"So shortly after you arrived here yesterday, Monette gave you and Kat a tour of the downstairs. As soon as the three of you went in the house Patrick, Lou and Kyle got busy snorting up a couple of thousand dollars' worth of coke. By now Patrick was so bombed that he told Lou the whole world was starting to spin. Lou promptly fed him some pills. Speed, I imagine." I glanced over at Lamp. "Are you with me so far, Lieutenant?"

He shook his neat blond head. "I'm afraid not, Hoagy."

"Hang in there. We're getting to it. After Monette had given Trish and Kat the royal tour, Kat went wandering off to the pool house with Boyd, whom she'd convinced to help her steal my vintage leather flight jacket."

"That's an unfair characterization," Boyd said defensively. "We were discussing a highly lucrative book deal. Kat Zachry is a very hot property for HWA right now and we—"

"Kindly shut the heck up, will you, Samuels?" Lamp said.

"Meanwhile," I continued, "Kyle asked Trish if she'd mind showing him around the house. Lou tagged along, after first asking Patrick for permission. It seemed plain to me that neither Kyle nor Lou had developed a sudden passion for interior decorating. It was you they wanted, Trish. Joey didn't. In fact, he seemed quite repulsed by the idea of you being offered to him as a birthday present."

Trish shrugged. "Whatever."

"After you, Kyle and Lou went in the house Patrick announced to Monette that he needed to take a 'humongous' piss and went inside, too."

"Hoagy, I still don't get where you're going with this," Lamp said.

"Not to worry. We're almost there. Tell me, Trish, where did you disappear to before you got busy in the billiard room with your duo of dead men?"

"I didn't disappear anywhere."

"Sure you did. Before Lou went inside Patrick ordered him to stay downstairs. He said that the upstairs was for family only. That made you curious, didn't it? You wanted to sneak a quick look around upstairs."

She shrugged again. "So . . . ?"

"So you left your two lover boys in the billiard room for a few minutes, didn't you? Told them you had to go powder your nose . . ."

"Powder my *what*?"

"And went scampering upstairs. Lou, who always followed Patrick's orders, stayed put in the billiard room. So did Kyle, who wasn't the least bit interested in anything but your slim, firm bod. Where did you go when you got upstairs?"

Trish didn't answer me. Just stood there in taut silence.

"Answer him," Lamp ordered her.

She rolled her eyes. "I just wanted to have a look at her things, I swear."

"Whose things, Trish?"

"Monette's. She's a really rich lady. I wanted to see what kind of stuff she had in here."

"Meaning you wanted to have a look at her wardrobe?"

Trish let out a laugh. "Meaning are you kidding me? She dresses like my mother." She glanced at her apologetically. "No offense, Mrs. Aintree."

Monette said nothing. Just stared at her with total hatred.

"I wanted to see what kind of mascara and lip gloss and stuff she uses," Trish explained. "I wasn't going to take anything. I was just curious."

"And what were you wearing, Trish?"

She frowned at me. "A white bikini. I just told you that."

"Now tell us what happened when you came in here to have a look at Monette's cosmetics."

Trish hesitated, her lower lip clamped between her teeth. "Do I have to?"

"You're asking for trouble if you don't," Lamp told her. "Obstructing a police investigation is nothing to fool around with."

"Well, okay," Trish said reluctantly. "When I came through the door, I found Patrick in here tossing the dresser drawers and babbling to himself like a total crazy person until . . ." She broke off, her chest rising and falling. "Until he saw me."

"What did he do?" I asked her.

"He got this huge grin on his face and he said, 'Hey, darlin', I was hoping you and your nice, long legs would show up. I've been wanting a piece of you.'"

"And did the two of you . . . ?"

"Get it on? No way."

"Why not?"

"He was Kat's boyfriend. She would have gotten pissed at me. Plus he was acting way too wild-eyed and scary. When I told him I had to go back downstairs, he got pissed off and made a lunge for me."

"Did he scratch you up?"

Trish shook her head. "He was so bombed that I was out the door before he got anywhere near me."

"So he didn't leave any scratch marks on you?"

"I just told you he didn't. Are you even listening to me?"

"And then you went back downstairs and got it on with Lou and Kyle in the billiard room, correct?"

"Well, yeah."

"Trish, how tall are you?"

"Five foot nine. Why?"

"And how much do you weigh?"

"Right around 110 if I don't party too much. I definitely look my best in a bikini if I'm at 110. But I can balloon to 120 real easy if I'm not careful."

I looked at Monette. Then over at Danielle, who stood next to Monette in her Brentwood High hooded sweatshirt and sweatpants. "Would you do me a favor, Danielle?"

"Me?" She seemed startled. "What is it?"

"Would you go stand next to Trish for a second?"

"Why?"

"I'm just curious about something. Please go stand next to her."

Danielle went over next to Trish and stood beside her.

"How tall are you, Danielle?"

"Five foot eight."

"And how much do you weigh?"

"I weigh 115 pounds."

I studied the two of them as they stood there shoulder to shoulder, both of them looking very uneasy. Facially, there was no resemblance between them at all. Danielle was a bright-eyed fifteen-year-old girl with good, high cheekbones and her father's strong jaw. Trish was seven years of hard partying older with a receding chin and eyes that were too close together and had seen too much. But they were the same height, same weight and same type—willowy, leggy, small-breasted California girls with long, shiny blond hair that both of them wore gathered in ponytails today.

"Danielle, did you have your hair in a ponytail yesterday?"

"No, it was down."

"How about you, Trish?"

"Same here."

"Would the two of you mind . . . ?"

They untied their ponytails and ran their fingers through their hair until it hung free and loose in front of their shoulders, framing their faces.

I studied them some more. "What do you think, Lieutenant?"

He thumbed his chin thoughtfully. "I don't know. I'd have to see Danielle in something other than those baggy sweats."

"That is *not* going to happen," Monette said angrily. "And I don't like where this is going *at all*."

"Neither do I," Reggie said. "Stop this right now, Stewie. *Please.*"

Lamp continued to study them. "But I can believe it. Sure, I can."

"I'm just a stupid little girl from Atascadero," Kat spoke up. "Would somebody please explain to me what you're talking about?"

"What we're talking about," I said to her, "is two tall, slim young women with long, straight blond hair who happened to be wearing the same color bikini yesterday. White. White's a popular color. Shows off one's tan. I know this because I read it in last month's issue of *Seventeen*. Shortly after Trish, in her white bikini, slipped free of Patrick's grasp and dashed downstairs to the billiard room, Danielle, in her white bikini, came up those same stairs with Reggie fresh from the swimming pool to change for lunch. Reggie went directly to her room. But you didn't, did you, Danielle? You noticed your dad was in here and stopped to say hello to him. Unfortunately, your dad was so bombed on tequila, coke and God knows what else that he mistook you for Trish. Thought Trish had changed her mind and come back for some action. And so he tried to have sex with you, didn't he?"

"Don't answer him, Danielle," Monette commanded her.

Danielle didn't answer. Just stood there, ashen-faced.

I moved over closer to her. "He thought you were Trish, didn't he?"

Danielle remained silent, her lower lip quivering.

"Didn't he?" I grabbed her by her left wrist and yanked the sleeve of her sweatshirt up over her elbow.

Her left forearm looked perfectly fine. No scratches or bruises.

I reached for her right sleeve.

"No, please don't!" she protested.

Gouges. She had fingernail gouges on her right forearm. Also angry bruises around it. Someone with strong hands had clutched her tight.

"It's *your* Type A blood and tissue that's under his nails, isn't it, Danielle? They found Type O. Your mother is Type O. They also found Type A. You're Type A, just like your father was."

Danielle let out a sob, her chest heaving. "He didn't even *know* me. He said these dirty, awful things to me and grabbed me and—and *kissed* me and started to tear my swimsuit off me. I screamed at him to stop. I screamed at him and I fought with him and he just laughed and said, 'So you like to play rough, huh?'"

"Danielle, did your father rape you?"

"No . . ." She gulped back her tears. "But he would have if he hadn't been stopped."

"Is that the truth?" I asked Monette.

She nodded her head. "He had her top off—that's all, thank God."

"But it wasn't you who stopped him, was it, Monette?"

Her gaze turned steely. "I don't know what you mean."

"Sure, you do. Someone in this house heard Danielle's screams. Someone who did something about it—unlike Elliot, who just stood out there on the patio doing absolutely nothing."

Elliot glowered at me. "You know what, Hoag? I've taken just about as much crap out of you as I'm—"

"I'm talking about Joey." I looked at him as he stood there next to Monette. "It's Joey who, in a weird way, is the hero of this twisted family tale. Joey who, just this once, wasn't trying to block out every sound in the house by blasting Nirvana through his headphones. You weren't reading *Journey to the Center of the Earth*, were you, Joey? And you weren't poking away at a term paper on your word processor. You were standing at your window peeking through the shutters at your dad while he snorted coke with Lou and Kyle out on the patio. An aspiring writer needs to observe human activity, after all. And when Kat and Trish came back outside with your mom after their little house tour, you were sneaking peeks at Kat, which is perfectly understandable. She does happen to be the sexiest nineteen-year-old girl on the planet. I'm guessing you were looking at Trish, too, and maybe having some second thoughts about telling Kyle you weren't interested in having sex with her."

"I—I was not," he protested, reddening.

"It's nothing to be ashamed of, Joey. I would have been having second thoughts myself if I were you. It's not every day that a red-blooded seventeen-year-old virgin is offered the sexual favors of a hot-bodied blonde, no strings attached. So you were standing there having yourself another look. That's when you heard your sister scream. And you came running. Ran right in here and found your very own father trying to rape your very own kid sister right there on your parents' bed. Your dad was an All-American at Notre Dame. Stood six foot four and outweighed you by at least sixty pounds. I'm guessing you'd tussled with him before. He knocked you around some. Am I right?"

Joey didn't say yes. Joey didn't say no. He didn't say anything.

"There was absolutely no way you were physically capable of pulling him off Danielle. You knew that. So you did the next best thing. You opened your mom's nightstand drawer, grabbed her loaded Beretta and fired off two shots at him, didn't you?"

"Don't answer him, Joey," Monette said.

Joey's eyes met mine. He nodded and said, "Yes."

"Your dad took one shot in the shoulder and the other in his side. There was blood spatter on the wall behind the bed, blood spatter on the bedspread and there was this . . ." I opened the suitcase now and unrolled the pale blue hand towel that I'd found in the black trash bag last night. Inside it was Danielle's white bikini, spattered with blood. "Lieutenant, you'll notice that there's also a yellow bikini wrapped up in this towel that has blood smears on it here and here, see? This would be the bikini that Reggie was wearing when she and Danielle went swimming before lunch."

The room fell utterly silent. No one said a word to contradict me. No one even seemed to be breathing.

"Now came that two- or maybe three-minute gap between shots," I went on. "I'm starting to think it was closer to three minutes, Lieutenant, because an awful lot had to happen. Everyone had to spring into action. By everyone I mean Monette and Maritza, who came dashing up the stairs from the kitchen immediately after the shots were fired. And I mean Reggie, who was down the hall in her room changing for lunch. Maritza, you tried to comfort Danielle, who was all scratched up and spattered with blood. That's how your uniform got blood smears on it." I unrolled the big bath towel and showed everyone the pale pink uniform that Maritza had been wearing. "Reggie, you got Danielle the hell out of here. Dragged her down the hall to her room so she could shower and change into something with long sleeves. That's how you got the blood smears on your bikini. You hid both of your bikinis in Danielle's room for Maritza to dispose of later. Maritza had to run downstairs to her own room so she could change into a different uniform. Monette, that left you alone in here with Joey and your wounded husband, who was lying there on the floor slumped against the bed. You have a very clear head, Monette. What you did next was, well, allow me to say I consider it pretty damned impressive. You took the Beretta away from Joey and then you told him to do something that mothers don't usually ask their sons to do—punch you in the nose. Hard. It was Joey who gave you the bloody nose, not Patrick. Then you told him to go to his room, change his clothes, wash his hands and face and put on his headphones. Which Joey did. Unfortunately for you, Joey, Lulu followed the gunshot residue trail right to your room. She smelled it on your shoes. Here are the clothes you were wearing . . ." I laid his jeans, flannel shirt and Nirvana T-shirt out on the bed. "Lieutenant, your lab people will find that they're covered with gunshot residue. Monette wiped Joey's fingerprints from the Beretta with this second T-shirt right here before she used the Beretta herself to pump two more shots directly into Patrick's heart. Monette, you told me that you and Patrick had quite some conversation before you shot him. You telling him what a horrible bastard he was. Him telling you what a rotten lover you were. You made that part up. There was no time for any such conversation."

"No time," she admitted hoarsely. "But I didn't make up the conversation. We'd had it several times before. Too many times."

"Did he say anything to you at all before you shot him or was he unconscious?"

"Oh, he was plenty conscious. He laughed at me as I stood there pointing the gun at him. He said, 'Don't forget to curl your pinkie finger when you pull the trigger, Queenie.' Those were the last words that the father of my children said to me before I shot him. Pretty sad epitaph, isn't it?"

"I think this is all pretty sad, actually. I'm curious about one thing, Monette."

She let out a weary sigh. "Yes, what is it, Hoagy?"

"Why did you do it?"

"Do what?"

"Why did you kill him?"

"I had to. I couldn't let him survive. Even if he'd kept his mouth shut, which I doubted he was capable of doing, the police would have figured out what had happened. Joey would have gotten in serious trouble. Danielle would have been subjected to the vilest sort of media scrutiny. I couldn't allow that to happen. They're my children."

The master suite fell into total silence again.

"Monette's your killer, Lieutenant, just as she's maintained all along," I said. "But it wasn't self-defense. Patrick didn't punch her. Nor did he gouge her with his fingernails. She gouged herself, didn't you, Monette? You took off your long-sleeved shirt, grabbed him by his dead hand and raked your own bare arms with his fingernails. Pretty gutsy if you ask me. Only a mother would do that. You, Reggie and Maritza—the three of you were protecting Joey, who'd fired two shots at his own father, and Danielle, who'd been sexually assaulted by him. When I came running upstairs after I heard the shots, Reggie and Danielle were standing in the hallway looking stunned and frightened." I glanced at them. "But you kept it together. Both of you. As did you, Maritza, when you came up the main stairs to find out what had happened. By claiming that the door at the top of the service stairs was locked, you bought yourself enough time to change uniforms. By the way, where did you hide all of this bloody clothing? I couldn't find it in the laundry room. Did you stuff it in the kitchen trash bin?"

"Under my bed," she said in a faint voice.

I turned back to Monette and said, "That wasn't an idle question you asked me before, was it?"

Monette frowned. "Which question do you . . . ?"

"You wanted to know whether the medical examiner's men were planning to strip us naked when they came here to take our blood and hair samples. You were afraid they'd find those gouges on Danielle's right arm, weren't you?"

She nodded. "I told her to make sure that she offered them her *left* arm when they asked to take her blood. Her left arm looks fine. You saw that for yourself."

"You're right, I did. But I wasn't being totally honest with you. The truth is that they were planning to subject each of us to a head-to-toe body search. Correct, Lieutenant?"

"Correct."

"So they *were* going to find those fingernail gouges in Danielle's right arm. And, well, you were never going to get away with it. Also correct, Lieutenant?"

"Also correct."

Monette started to speak but no words came out of her mouth. She just stood there with her mouth open, glaring at me.

"Reggie, you visited me in the pool house last night to find out how much I knew. You needed to find out whether or not I was going to cause you trouble."

She gazed at me, her huge eyes shimmering in the sunlight

that streamed through the open windows. "I visited you because I wanted to be with you."

"You're a part of this. You helped cover up what really happened."

"Danielle and Joey are *family*. Are you trying to tell me you wouldn't have done the same thing?"

"I don't know."

"I begged you to leave it alone. Why couldn't you leave it alone?"

"Because you can never bury the truth. It has to come out."

"Why?" she demanded. "What good comes from this? Who's better off?"

I didn't answer her. Didn't have an answer. Instead I turned to Elliot and said, "How much did you know?"

He shrugged his soft shoulders. "I heard the screaming, sure. But Monette asked me to keep quiet about it, so I did. I don't ask questions. I've been managing talent for thirty-five years. They come, they go. Hardly any of them last. All that lasts is loyalty. I'm here for Monette, same as she's here for her kids." He looked at Lamp and said, "And I'm 100 percent with the kid sister, Lieutenant. What's to be gained by pursuing this? Who's better off?"

"My job is to enforce the law, Mr. Schein," Lamp said to him quietly. "I can't look the other way. New charges will have to be filed against Monette Aintree. And Joey will have to be taken into custody."

"Why?" Elliot demanded. "He was saving his sister. That boy's a hero."

A loud buzzer went off downstairs in the kitchen. Someone was ringing the house from the front gate.

"That'll be my men," Lamp said. "I called for more backup."

"I will go down and let them in," Maritza said. "If that is okay."

Lamp nodded to her and she went down the stairs to the kitchen.

"I'm with Elliot," Boyd said. "There was only one crime committed in this room yesterday—that drunken creep trying to get over on his own fifteen-year-old daughter."

"Personally, I don't disagree," Lamp said. "But professionally, I can't. You committed a calculated act of murder, Mrs. Aintree. You concocted a lie about it and you involved your children, your sister and your housekeeper in that lie. By doing so you made all of them party to the willful obstruction of a police investigation. I understand why you did what you did. Believe me, I do. And I'll do everything within my power to keep Danielle's name out of this. My report will simply state that the victim was making improper advances toward an underage guest whose identity is being withheld to protect her privacy. That'll be the official version. The press will never get hold of Danielle's name. Not if I have anything to say about it. And I do."

"Thank you, Lieutenant," Monette said, her voice barely a whisper.

Maritza came back upstairs now from the kitchen with an odd, puzzled look on her face. "I let him in, Senora. He is coming in."

Monette frowned at her. "Who is, Maritza?"

"The postman. He says he has an express mail delivery for you and Senorita Reggie."

Monette drew in her breath. "Oh, God . . . ," she said to Reggie. "Please tell me this isn't happening now. It can't be happening."

"Sorry, Olive." Reggie reached over and gripped her sister's hand tightly in her own. "It's happening."

CHAPTER ELEVEN

Dear Olive Oyl and Sir Reginald—

First of all, please allow me to apologize for the pain and heartache that these past twenty-four hours have brought you. I cannot help but feel that everything that has happened in regards to Patrick has been my fault. That if I hadn't written to you, your lives would not have been torn asunder yet again. I seem to ruin everything I touch. I always have. By reaching out to you, I have managed only to bring you more pain. Please believe that this was never my intention. My heart aches for you right now. And I do have a heart, hard as that is to believe.

Obviously, it was a mistake to think that I could come back into your lives after so many years. Even the mere possibility that I might return has proven to be utterly disastrous. This is the price I pay for being the evil creature that I am. I will not burden you any further. This is the last letter you will receive from me. I will continue to stay far, far away from both of you. That is a promise.

But before I go I do wish to explain myself to you. Or at least try. This old man's purpose in contacting you was that I was hoping for forgiveness as my own end draws near. Not that I deserve any. Forgiveness for what, you may ask. Your mother, God rest her soul, did not take her own life on that East Village rooftop back in 1970. Eleanor didn't jump. I pushed her. She had caught me making love to another woman earlier that evening, which was nothing unusual, believe me, but for some reason it set her off and she said some very accurate, painful things to me. She reminded me that if she hadn't rewritten Not Far from Here *for me after Alberta Pryce initially declined to represent it, that Alberta would never have agreed to take me on, never have sent the manuscript out, never have sold it and I would never have become rich and famous.*

No one has ever known the ugly truth that it was your mother who rewrote the novel, not me. I was too proud and stubborn to do it. I also didn't have the slightest idea how to go about it. I was, and still am, a no-talent fraud. No one could ever figure out why I never wrote a second novel. Only your immensely gifted mother understood why. Your mother who loved me and never, ever revealed our secret to anyone. Not even to Alberta. But when she caught me cheating on her that night, Eleanor decided she'd had enough. She told me she was sick of my selfishness, sick of my inflated ego, sick of me. And that she intended to set the world straight, come morning, on who was really responsible for the success of Not Far from Here. *I couldn't allow that. I was Richard Aintree, after all. The* Richard Aintree.

So I pushed her off the roof.

The authorities found drugs in her system and concluded it was suicide. I encouraged that conclusion. I told them she'd been despondent. But that was never the truth. The truth is that I murdered your mother because she was going to expose me. The truth is that every awful word she'd said about me was valid and warranted. I was not worthy of her love. Or yours. Or anyone else's. And so, once the business of her death was completed, I fled.

I should have just killed myself. I did try to jump in front of an oncoming freight train on the trestle in Gaviota, California, one night a long, long time ago. But I lacked the courage to do it. I still lack the courage. So I'll just keep on keeping on, waiting for time to take care of what needs to be done to me. My health is poor. It won't be long now.

Please don't bother to look for me. You'll never find me.

I apologize to Eleanor for never being willing to acknowledge how much her help meant to the success of Not Far from Here. She was its co-author. Her name should have been on its cover right there next to mine. I apologize to Alberta for deceiving her about Eleanor's contribution and for lacking the courage to tell her what really happened to her dear friend on that East Village rooftop. I apologize to Stewart Hoag for dragging him into this project, which I now realize was the desperately misguided gesture of a foolish old man.

But, mostly, I apologize to you, my darling daughters, because all I've managed to do is make a mess of things yet again. I would ask you to try to forgive me, but I know you never will. I do not deserve your forgiveness. The painful truth is that I am not a very nice man. Feel free to hate me if you wish. I won't blame you one bit if you do. And now I will say goodbye.

With all my love,
Dad

THEY WEPT.

The two sisters stood there in the front hallway with the express mail letter that had been sent from a post office in Teaneck, New Jersey, and hugged each other and wept as Danielle and Joey watched them with curious looks on their faces. Kat and Trish had been escorted out by the tall, tanned cop and were being driven to their respective homes. The medical examiner's lab rats had evaporated. Boyd and Elliot had stuck around, as had Lamp.

"I—I knew it," Monette sobbed. "I just . . . I—I knew she'd never abandon us that way. A mother doesn't do that to her children. They're our babies. We always take care of them. Always. We never, ever stop."

"Never, ever," Reggie sniffled, tears streaming down her cheeks. They were talking about Danielle and Joey now, about what had happened upstairs in the master suite yesterday. "But I feel sorry for Dad, I have to admit."

Monette gaped at her in disbelief. "How can you? He *killed* Mom!"

"I know he did. But he's been out there by himself for all of these years, living with his guilt, suffering . . ."

"We don't know that," Monette said. "Maybe he changed his name and started over again with a new wife and kids. For all we know he's been managing stock portfolios in some posh New Jersey suburb for all of these years."

"I don't believe that," Reggie said. "And neither do you. He's been alone this whole time. Alone and miserable."

"Well, shit on a stick," Boyd grumbled at me. "No Richard Aintree means we have no book. Guess I wasted your time, Hoagster."

"Oh, I wouldn't say that. I got a free trip to L.A. Rode a terrific bike, reconnected with a dear friend *and* made a hundred thou."

He raised his eyebrows at me. "You did?"

"My kill fee, remember?"

"Oh, right," he acknowledged glumly.

"No, I can't complain one bit."

"Well, I sure can. I lit a ton of media heat under this. I thought we had a major, major literary event. Instead, all we have is one dead TV star, two dead flunkies and an epic flop. I'm going to look like the putz of the century now. The *Times* is going to kill me. *Publishers Weekly* is going to kill me. And Mr. Harmon Wright will probably fire me."

"There, you see? Some good may come out of this after all."

Boyd looked at me with a hurt expression. "You really detest me, don't you?"

"I might if I gave you enough thought. You're like one of those flesh-eating viruses that can be picked up from any delicatessen counter or public lavatory. I know you're out there, but I prefer not to dwell on you for fear of going insane."

"You're living in the past."

"Thank you, I try."

"I'm the future of American publishing," Boyd proclaimed. "And one of these days, amigo, I am going to win you over."

"No, you're not. And I am *not* your amigo."

I SAW NO point in sticking around so I didn't. Lulu and I caught the red-eye out of there that very evening.

I did call Alberta to let her know that her dear friend Eleanor Aintree hadn't killed herself that night back in 1970.

The Silver Fox listened to my news about Richard's confession in silence. And remained silent for a long moment before she said, "Thank you for letting me know. I never dared to say the words out loud, but I always thought that he killed her. In fact, I was positive that he did. Call me when you get home, will you? We'll toast Eleanor's memory properly at the Algonquin. Two martinis, very dry. Safe trip, dear boy."

It took me less than thirty minutes to pack and then I was ready to leave. I didn't have a whole lot to say to Monette, Joey or Danielle. I'm not big into long goodbyes. Besides, the odds were excellent that I'd be back in a few weeks to testify at Monette's trial. Joey's trial, too, if there was one. I did remind Danielle to work in some sprints every day so that her legs wouldn't get heavy on her. And I thanked Maritza for taking such good care of Lulu and me. I gave her a kiss on the cheek, too. She blushed.

It was no problem to drop the Roadmaster off at Dirk Weir's vintage car warehouse on a Sunday evening. Dirk was there working on a rush job for a film shoot in the morning. I was sorry to bid the bike goodbye, though not as sorry as Lulu was. Reggie followed us there in Joey's red Jeep Wrangler with my Olympia and my bags stowed in back.

I joined her out front on La Brea after I'd returned the keys and discovered that Emil Lamp's white Chevy Caprice was parked there behind her. He and Reggie were standing on the sidewalk chatting. When she spotted me, she got in the Wrangler so that he and I could talk.

"I couldn't let you leave town without saying a proper goodbye," he said to me. "And to thank you for your help. When they call you back to testify, I'd love for you to meet Belinda. Bring your lady friend over there. We'll make a foursome out of it," he suggested, which prompted Lulu to let out an indignant snuffle. "Fivesome, I mean. Sorry, Lulu." He bent down, patted her and thanked her, too. Mollified, she got in the Wrangler with Reggie to wait for me.

I stood there watching the traffic go by on La Brea for a moment before I said, "What will happen to these people?"

"As little as possible, if I have anything to say about it."

"Do you?"

"Not really." He grinned at me boyishly. "But it sounded good, didn't it?"

"It absolutely did. I bought it."

"Joey's old enough to stand trial as an adult for putting those two bullets into his father. But he does have that history of setting fires and he's been under a therapist's care. My guess? He'll be sentenced to hospitalization in a state mental facility and released within a couple of years. He was trying to protect his sister, after all, and it's not as if he's the one who killed his father. His mother is."

"What will happen to her?"

"She'll still plead self-defense, only with a different wrinkle. They call it the Mama Bear defense. She was protecting her cubs—which isn't a legitimate argument in a court of law except for the fact that it is. She has a God-given right to do what she did. No jury will convict her. She'll win in the court of public opinion, too, I imagine, when the public finds out what sort of a guy Patrick was." He glanced over at the Wrangler, where Reggie was engaged in a serious conversation with Lulu. For the record, it was Reggie who was doing all of the talking. Lulu was strictly listening. "As to the matter of certain individuals obstructing our investigation and flat out lying to us, I don't believe there'll be any appetite to pursue that."

"I'm glad to hear that. And what will happen to Richard Aintree? He's confessed to murdering his wife. You have it in writing. And there's no statute of limitations on murder."

"I expect the NYPD will reopen the case and issue a warrant for his arrest."

"No one's been able to find him before. Do you think they'll find him now?"

"They will if they really want to."

"Would you want to if you were in their shoes?"

Lamp studied me curiously. "Why are you asking me that?"

"Just wondering."

"Yes, I would, Hoagy. Murder is murder." Lamp stuck out his hand. "I'll catch you when you get back."

I shook it. "Take it slow, Lieutenant."

Then I got in the Wrangler with Lulu in my lap and Reggie steered us toward LAX. Somehow, I'd forgotten just how truly awful a driver Reggie was. The woman was totally oblivious to such things as speed limits, traffic lights and other vehicles as she sped down La Brea to the Santa Monica Freeway and floored it, squinting out at the road before us as she changed lanes restlessly, her seat shoved so far forward that the steering wheel was practically flush against her chest.

"You could have told me what really happened, Stinker."

"I was protecting you. I lied to the police. We all lied. I'm not the least bit sorry we did." She glanced over at me. "But I didn't want to pull you into it."

"Please keep your eyes on the road, will you? I'd like to make it to the airport in one piece. And I don't want you looking at me while I'm saying what I'm about to say."

"Which is . . . ?"

"Thank you."

"For what?"

"For being the first great love of my life. I'd lost you there for a while, but I feel as if I've got you back now."

"You're not getting all sloppy and sentimental on me just because we had fabulous sex last night, are you?"

"Just being honest."

"Well, in that case I want to say something, too, Stewie. I'm sorry."

"For . . . ?"

"For being so terrified of losing you that I drove you away."

"You didn't drive me away. I told you that last night. What happened to us was about me, not you. You're fine just the way you are."

"I'm *not* fine. No one in my whole family is fine. Just take a look at us, will you?"

"That's exactly what I've been doing, and I think you handled yourselves amazingly well these past two days. You watched out for each other, stuck together. That's what families are supposed to do, isn't it?"

"I guess," she conceded.

"How long are you planning to stick around?"

"For as long as I'm needed. Monette has a major ordeal ahead of her. So does Joey. And Danielle is going to be under a huge emotional strain. Someone has to be here for them."

"What about the Root Chakra Institute?"

She sped up onto a Toyota's tail, abruptly changed lanes, got honked at by a guy in an Econoline van, changed lanes one more time and punched it up to eighty-five. "The institute doesn't need me. My family does."

"And what about your work? Will you start writing again?"

She shook her head. "The words are gone."

"They're not gone. Not yours, not mine. I refuse to buy into that."

"How come?"

"Because if I'm not writing, then I have no idea why I'm here."

"You find other things that matter to you. You move on."

"I'm not going to move on. I call that giving up."

"Really? I don't call it that at all." Reggie shot a glance over at me before she looked back at the freeway and said, "I call it life."

MY OVERNIGHT FLIGHT home was quiet. I spotted no celebrities in first class. Celebrities don't fly the red-eye. Not if they can help it. I slept most of the way with Lulu curled up in the empty seat next to me.

It was still December in New York. There was a dusting of snow on the pavement. The morning wind had an arctic bite to it. I made it to my crummy old brownstone on West Ninety-Third Street by 8:30 and collected my mail, what little there was of it. I'd only been gone for three days, even though it felt like a month. Then I climbed the five flights up to my drafty apartment and put down some fresh 9Lives mackerel for Lulu.

When I checked my phone messages, I discovered that Merilee had finally checked in while I was somewhere over Iowa: "Hello, darling, it's me. I've just been reading all about you in the *International Herald Tribune*. I do hope you and Lulu are both okay. How awful for you. Speaking of awful, it snowed nonstop for two days in Budapest and the phone lines were down and then our financing fell through. They've sent us home. I'm in London right now to see a Stoppard play that might be a good fit for me when it comes to Broadway. I'm catching the Concorde in the morning. I'll call you when I get in. Let's have dinner at Tony's, okay? We'll cheer each other up. I love you both."

I played it twice so that Lulu could hear her mommy's voice. She was very excited. Also very happy to be home. As much as Lulu likes L.A., she's still a New Yorker at heart.

I unpacked our bags, pausing to give my old leather flight jacket an affectionate pat after I'd hung it in the back row of my closet. I showered, shaved and dressed in the cheviot wool tweed suit with a burgundy Italian flannel shirt, the powder blue knit tie and my shearling-lined brogans. Then I helped Lulu wriggle into her Fair Isle wool vest, put on my shearling greatcoat and fedora and out the door we went.

We strode briskly over to Amsterdam Avenue in the morning cold, pausing to pick up the papers from the newsstand on Broadway, and made our way up Amsterdam to the Blue Tea Cup Café on West 104th. The Blue Tea Cup is owned by two mountainous black women from South Carolina who make *the* best buttermilk pancakes in New York City—though I'd appreciate it if you kept that to yourself because they can only seat twenty people at a time. They offer an exotic assortment of sides. I opted for fried chicken livers with my stack of pancakes. Lulu had some fried catfish, minus the pancakes.

I read the newspapers while we ate. Lamp was true to his word. Danielle's name didn't appear in any of the accounts of the events leading up to Patrick Van Pelt's murder in the master bedroom suite of Aintree Manor. Neither did Trish Brainard's, I noticed. Since it was Trish whom Patrick had mistaken Danielle for, it worked out much tidier if Trish's presence at Joey's birthday party was erased from the picture. Trish's brush with fame was a fleeting one. So fleeting it never happened at all. All she had were her memories and her knee abrasions from the Eartha Kitt sofa.

Thanks to a swiftly deployed team of high-priced public relations wizards, Monette was already winning big in the court of public opinion. Just for starters, it turned out that no one who'd worked with Patrick on *Malibu High* had a nice word to say about him. Executive producer Marjorie Braman went so far as to label him a "ticking time bomb" in the *New York Times*, adding, "Patrick was a fine actor but he was temperamental and prone to violent outbursts. I was also frightened by the company that he kept." Meaning his 320-pound personal assistant, the late Lou Riggio who, according to highly placed sources in the LAPD, was a "major" drug trafficker as well as the chief suspect in Kyle Cook's murder.

Meanwhile, two young actresses had already come forward in

the *New York Daily News* to accuse Patrick of being a "sexual predator." One of them claimed that he tried to rape her at a pool party in Malibu in October and would have succeeded if two members of the L.A. Lakers hadn't pulled him off her. The other alleged that after she'd let Patrick buy her a drink at a West Hollywood nightclub last month he'd forced his way into her apartment, demanded she perform oral sex on him and given her a black eye when she refused. She had the photos to prove it. Neither woman had come forward publicly until now because they said that Lou Riggio had threatened to "mess them up" if they did.

And Kat Zachry, who was nothing if not a survivor, already had this to say on page one of the *New York Post*: "PAT SCARED ME WHEN HE WAS HIGH." Kat revealed that she'd tried repeatedly to get Patrick to go into rehab for what she described as a "major cocaine problem." She acknowledged that he'd undergone a vasectomy and that the baby she was carrying wasn't his but that he'd "forced her" to say it was because he was trying to pressure his wealthy wife into a lucrative divorce settlement.

In the days to come, Boyd Samuels would land the nineteen-year-old bad-girl star of *Malibu High* a major six-figure deal for a tell-all book about her very public love affair with the late Patrick Van Pelt. I would be offered the job to ghost it for her but would choose to exercise the "life is too short" option.

But that was in the days to come. Right now, my attention was focused on putting away a second stack of buttermilk pancakes.

After that I strolled over to Broadway and started home, Lulu ambling along happily beside me. Burly young men from Maine were out on the sidewalk at West Ninety-Sixth Street with their fragrant, fresh-cut Christmas trees for sale. And the mad scribbler and the jabbering kid were parked in their usual spot on the corner of Broadway and West Ninety-Second, peddling their meager stacks of used paperbacks and LPs. The kid was trying to convince someone walking by, anyone walking by, to show an interest in his priceless collection of Grand Funk Railroad on vinyl. He was getting no takers. Not one. The gaunt, bearded old man was seated in his folding chair wearing my old Harris tweed overcoat and cashmere scarf, eyes glued to his long yellow notepad as he scribbled and scribbled, oblivious to the world around him. I reclaimed my copies of *Sneaky People* and *Giles Goat-Boy* and put a five-dollar bill in the cigar box before him.

As usual, he paid me no mind.

As usual, the kid grinned at me and said, "Have a good one."

As usual, Lulu growled at him as we started to walk away.

That was when something highly unusual happened.

"Thank you for what you did," a hoarse, rusty voice called out to me. It was the old man. He'd lifted his eyes from his notepad and was staring at me.

"No problem," I said, trying to keep the look of surprise off my face. Because he'd never spoken to me before. Not once. "You knew there would be trouble, didn't you? How did you know?"

"A father knows things. It's in the blood." He shook a grimy, crooked finger at me. "I want you to stop wasting your time. Just close your fucking eyes and start writing, will you?"

"I'm sorry, did you say *close* them?"

He didn't answer me. He'd lowered his gaze and retreated back inside of the lonely prison where he was serving a life sentence, scribbling and scribbling.

I strode back to my drafty apartment and put on the coffee and some Garner. Turned on the electric space heater and positioned it next to my desk. Changed into my Orvis shirt, jeans and mukluks. When the coffee was ready I poured myself a cup and sat down in front of my Olympia, rolled a fresh sheet of paper into

ACKNOWLEDGMENTS

It's been twenty years since the dapper celebrity ghostwriter Stewart Hoag and his faithful, neurotic basset hound, Lulu, last appeared in print. I can say with total confidence that you wouldn't be reading these words right now if my name hadn't come up by chance one day when my literary agent, Dominick Abel, was having lunch with Dan Mallory, executive editor of William Morrow. Dan happened to mention that the Hoagy series had long been one of his family's favorites and wondered if I'd ever considered reviving it. Dominick gave him my standard response, which was that in our modern Internet age of twenty-four-hour-a-day tweets and viral videos there are no longer such things as celebrity secrets, certainly not the kind of juicy secrets that would make readers keenly interested in a star's memoir and the failed novelist whose second career was penning those memoirs. The Hoagy series, I felt, belonged to a bygone era.

It was Dan and a young editor at HarperCollins named Margaux Weisman who offered up the bold suggestion of going back to that bygone era. It was their idea, not mine, to set this novel a quarter century ago in 1992. I am incredibly grateful to them for the idea. And grateful to Dominick for urging me to go ahead with what has turned out to be a labor of love from start to finish.

Which is not to say it was easy to summon up the voice of a character I hadn't written for two decades, especially when that character's views and observations are so crucial to the telling of the story. I would never have found Hoagy's voice again without the tireless support and patient feedback of my longtime companion, Diana Drake, whose belief in this project—and me—never faltered. I am also indebted to Elaine Pagliaro, Peter Dixon, Brittany Finkeldey, Liza Dousson and Emrys Tetu for their expertise, advice, encouragement and support these past many months.

Two different independent publishers, Byron Preiss and David Thompson, labored tirelessly over the years to keep paperbacks of the eight Hoagy novels in print, particularly my Edgar winner, *The Man Who Would Be F. Scott Fitzgerald*. Both men have passed, but I have not forgotten their faith in me. And I'm hugely grateful to Otto Penzler, who in 2012 made the entire Hoagy series available as e-books on his MysteriousPress.com so that a whole new generation of readers has been able to discover it.

I can't mention Hoagy without a tip of my fedora to my first literary agent, the late, great Roberta Pryor—the real life Silver Fox—who sent the manuscript of my very first Hoagy novel, *The Man Who Died Laughing*, to a mystery editor at Bantam named Kate Miciak. Kate loved the writing but rejected it because the plot was woefully thin. The woefully thin part didn't surprise me. I had never written a mystery before. Roberta convinced Kate to sit down with me and explain how to make it, well, less woefully thin. I rewrote the novel from scratch, Roberta resubmitted it, Kate bought it and it went on to be nominated for an

Anthony Award. I wrote all of the Hoagy novels before this one for Kate. There would be no Hoagy and Lulu if it weren't for her.

Lastly, I would like to thank the countless readers who've written me over the years to beg me to bring Hoagy back. Consider it done. He's back.

David Handler
Old Lyme, Connecticut